LONE WOLF WITH A GUN

WARBONNET was a boom town waiting to explode. There was money to be made here—big money—but not for McMahon. He was a manhunter, a bitter, proud man doing a lonely, dirty job—the last job—and the biggest.

• Frank O'Rourke tells the story of a lone wolf with a gun who crashed headlong into the bloody struggle for the vast range lands of the Kansas-Colorado territory. It is a story of courage and violence torn from the history of a raw and lawless land.

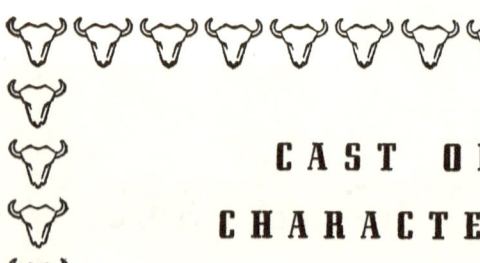

CAST OF CHARACTERS

JOHN McMAHON came to Warbonnet as a manhunter, but his job changed.

RED EGAN was tough, but not too tough to serve as bait or a killer.

FERRIS BUCHANAN had a big deal working —one of the biggest.

PAUL MASON remembered where he had seen a man before. He planned to use that memory.

TRUMBELL thought he had bought McMahon when he hired him.

ALICE TRUMBELL was ambitious, and she had never failed to get her way.

THE FLETCHERS owned a piece of land that was the key to the whole scheme.

WARBONNET LAW

by
FRANK O'ROURKE

WILDSIDE PRESS

WARBONNET LAW

Originally published under the title *The Gun*

Copyright, 1951, by Frank O'Rourke

For Marion Broman

One

AT THAT mid-winter time of early morning between the last ragged curtain of darkness and gray dawn, the town lay invisible beside the river, smoke rising thinly from roughly mortared chimneys, breakfast lamps hidden behind closed shutters and veined green shades, frost mist lifting slowly to mingle with the river fog that covered the valley, blanketing earth and buildings with impersonal coldness.

This was Warbonnet in the high plains country, closer to the rampart of the Rockies than to the rich farming country farther east. It was arid, bleak, lawless, dominated by the cattlemen, and the law was the six-gun. But it was the time when the farmers—nesters, they called them— were beginning to come in to break the age-old sod. The transcontinental railroads were to come later, but even now the little branch line feelers were probing out into the wilderness, with their owners sensing an empire to be gained.

The morning train, finishing an all-night run from the main line on this branch track, rumbled across the spidery river trestle and halted at the depot as the engineer cracked his whistle with a last vestige of sleepy spirit. With the train's arrival, an everyday but always fresh link with the outside world, shutters banged open and people trickled reluctantly onto Front Street for another day in Warbonnet's brief life.

John McMahon had huddled behind the pot-bellied stove in the depot waiting room since two that morning, dozing fitfully, waking whenever the fire burned low and his feet chilled. The night watchman, a red-nosed old busybody in an ancient, coal-smeared overcoat, had retreated to the agent's private office after exacting McMahon's promise to tend the waiting-room fire.

He had prepared for this night by appearing the length

1

of Front Street in a familiar condition, that of the cheerful drunk who visited every saloon and, as had happened often in the past six weeks, wobbled into the depot to sober up before returning to his hotel room. Now, at dawn, McMahon heard the agent come on duty, kick the night watchman from his office, shake up the fire, cough with the thick grogginess of awakening, and stamp into the express room for the high-wheeled cart moments before the train crossed the river trestle and whistled its arrival. McMahon heard the sanded wheels grit and squeal on slick rails, and lifted himself from the bench to stand beside the cooling stove, hands thrust deeply into his mackinaw pockets, face caked with the oily crust of another bedless night. He waited, slack-faced, while the agent and conductor offered sparse directions to six well bundled-up passengers who had gotten down and stood uncertainly on the platform, tired eyes flinching at Warbonnet's frontier drabness in early morning light.

McMahon walked unsteadily from the waiting room and glanced beyond the passengers at the hills, his face blurred and coarsened from lack of sleep and too much liquor. He saw a plump, apple-cheeked man in a greatcoat, two dog-tired ranchers home from an Omaha whirl, and three other people standing close together in a tight, aloof knot. One was a girl muffled in furs, wearing stylish black buttoned overshoes, and shivering uncontrollably between two large men. McMahon ignored them and went around the corner toward Front Street and the hotel. Five minutes later he moved through the lobby to the stairs, unbuttoning his mackinaw and shaking his head with some weighty personal problem. The night clerk smiled with understanding and said, "Tough night, Johnny?"

"Too damned cold," McMahon said thickly. "I ought to be fat in the cheeks like you, Will."

"Man can't be too fat for this weather," Will Overton said. "How many passengers?"

"Six," McMahon said. "Tell 'em to be quiet coming upstairs."

McMahon mounted the stairs and shuffled to his room at the north end of the hall. The six passengers would come shivering into the hotel and sign the register. Someone would be sure to mention the drunk at the depot and Will Overton would say, "He's all right. Just snowed in for the winter and enjoying life."

But that was enough. McMahon stood at the window, shaking off his slack-faced dullness, rolling a cigarette with quick fingers. If the passengers judged him in that manner, he had finished another successful night in a tough, miserable job. Below his window along Front Street, the stores were opening and smoke poured greasy black from all chimneys. Last night's debris was swept into the gutters and shades went up with a flickering snap. Abe Bloom, always first to open, lifted his pusher broom and knocked the hoarfrost from the sign above his door. McMahon turned from the window and washed his hands and face in the tin basin. Three light taps sounded on his door. McMahon said, "Come in," and began to dry his face and hands.

The plump passenger stepped into the room and closed the door gently. McMahon rubbed his left ear with the towel's frayed edge and asked, "Chambers?"

"Yes," Chambers said. "Glad to know you, McMahon."

Chamber's handshake was strong for a small man. He blew wearily through full lips and opened the greatcoat to reveal a mountainous assemblage of undercoats and sweaters. He searched through the slant-cut pockets of a checked blue flannel vest and removed a long cigar, found a gold knife on a gold chain, nipped the cigar end, licked it gently, and regarded McMahon with placid eyes. Chambers was the complete and smooth-faced drummer with his apple cheeks and guileless smile and expensive clothing; only in relaxation, when the eyes became round and shiny, did the true man appear.

"What a town!" Chambers said. "Cigar?"

"No," McMahon said. "Can't the Colonel stand pat? I thought this case was to be handled my own way."

"Time," Chambers said. "You've been here six weeks. No luck yet. I don't mean that as an insult. I know you're the best. But the Colonel figured you must need help. That's why I'm here."

"If you want to help," McMahon said, "take the night train back."

"I can't do that. I have my orders."

"This is a one-man job," McMahon said patiently. "You can't come in cold and help. Make one mistake and they'll store you in the ice house until spring thaws out the cemetery dirt."

Chambers smiled kindly. "I cut my teeth on worse horrors. Now tell me the facts and I'll get some sleep. I should sue that railroad for attempted murder. I've never spent a more miserable twelve hours in my life."

McMahon opened his shirt front and scrubbed his chest with the towel, distrusting Chambers as he had always disliked the Colonel's other employees. Too many of them had acquired a twisted feeling toward life that made them mulishly stubborn and mentally incapable of accepting rebuke or instruction. Through the years this significant attitude had come to mean one thing for McMahon: it was the sure sign of a man-hunter's undeviating philosophy and tottered but a short breath from the step beyond the man-hunter—the killer. That was why the Colonel's agency had been successful; it was based almost entirely on the ability of such men, lone wolves. McMahon had wondered often in the last two years if he wasn't that way himself, for he had never worked with another man. He knew everything about Chambers from the Colonel. Chambers was an op of the old school, smart and careful, colorless as a chameleon or flamboyant as a peacock, depending on the situation; and most of all, according to the Colonel, who was seldom wrong, faithful to all commands and orders. One difference in Chambers was pleasantly apparent: he understood the change in location and living conditions, and recognized McMahon's skill in this sort of country. McMahon studied him deliberately, reached a decision, and sat loosely on the bed. He spoke while undressing.

"Our man is somewhere in or around this town. That name he used in St. Louis—John Ryan—naturally has not been used here. There are around eight hundred people in town. I can't break into every house to find that trunk. But I'll get our man by spring. I wrote the Colonel that. Didn't he believe me?"

"Certainly," Chambers said, "but spring is two months off and we don't have the time."

"Time!" McMahon said. "What difference does two months make if I get him?"

"None to us but a great deal to the man who pays us," Chambers said. "He moved his deadline up. We've got to work faster."

"This Trumbell," McMahon said. "I didn't meet him. Does he think I can work a miracle? Why did he move the time limit up?"

"I don't know," Chambers said gently. "We're hired to do a job. The Colonel gives the orders."

"That's fine," McMahon said sarcastically. "Very well, I'll run outside and find his man—after I sleep."

Chambers smiled and relaxed perceptibly. "Good boy. Now, Trumbell is here, his daughter with him. They want to see you as soon as possible."

McMahon lifted the towel and wiped his face roughly, swallowing a deep, sudden anger. "Here?"

"You saw them at the depot," Chambers said. "Trumbell, the girl, and his right-hand bower, a lawyer named

Mason. I argued against their coming, told them it was dangerous and foolish. No use. Trumbell is one of those wealthy men who can't stand delay of any sort."

"Then I'm to take orders from Trumbell?" McMahon asked.

"Well, not exactly."

"Listen," McMahon said. "This Trumbell can ruin in six minutes what I've spent six weeks setting up."

"Meet Trumbell," Chambers said. "Listen to him, and then do as you please. You understand?"

McMahon smiled faintly. "I take it you aren't strong for Trumbell?"

"A man's opinion is his own," Chambers said. "I'll keep mine to myself, but you can guess. By the way, I'm selling a line of ladies' and gents' furnishings. When will you see the Trumbells?"

"After supper," McMahon said. "Where are they?"

"Directly across the hall. I'm on your left."

"Get your sleep," McMahon said. "Knock at six-thirty."

Chambers watched him worriedly for a moment and then said, "Very well," and slipped from the room. McMahon braced the doorknob with a chair and crawled immediately beneath the blankets; shaking from chill and anger, he spent fifteen minutes warming the long, narrow section occupied by his body, thinking with a small, cold part of his mind about this case and its unknown qualities. Ten weeks ago the Colonel had wired him from Kansas City, catching McMahon in Cheyenne, where he was enjoying a quiet week of doing absolutely nothing. The wire was cryptic, as were the majority of Colonel Sloane's messages: "Meet me in Omaha soon as possible." McMahon packed his valise, kissed a dark-haired woman good-bye, and caught the next train east. In Omaha, meeting the Colonel in a hotel room, McMahon was given the case.

A wealthy financier named John Trumbell had been robbed, in his St. Louis offices, of a great many valuable

papers pertaining to various business deals. Working in
St. Louis, the Colonel's men had uncovered all known
facts. A man named John Ryan had made the acquaintance of Trumbell's head bookkeeper; this much was gathered from the rooming house where the bookkeeper lived,
but no one could offer a clear description of John Ryan.
The bookkeeper was found in Trumbell's private office
the morning after the robbery occurred, killed by a knife
thrust to the heart. A small trunk was missing from the
big office safe; the trunk, a memento of some western trip
Trumbell had taken years earlier was made of redwood
and buffalo hide, carved intricately with scenes of hunting
and fishing. It was two feet long, one foot wide, and fifteen
inches deep, with a shallow top drawer fitted into the
upper flange, and the bottom cavity, an open receptacle,
filled with the important papers. Trumbell wanted those
papers badly enough to pay a large sum for the Colonel's
services. McMahon knew this when the Colonel gave him
carte blanche on expenses and time. It came belatedly to
McMahon, once he had traced the trunk half-way to Warbonnet, that Trumbell had made no mention of bringing
the killer back for justice. Bookkeepers were a dime a dozen
to Trumbell, it seemed, but the papers meant everything.

McMahon had spent a month tracing his man north
and west, and finally north again on the branch line to
Warbonnet. John Ryan had changed his name long before,
but the trunk was too large to hide effectively, and too
small to be careless with in shipping and packing. Mc-
Mahon found a baggage smasher in Bent Fork who remembered the trunk, but not the man who carried it. Ryan
had bought a ticket on the branch line north to end of
track at Warbonnet. The smasher passed, pulling a load
of freight, and saw the trunk, partially hidden by an overcoat. He stopped and looked at the trunk and made some
remark about its beauty, and the man, Ryan, standing in
the night shadow beneath the depot roof, growled some-

thing about minding his own business, and covered the trunk fully with the overcoat. That was enough for Mc-Mahon, who had followed a tenuous trail too long for comfort; he caught the next train to Warbonnet after wiring the Colonel. Arriving in Warbonnet, two weeks before Christmas, he took a room at the hotel and began playing a difficult role. Remembering the past weeks now, with the work and danger and the rotgut whisky he had been forced to drink, McMahon thought of Trumbell with sour anger and fell asleep in the warming bed.

McMahon woke at six o'clock and lay beneath the blankets, squinting into the early dusk blurring his window. Another night, he thought dismally, in Warbonnet. Go down and play his part, follow the pattern of six weeks, and come upstairs and curse his failure. Actually, he hadn't failed. He knew the town and its people. Warbonnet was young and wild and unsettled, overflowing with drifters and long riders and petty thugs, all deposited like so much stagnant backwater by the branch-line construction of three years ago. But the town claimed a good share of honest, solid people, and it would change for the better, as did all towns in the course of time. McMahon had made his own place in this small world. To the town he was a drifter holed up for the winter, a big easygoing man who drank too much, paid his bills, and avoided trouble. Come spring he would feel the itch, the fiddle-foot blues, ride away and be forgotten. All this was to ensure that Ryan, who was almost sure to see him, would give him no more than a passing glance.

Outside the town had spent another day and night was coming on. Front Street was stirring sluggisly along a three-block stretch, preparing for another evening of come what may. Beyond the town, on the frozen, snow-drifted river, lanterns moved yellowly as the fishermen settled in their tiny huts over the ice holes. Abe Bloom closed his shutters and locked his front door, glanced appraisingly at his competitor across the street, and hurried homeward, a bent, alpaca-coated shadow on the dirty snow, soon vanishing into the up-street gloom. The Antlers saloon lit all gas lamps and cast bold blocks of inviting light over the street. People called and someone dropped a wash basin from a second-story window, the tinny sound echoing clearly. McMahon was dressed and checking his gun when Chambers knocked.

"Six-thirty," Chambers called softly. "Come on over."

McMahon buttoned his brown-blanket mackinaw, opened the door, and stepped swiftly across the hall into the opposite room. Behind him, Chambers closed the door and coughed gently, clearing his throat for introductions. The big man standing beside the bed made a curt motion with one hand and said, "McMahon?"

"Keep your voice down," McMahon said softly. "These walls are about the thickness of a knifeblade."

Trumbell flared up immediately. He was, as Chambers had described him, the arrogant picture of a man unaccustomed to delay and mentally unsuited to accept any rebuke. He would weigh two hundred and twenty, McMahon estimated, with forty pounds of excess suet packed about his waist, forming a round, thick bulge in his clothing. His face was square and strong, and he affected side-burns and a thick mustache, almost gray and showing the man's true age of sixty or more. He would be a dangerous man to buck, McMahon judged, capable of buying and selling anyone to suit a purpose. He scowled at McMahon, then mastered his anger and relaxed his wide, thick mouth, but not his eyes. Small and black, they held his resentment. It was unfair to judge him completely on first look, for he possessed great strength and power, and possibly, beneath the arrogant surface, common sense and good judgment.

"Sorry," Trumbell said curtly. "Now, what's going on here, McMahon? Colonel Sloane told me you were the best man at this business. I've paid a lot of money, wasted precious time, and you've given me nothing."

"Are you saying I've laid down on the job?" McMahon asked.

"I didn't mean that . . ."

"Then get off the fence." McMahon said bluntly.

"What do you mean?"

"If you don't like my way," McMahon said, "just say so. I'll quit and save argument. I think we had better understand one thing right now. I do my work my own way, without advice or criticism. When the Colonel gave me this case there was no time limit. I worked blind from the start. It has taken me six weeks to establish one fact— your man is here and I'll get him in the spring. Now you come running and give me a month. Very well, I'll do my best. I may get him, maybe not. It's a fifty-fifty gamble. But I know one thing. Coming out here, bringing your daughter along, is a damned fool play."

Trumbell's face, above his stiff white banker's collar, turned beet-red. The other man stepped forward then and rapped his knuckles sharply on the bureau and said, "Watch your tongue, McMahon."

He had not considered Mason after the first quick look. The man was about McMahon's age, thirty-three, well dressed and sharply handsome, undoubtedly an excellent judge of wine, profits and women. Mason would possess these traits of the eastern businessman gone west for advantageous reasons, but he lacked something which had no name and did not show until he entered this wild, rough country and stepped foolishly beyond his depth. He was Trumbell's man and no doubt a good one in the way Trumbell used him, but he was a definite, clearly exposed degree below Trumbell's own stature. But then, McMahon thought, that was exactly the way Trumbell would pick his men.

"When I want your advice," McMahon said, "I'll ask you."

The girl touched Mason's arm and stopped him after one bold, angry step. She was tall and well formed, with her father's eyes and a full, softly stubborn mouth that lacked Trumbell's hardness. She studied McMahon calmly, the small hint of laughter touching her mouth and rising to her eyes.

"Don't quarrel," she said. "Father, hear Mr. McMahon out."

"Very well," Trumbell said shortly. "Concerning our presence, we can take care of ourselves. What are you going to do, McMahon?"

"Have a drink," McMahon said. "I can't make you go home, but stay away from me in public. If you want to talk, arrange it with Chambers. This isn't a child's game."

"I'm aware of that," Trumbell said impatiently. "I want to hear your plans."

"You know them," McMahon said. "I'm to find a man, and a trunk. Tell me why you've placed a time limit and I'll tell you how I'll do it, step by step."

Trumbell had the grace to smile wryly. "Go ahead. We'll wait."

"One more thing," McMahon said. "You've got to have a legitimate reason for coming here. Think one up before you go downstairs. Good night."

McMahon stepped quietly into the hall and turned to the back stairs, a narrow corkscrew flight that dropped steeply around a rough timber center pole, past the kitchen wall into a tiny, unheated vestibule opening onto the alley. He went through the back door into the total darkness of the alley and walked north five blocks to the edge of town, then moved northwest toward one of several scattered houses. He tapped softly on the bedroom window and heard Abe Bloom pad from the kitchen in his felt slippers, pause against the wall beside the window, and whisper, "John?"

"Open up, Abe," McMahon said. "It's cold out here."

Abe Bloom laughed gently and raised the window. McMahon lifted himself over the sill into the bedroom and followed his host down a short hallway into the kitchen which was all things to the merchant in this raw town. Abe was dreaming of a big home filled with children and beloved possessions, but now, from necessity, lived in a two-room shanty that contained the bare essentials of mean living. Abe had opened his store a year ago and was not yet ready to bring his wife and three small children out from Omaha. Meanwhile, with quick trips back for happy visits, Abe lived a monastic, lonely life. He was a short and heavy man in his late thirties, with the keenly intelligent face of the shrewd businessman and the liquid, thoughtful eyes of the dreamer. Sitting across the table from McMahon, he filled his pipe and smiled warmly.

"Any luck last night?"

"No," McMahon said. "Chambers arrived. Short and heavy, like you. He's selling ladies' and gents' furnishings. He'll call on you."

"He already has." Abe chuckled. "What a salesman! Even knowing, I bought suits and shoes. Tell me, will I actually receive the goods?"

"Yes."

"But you are worried, John?"

"Everything has changed," McMahon said. "The Trumbells came with Chambers, plus a man named Mason. Trumbell has placed a time limit of one month on the case. That's why I had to see you tonight. I've got to rush it now, do it different. From tonight on, forget that you know me."

"Now wait," Abe said mildly. "You don't want my help, eh? A little danger—pshaw! Life is a danger every day. I like you. Are you forgetting we've known each other five years? I insist on helping if you need me, if you need my friends. My mind is made up. Don't argue with me. I'll get mad, and I'm terrible then. I warn you."

McMahon smiled. "All right, Abe. I won't argue with you."

"Good," Abe said. "Now, what is this change of plan?"

"You know how I've gotten in good with some of the boys," McMahon said. "Tonight I'll get real friendly with one of them. He's been wondering about me, trying to figure me out. He's a penny-ante drifter who can rustle a few cows, rob a crossroads store, roll a drunk. Maybe a little more if somebody shows him the way. The important thing is, he knows his own kind in this town. I'm betting he takes orders from somebody bigger. I've got to get inside that bunch and then trust to luck."

"But why?" Abe asked. "It doesn't make sense. You risk your life, John. Your first plan is the best, to work in slowly and find your man, or men, and then search their houses this spring."

"Can't now," McMahon said shortly. "Look, this is my business. I'm after a man. I've never failed. It's not the money so much as my pride. I guess a man is mostly pride when all's said and done. What else do we have?"

"Yes," Abe murmured. "Yes, pride is a great and dangerous blessing. But you can do it. Luck be with you. Are you hungry? Have you time for one game of chess?"

"Sorry," McMahon said. "I've got to go. Don't forget now—no help until I let you know. See you tomorrow."

McMahon returned to his room by the same alley route and walked downstairs ten minutes later. He paused in the lobby for a few words with Will Overton and a glance at the old men playing checkers in the front corner, spitting into the copper-colored cuspidors and moving the red and black checkers over the inlaid board with a seriousness bordering on insanity. McMahon studied them for a brief

moment and then moved with the unabashed desire of the
steady drinker straight through the connecting door into
the hotel barroom. He had one quick drink and slouched
against the bar, drinking his second glass slowly and glancing around with restored good humor. The fiddler came
from his back stool and sawed energetically into the night's
first tune, the snake rattles inside his violin bouncing dryly
with the rhythm. A sad-eyed half-breed, snowbound between fall work and his little north hills ranch beyond the
Gap, hunched against the wall behind the piano, shoulders
hidden under a greasy Chimayo blanket. McMahon waved
to several men, spoke casually with others and finally wan-
dered from the barroom, through the lobby, and into the
street. He had created his nightly impression and now he
would cross to the Antlers and have two drinks and get in
a game for half an hour so that, later in the evening, moving along Front and visiting all saloons, he could have a
drink in each and exaggerate his drunkenness without losing his wits.

This was the price paid for getting the feel of Warbonnet, meeting the men who caused the undercurrents and
small blusters that upset the town. Cattlemen in Stetsons
and chaps passed overalled farmers on the street and no
words were exchanged but a quiet gust of anger swirled between them. Townsmen in more or less city clothes
watched a woman in velvet dress and ostrich plumes and
grinned knowingly. Another woman stopped a man and
spoke for his ears alone, pleading for some lost token, something held dear by the man and now finished. In certain
houses men talked behind drawn shades; in the lamp-
lighted saloons men played poker, drank and did not invite
strangers into their circle. All these separated incidents
were part of the town and would bulk more important in
the spring. McMahon had watched certain men and
weighed them closely, until he possessed a picture deco-
rated with special faces and names, each man placed in his

proper rung on the ladder of McMahon's understanding. Such a man was Red Egan; in a lesser degree such a man was Casey, who owned the last and worst saloon on Front Street. Of a hundred such men, McMahon was absolutely certain about Red Egan and Casey; and seeing other men with them at the poker table, over a bottle, riding through the street late at night, was stamping those men with the same brand as surely as if they had admitted the fact. McMahon had gathered all this for spring use; but now he could not wait to play the game his own safe, sure way.

Two

AT MIDNIGHT McMahon stepped into Casey's, moving through the door into a hot, odorous mixture of smoke and sweat and damp sawdust. He grinned at Casey standing behind the bar in a checkered vest, his sleeves rolled halfway up to his elbows. Red Egan was playing cribbage with a small, ferret-faced man named Mathews. Red was dressed like a cattleman in town on business, heavy wool pants stuffed into high-heeled boots, wool shirt, and Stetson hat. A short sheepskin overcoat hung on a peg in the wall behind him. They were drinking and Mathews had the larger stack of chips between his thin white hands. Mathews habitually wore a celluloid collar, a black string tie, and a derby hat, his face compressed between the hat and collar into a shadowed, sharp-planed triangle of quick eyes and hard, twisted mouth. McMahon had instinctively disliked the man from their first meeting a month ago; tonight he was pleased to find three of a kind under the same roof. He slapped the bar and called, "Have one with me?"

"Come on back," Red Egan said. "We're dying on the vine."

McMahon said, "Pour a round, Casey." He kicked out a chair and sat unsteadily, spilling whisky on the cards. He said, "Cold tonight," and pushed the glasses around and went on in the same breath, "How do you stand it here all winter, Red? I'm goin' crazy, doing nothing."

Red Egan tilted his flat-crowned cattleman's hat on coarse red hair and grinned, showing discolored teeth and the nearly vanished goodness of a laughing face no longer young and clean. He said, "Drink up—luck. What do you mean, doing nothing, Johnny?"

"Just that," McMahon said. "Some poker? Casey, make it a foursome."

Casey dropped his flabby weight into a protesting chair, making a four-handed game that moved slowly with small pots and only their mechanical interest keeping it alive. McMahon played carelessly, dropping pots to Red and Mathews; two hours past midnight he lost a ten-dollar pot and held up both hands in surrender.

"No luck," he said thickly. "I've had enough."

"Why worry," Red Egan said, "if there's more where it comes from? Casey, get us a drink."

"No worry," McMahon said. "Always more, Red, come spring."

"Now that's an interesting subject," Red Egan murmured.

"Spring?" McMahon said. "Mighty interesting, Red. Best season of the year."

"I was talking about more money come spring," Red Egan said easily. "You never did say what you do for a living, Johnny."

"My business," McMahon said sharply, and then smiled. "No offense. You never asked. Maybe you wouldn't understand, Red."

Red Egan pursed his lips and spoke softly, "No? I might at that."

"So you say," McMahon said. "Come to remember, when do you work, Red? Got a rich uncle?"

"A lot of them," Red Egan said. "They come along."
McMahon said, "Mathews got a rich uncle?"

"Could be."

"And Casey?"

Red Egan moved his cigarette in slow, tight circles before his thin face. "And Casey. Are you too drunk to understand me, Johnny? I say Mathews and Casey are all
right."

"I'm not drunk," McMahon said, with dignity. "Glad
you've got friends. I've got none to talk with, to plan with
. . ." He lifted his glass suddenly. "How the hell do I
know who you are? I'm goin' to bed."

"Sit back," Red Egan said. "We talk the same language.
About that rich uncle. How's he holding out?"

"Poorly," McMahon said. "Come spring I'll have to tap
him. And yours?"

"Always good for a tap," Red Egan grinned. "Depends
on how a man goes about it. Two or three of us could make
it worth while."

Mathews murmured, "Easy, Red."

"Ah," Red said impatiently. "I know what I see and
hear. I told you three weeks ago Johnny was our man.
Casey . . ."

"Ho?"

"Close up. We'll go back and talk."

"Very well," Mathews said pettishly. "Do it your way."

"That I will," Red Egan said tolerantly. "Come along,
Johnny."

Casey locked the front door and capped his lamps, and
Red Egan led the way down a short, dirty hall to a back
room facing the alley, a small cubicle heated by a Franklin
stove with an open can of stale water steaming on the top,
giving the air a damp, wet smell. Casey brought one kero-
sene lamp and hung it from the ceiling hook, and placed a
bottle and four glasses on the table. Red Egan sighed and
poured four drinks and said, "Cards on the table, Johnny?"

"Face up," McMahon said. "I'm all ears, Red."

"What can you do?" Red Egan asked bluntly.

"Damn it," Mathews said. "Cut it out, Red."

There was a time to make the bold move, a time to smash all uncertainty and force the play. McMahon took Mathews by his coat front and lifted him roughly from his chair.

"How do you mean that?" he said.

"I mean . . ." Mathews began.

"You remind me of a pimp I knew," McMahon said. "The scum of the earth."

Mathews cried, "You . . ." and struck at McMahon's face with both fists. McMahon moved inward between the forearms and slapped him twice, full and solid blows, and threw him across the room. Mathews hit the wall and dropped limply. McMahon followed, lifted him and slammed him against the wall again, then cuffed his head until it bounced and swiveled loosely. McMahon carried him to the woodbox and dropped him inside and turned to speak without anger. "Never liked runts who wore dude collars and talked too much. I'm all ears, Red."

He had spoken Red Egan's language, not in words but in the brutal action Red understood above all things. He saw the rising admiration in Red's eyes, the envious look of a man who wanted to act this way against all men, and lacked the courage. Red Egan would follow a man like that to bask in reflected glory.

"He's out," Casey said. "Plumb out."

"A sneak," Red Egan said. 'Watch him, Johnny, from now on."

"Then why do you sit with him?" McMahon said.

Red Egan opened both hands, palms up, and moved the thumbs across the palms. "Easy money, Johnny. I don't like him, but a man has to eat."

"Why put up with him?" McMahon said. "If he can't stand the music, why let him dance? What does he know?"

Red Egan said, "How do you mean that, Johnny?"

"I like your style, Red," McMahon said. "Casey will do. But not this pimp. Whatever we cut between us, he's out. I can't trust a man who can't trust me. Finish him and push him through the ice. Kick him out of town. Just don't let him hang around me—you hear?—or I'll do it myself."

"By God!" Red Egan said. "You mean that, don't you?"

"Certainly," McMahon said. "Well . . . ?"

Red Egan glanced at the woodbox and said, "You want some easy money?"

"Bad, Red."

"Then listen to this. There's a spot we can tap any Saturday night."

"For how much?" McMahon asked.

"Not big, not too small. You know Bloom?"

"The store?"

"Yes," Red Egan said. "He stays open Saturday nights, has good business, can't take it to the bank until Monday. I've watched him. The cash is in the back office. An easy job. What do you say?"

McMahon detested them for the niggardly scope of their ability, even in this petty crime, but most of all for their lack of courage. They were unable to think and act big in their own field. He said, "It's penny-ante, but I need quick cash. Three-way split?"

"Three-way," Red Egan said. "Casey will stand lookout."

"One thing," McMahon said softly. "You understand why I'm doing this? Not for a few dollars, understand that now. I want to work with you, judge you, and then I'll show you some real action. Does that sound good?"

"I'm your man," Red Egan said eagerly. "I knew we'd see eye to eye. Now listen . . ."

Sore from his beating by McMahon, George Mathews

walked cautiously through the night's blackness, turning east from Casey's and picking his way toward the river. Reaching the bank he turned south into the first grove of cottonwoods surrounding a large house. He jerked the knotted end of a thin cord that hung from the side door, and let himself into the hallway with his own key. He stepped quickly along the hall to an end door in the rear of the house, tapped gently three times and waited, blowing on his chilled hands and feeling the bruised, puffy marks on his face. The door swung back soundlessly and Ferris Buchanan appeared, holding a lamp, dressed in his knee-length Canton flannel nightgown with a gold brocade robe tied snugly around his middle.

"Come in," Buchanan grumbled. "Too cold for talk out here."

Mathews slipped inside a library walled with books and distorted by misshapen shadows cast from an over-hanging globe of the world and the high backs of stiff chairs placed around a huge walnut desk. He made his own tiny shadow against Buchanan's bulk and shivered with pain and cold.

"I'm freezing," Mathews said. "I need a drink, Ferris."

"So it happened?" Buchanan asked.

"Yes. He jumped the gun, like you said he would when Trumbell pulled in. A drink . . . ?"

"On the desk," Buchanan said. "So McMahon couldn't wait. How did he work it?"

"At Casey's," Mathews said. "He worked on Red and Casey. They're tapping Bloom's till tomorrow night. I tried to steer Red off, just like you said, but you know Red. McMahon gave me a beating, damn him. I'll . . ."

"Forget it," Buchanan said. "At least for the present. So he made his move."

"Sure, and Red's the fool. He'll be bringing McMahon out to meet Timberlake next thing you know."

Buchanan padded noiselessly around the desk and poured brandy and sat in the big leather chair with the tiny glass warming between his hands. His face, roused from sleep, was expressionless and heavily layered with drooping fat, his eyes alone bright and thoughtful, staring beyond Mathews at the wall. He sipped brandy and pushed his nightcap back and off a shining bald head, round and pink and small, the ears set obliquely against this hairless egg, protruding an inch on each side and giving him the appearance of a cast-metal Buddha brought to life.

"They cut you out of the deal?" he asked.

"You wanted it that way," Mathews said. "Didn't you?"

"Good. Now pay attention. To rob Bloom's they'll come down the alley from Casey's and enter the store through that back door. Can you throw a knife from my warehouse window across the alley?"

Mathews leaned forward, smiling a ferret's sly joy. "Twice that far, Ferris."

"It's twelve feet. Are you sure?"

"I'll show you tomorrow if you want."

"All right," Buchanan said. "Now, Casey will be lookout, of course."

"Yes. Up the alley by Jensen's livery barn."

"Let them go inside. When they come out, you get McMahon. Leave the small door open on the river side of the warehouse. Make your throw and get away, lock the door, and run for the river. Put your horse in my barn after dark. Come up the river under the bank, get your horse, and ride straight to Timberlake. Can you do that in three minutes' time?"

"Easy, Ferris. But listen, I can do it a better way. Some people in town know I throw a knife. But we know fifty men who ice fish and use a fish spear. Let me use a fish spear. I can't miss, even in the dark. Think what a fish spear'll do to him, Ferris!"

Buchanan laughed softly, almost benevolently. "You're a cold-blooded devil, George. Very well, use a fish spear. It is the best, and safest. Don't worry about Egan and Casey.

They'll run like scared rabbits when McMahon drops. Now, you stay at Timberlake's a week, then send Sid in for a report before you come back to town. Understand?"

"All right," Mathews said. "Good night, Ferris."

Buchanan watched him go and sat motionless until the tiny bell tinkled in the library as the outside porch door opened, closed, and locked itself from within. He sat lumpily at the desk and scowled upon his hands, considering the swift change in his plans, weighing the danger and chance of exposure, and finding himself satisfied on all counts. He had grown to respect McMahon as a fearless and intelligent man who planned well and waited for the proper time; now he visualized Trumbell upsetting that timetable and forcing McMahon to act prematurely. Buchanan wished it was possible to tell McMahon how he had been used, how those papers were important for reasons Trumbell would never explain until the right time. Trumbell had planned exceedingly well, but those papers had been his weak point, and through their possession had come all Buchanan needed to know.

He thought of spring, two months distant, and Trumbell's plan for the branch line railroad that would leap suddenly sixty miles north of Warbonnet across the Willow Gap into the open country beyond. Three years ago the railroad had built the branch north from the main line to Warbonnet and stopped. The valley north for twenty miles was rich black farm land, lying deep over porous sub-soil just being developed, and the railroad had figured rightly that wagon roads would bring all produce south to Warbonnet for shipping, thus saving the expense of extending the branch line. Trumbell was a major stockholder in the railroad, and it was not accidental when construction stopped at Warbonnet. For three years Trumbell had been purchasing, through agents, a right of way north from Warbonnet, twenty miles up the valley to the Willow Gap, over the Gap, and twenty-five miles beyond into the plateau country. There was the real fortune for the taking, lying dormant now, needing only a railroad to open it wide.

At this moment Trumbell lacked only a mile stretch belonging to Fletcher, who owned the section of farm land lying just below the southern entrance to the Gap. Fletcher would not sell; at least, he had not showed any disposition to sell so far. Ferris Buchanan had gathered these facts a year ago in his own way, had sent Mathews to St. Louis for proof, and Mathews had brought that proof—all the titles to the right-of-way land. Mathews had made friends with the bookkeeper, and tried to get into Trumbell's offices by trickery; failing that, with time running short, he had knifed the bookkeeper, found the papers, and returned to Warbonnet immediately.

When Buchanan studied the titles to the right-of-way land, he had chuckled joyously for a week. He had every reason to laugh. Trumbell's agents had paid top prices for post-dated bills of sale and titles to the right of way, and paid each farmer more to keep the secret until Trumbell had a through route and was ready to start construction. There was no record of the sales in the county courthouse of Warbonnet County; hence the sales were null and void unless Trumbell could produce the titles.

Buchanan had thereupon acted swiftly, buying a dozen quarters of land from farmers anxious to sell and return east; the quarters lay end to end, from west to east, across the valley, ten miles north of Warbonnet; and the key quarter bordering the river was the one from which the former owner had sold Trumbell's agent a through strip of land from south to north, three hundred feet wide and the full quarter mile long. That man had sold out after Timberlake and several others paid him a midnight visit; now Buchanan owned the land and had the title and bill of sale from the previous sale, and Trumbell was completely blocked across the valley on the west side of the river. He could not build on the east bank; there the bluffs came down abruptly and made construction impossible.

Sitting at his desk, Buchanan smiled at his empty glass, recalling the past the the manner in which he had discovered this potential bonanza. Three years ago he had foreseen the wisdom of building an independent line north through the Willow Gap. Such a project was beyond his own financial capacity, but not beyond his desire and ability. Now he held the aces in a tremendous pot; now Trumbell would eventually be forced to meet his demands when he showed his cards. And when he did—Buchanan smiled again—he would cut Buchanan in for a generous share of the profits with none of the risk, or do without the railroad and the millions waiting to be taken. And Fletcher remained at the foot of the Gap, unwilling to sell. That would be the biggest talking point. Buchanan could force that sale, but Trumbell couldn't; and once Fletcher sold right of way, the road was open.

Walking daintily, Buchanan crossed to his bedroom and trimmed the lamp wick to a tiny, bright glow. He could not sleep in total darkness, and this very real fear was the only human weakness he admitted to his secret conscience. He adjusted his nightcap, removed the robe and crawled ponderously into bed. Tomorrow would be a busy day. Trumbell was certain to call at the bank. That night McMahon would leave the picture, which was now developing rapidly into a full-blown portrait Buchanan loved with all the fervor of an artist preparing final colors and limbering brushes for the last-minute strokes.

McMahon entered Abe Bloom's store late the next afternoon and pawed over woolen work shirts and thick-knitted boot socks while Abe waited on a customer, wrote the sale in his day book, and looked up sharply. "We're alone."

"Listen," McMahon said casually. "Leave three hundred in your cash box tonight. No more. It'll be gone Sunday morning. Where do you keep it?"

"Behind the desk in the back office," Abe Bloom said. "What . . . ?"

"Close up at nine tonight," McMahon said. "No later. I'm baiting a trap, Abe. You'll have to help. You'll get the three hundred back."

"Can you tell me more about this?" Abe Bloom asked.

"Not now. Later tonight. If I can't make it, Chambers will come. He knows the deal."

McMahon paid for the shirt he had selected, smiled at Abe Bloom's worried face, and stepped into the street, pausing to glance at the sky. Another storm, he thought, about twelve hours north. He saw Trumbell, his daughter, and Mason come from the hotel and move cautiously along the warped plank sidewalk to the bank building on the corner. He saw Buchanan appear in the big front window, nod in greeting, shake hands suddenly with a broad smile, and lead all three into his private office. Trumbell was showing common sense; nothing could be more logical than visiting the local banker on supposed business. McMahon crossed to the hotel and entered the lobby with a following wind that curled his hat brim and blew powdery snow from swinging door to desk.

Will Overton was talking with a stocky man and a slender boy in the warm alcove behind the big stove. Not until he reached the stairs did McMahon see the fair blond hair beneath the home-made raccoon fur cap and note the subtle difference in the boy's form. Will Overton looked up and smiled.

"Snowing, Johnny?"

"Not yet," McMahon said. "Storm's coming."

"Say," Will Overton said. "Meet Sam Fletcher and his daughter. Sam, Mary, this is John McMahon."

"Happy to know you," McMahon said.

Fletcher's handshake was firm and sharp, and the girl's

equally solid. He remembered the night before when Trumbell's daughter offered no more than a nod and a reserved smile. The girl was still brown from past summer sun, pleasant and quiet, thoroughly comfortable in her boy's winter clothing and heavy boots. Her father appeared to be the typical frontier farmer dressed up for town.

"Storm coming," McMahon said. "Which way do you live?"

"North," Fletcher said. "It'll wait for us."

McMahon smiled. "How long?"

"Twelve hours."

"I say ten before it hits town," McMahon said. "I would make a small bet."

They laughed together, easily, and Fletcher lit a cigar. "Maybe you're right, McMahon. Give me time and I'll think of a good bet."

McMahon rarely met the counterpart of this man. Fletcher was realistic and plainly a hard worker, yet the owner of a great appetite for living that showed in his eyes; and behind this love for life was humor, a bubbling well of laughter that showed in the girl's face when she moved too near the stove and jumped forward with a little yell. McMahon was ashamed to meet them posing as a drifting loafer, drinking away the winter while they bucked snow on some homestead miles to the north.

"I was just telling Sam," Will Overton said, "that you might stick around in the spring. Sam says he can use a good man then."

"Doing what?" McMahon asked.

"What can you do?" Sam Fletcher asked.

"A little of everything," McMahon said.

The girl was studying him as he spoke, judging his face, his clothing, his speech, reaching some decision but reserving any final appraisal. Fletcher said, "You know farm work?"

"Fair," McMahon said. "How big is your place?"

"Section," Fletcher said. "Twenty miles north at the foot of the Gap."

"Prettiest farm in the valley," Will Overton said. "And one of the best." Will Overton glanced shyly at Mary Fletcher and added, "And the best cooking I know."

"I better explain," Fletcher said patiently. "We run a few cows, but the land is too good for that. I'm figuring on breaking more ground this spring for crops. If you want to start right now, there's enough to do before spring."

"Not yet," McMahon said. "But I'll sure keep your offer in mind."

He nodded to the girl, wondering if she cared for Will Overton and saw pity and resentment in her smile. Going upstairs, dozing through the remainder of the afternoon and early evening, McMahon thought of her and was ashamed. How many times had this happened to him, he remembered bitterly, how often had good people met him while he played a role. Sighing, he turned over and eventually slept.

The wind was strong and bitter cold at midnight. Red Egan shivered and blew on his hands, dressed inadequately for the night's work in a thin poplin jacket, slouch hat, and wearing leather gloves that chilled rather than warmed his fingers. They had walked from Casey's back door, down the alley, and stood in the shadow of Jensen's livery barn some fifty yards north of Abe Bloom's. Red Egan flexed his thumbs and whispered, "Casey stands lookout here. All ready, Johnny?"

"You're half froze," McMahon said. "You can't work like that. I told you to get more clothes."

"I like to be loose," Red Egan said. "But it is cold. Maybe I ought to run back and get my mackinaw and mittens."

"No time," McMahon said curtly. "From now on, think before you leap. Here, put my coat and cap on. I want no fumbling on this job."

"No," Red Egan said. "That ain't right, Johnny."

"Shut up," McMahon said. "Get 'em on."

He shucked off his mackinaw and fur cap and forced them on Red Egan, boosting the coat high on the skinny shoulders and pushing the cap well down over Red's big ears. He murmured then, with a streak of perverse humor, "Fits you like a glove, Red."

Red Egan chuckled softly and hunched himself comfortably within the mackinaw. McMahon placed Red's light hat on his own head and grinned.

"Time to move," McMahon said. "You certain that key will fit?"

"Fit?" Casey replied. "Red's got a key for every lock in town. Get on with it. Now I'm getting cold."

"Under that blubber?" Red Egan snorted, "Come on, Johnny."

Warbonnet was sleeping soundly at midnight. Egan followed a well-learned path between garbage cans and boxes frozen drunkenly in the manure-stained snow. They reached Abe Bloom's back door and huddled together over the lock. McMahon glanced across the alley at the dark bulk of Buchanan's warehouse which cut off all wind from the river, standing black and rectangular, some thirty feet long on the alley and a full two stories high. McMahon wondered why Egan had not suggested looting the warehouse; it was sure to hold more quick profit than a dozen petty cash boxes. He was reflecting on this short-sightedness of Red's when Egan whispered, "Come on."

McMahon followed him into the small office that smelled of fresh cloves and good cigar smoke. Red Egan closed the door and ran quick fingers over the window shade before lighting a short candle, shading the flame with both hands.

"Get at it, Johnny," Red Egan said. "I'll hold the light."

McMahon searched the office thoroughly, spending five minutes on drawers and cabinets before pulling the roll-

top desk out and discovering the small cubby-hole in the
wall. He lifted the cash box to the desk and counted the
money.

"How much?" Red Egan murmured greedily.

"Around three hundred," McMahon said. "Pinch the
candle."

He replaced the empty cash box, pushed the desk against
the wall, and crossed to the door. Red Egan snuffed the
candle and said, "Easy now, Johnny," and opened the door
wide enough for one man to slip through. McMahon said,
"Go on," and followed him outside on the single step and
dropped off into the packed snow on the north side,
crouching against the wall while Red Egan closed the door
and turned his greased key in the lock.

"Told you it was easy," Egan said.

"Why not?" McMahon murmured. "What's hard for
two good men?"

Egan laughed deep in his throat and said, "An easy way
to make a living," and suddenly expelled his breath in an
agonized, choking cry and dropped heavily on the step.

McMahon heard the swishing sound as Red Egan spoke,
then cried out, and was three steps away from the door
with drawn gun before Red fell. McMahon reached for
the body and felt the long shaft of a fish spear and ran
straight across the alley against the warehouse wall and located what had to be there—a window set high in the wall,
directly opposite Abe Bloom's back door. McMahon
turned up the alley at a full run, rounded the corner of the
warehouse, and moved with decreasing speed and more
caution toward the northeast corner facing the river.
Rounding this corner slowly, McMahon found the door
twenty feet south closed and locked. The river bank was
some forty feet from the warehouse, with a narrow, well-
tramped path leading from the back door to the bank, and
down the steep bluff to the river's edge and the snow-covered ice. McMahon turned to the door, removed one mit-

ten and ran his bare hand along the crack between door and casing. The wind was blowing against this door, throwing a fine snow dust into all cracks, but the long, thin line between the door and the casing was clean. McMahon swore quickly and ran around the warehouse, thinking now of Red Egan and Mathews and Casey, but mostly of Mathews. His man, whoever he was, had thrown the fish spear and gotten away by a minute's scant safety, but a minute was enough in darkness along the river. McMahon came into the alley and knelt beside Red Egan. The warehouse was pitch black and the wind was rising. Egan was dead. McMahon drew the key from the lock, lifted the body, and ran up the alley until Casey asked, "What . . . ?" and stepped timidly from the livery barn shadow.

"Hold him," McMahon said harshly.

"Red!" Casey said. "Who . . . ?"

"Fish spear," McMahon said. "From the warehouse."

Talking, he stripped his fur cap from Red Egan's head, shoved Red's hat into Casey's coat pocket, and said, "Get the body out of sight. Hide that spear. Burn my mackinaw. No good with that hole in the back. I'll see you tomorrow night if I can."

This was too much for Casey, already reduced to a mass of quivering, fearful fat. Casey said, "I never bargained for nothing like this. I don't . . ."

"Shut up!" McMahon said. "It's a two-way split now. I'll bring yours tomorrow night. Get going, man!"

Casey said, "You think it was Mathews?"

"I think nothing," McMahon said. "Go about your business and keep your mouth closed. Anybody asks for Red, tell them he took a trip. And you damned well better hide the body good. Now move!"

Three

ANGRY QUESTIONS were crowding his mind as he came from the alley and stood on the warped sidewalk beside the cubbyhole office of Jensen's livery barn. He had forced this game and played for a break, expecting a long, thankless job of robbing cash boxes and rolling drunks with Red Egan, in the hope that Red would eventually lead him to someone who gave the orders in this town; and by the grace of God, the exchange of a mackinaw and cap, he was alive and slowly fitting together the misfit parts of a crazy quilt. McMahon wondered about Mathews and entered the smelly, overheated office. He called, "Tom, you asleep?"

The night man burrowed instinctively away from the voice, grunting thickly and speaking from the bunk depths, "Go 'way."

"Wake up, Tom," McMahon said. "This is McMahon."

The night man turned reluctantly. "What you want, Johnny?"

"Does George Mathews own a horse?" McMahon asked.

"Sure. Keeps it here. Say, Johnny, got a little snort on you?"

McMahon found a chair beside the stove and straddled it, reached into his back pocket for the bottle and passed it wordlessly to Tom, who drank deeply and coughed with agonized pleasure.

"Hits the spot," Tom said. "Thanks, Johnny."

"That horse in the barn?" McMahon said.

"He took it after supper," Abe said. "Told me he was going on a little trip. Why?"

"Between us," McMahon said softly, "he took me in a game two nights back. I just found out how he took me."

"I'll be damned!" Tom said. "Nobody ever complained, but I always figured him that way."

31

"I've been hunting him all night," McMahon said. "I want my money back. Where did he go, Tom?"

"Well . ..." Tom said hesitantly.

"Don't worry," McMahon said. "This is between us, Tom. I'll make it worth your while."

"I never meant that," Tom said. "You know Roy Timberlake?"

"No."

"Him and Mathews are good friends," Tom said. "Timberlake owns a spread in the hills, way to hell and gone in the wild country. To get there, you head north to the Gap, turn west at Fletcher's and it's about twenty miles. George didn't say where he was goin', but nine out of ten it's up there."

"Thanks, Tom," McMahon said. He pushed a gold piece under the pillow and stepped to the door. "I won't say a word."

He heard Tom's fingers rustle, moving under the pillow and feeling the coin. Tom said, "Many thanks, Johnny. Sure hope you get that money back. I'll forget I saw you tonight."

McMahon said, "Do that," and walked south toward the hotel, thinking of Mathews and his horse. Mathews had taken the horse six hours before Red Egan was killed. The horse couldn't stand outside that long in this weather; therefore Mathews had access to a private barn somewhere near the warehouse and close to the river. That fact could mean everything or nothing, depending on who owned the barn; it was one of the puzzle's odd pieces to be fitted into the pattern. McMahon considered his next move and barely remembered his own role as he entered the lobby. He walked unsteadily toward the stairs and grinned sleepily at Will Overton who looked up from the barrel chair behind the big pot-bellied stove in the alcove. Will was reading and smoking a cigar, lost in the story and looking pleased with himself. McMahon remembered Mary Fletcher and said, "Storm coming, Will."

"Bad one," Will Overton said, "from the sound."

"The Fletchers start home?" McMahon asked.

"Yes. They'll make it in time."

"Nice people," McMahon said. "Good night, Will."

He climbed the stairs and went down the dark hallway and tapped softly on Chambers' door; moments later it swung back and Chambers murmured, "Come in, John."

"Trouble," McMahon said. "Light a candle."

Chambers fumbled beside the bed and lit a stubby candle, dripped wax on the floor and stuck the candle upright between their feet, the flame showing his round, apple-cheeked face huddled into the top folds of his blankets as he sat cross-legged on the bed and said, "So soon?"

"Have you played cat," McMahon said, "and discovered you were the mouse all the time?"

Chambers said quickly, "Someone knows you!"

"Yes. You knew tonight's game. Luck saved me. Egan was cold and I gave him my mackinaw and fur cap. I wore his hat. Somebody threw a fish spear into him from the warehouse window across the alley. Egan's dead!"

"Mathews," Chambers said. "It has to be him."

"Yes," McMahon said. "I tried to get him, but he ran through the warehouse and down to the river. Trailing him in this storm is foolishness. But I stopped at the livery barn. Mathews keeps a horse there. He took it at six tonight, told the night man he was going on a trip. The night man says he goes north to a place owned by Timberlake. There's our second name to remember. What does this mean to you?"

"Two alternatives," Chambers said shrewdly. "He tried to kill you for that beating, or someone in this town knows your real identity and Mathews is working for him. Naturally, if that is true, killing you was the logical step. Either way we've got to find Mathews. When do we start?"

"Wait here," McMahon said. "I want to search Mathews' house.

"And then?"

"Abe Bloom expects us. We need him now. He's got to gather information from his friends. I'll take an hour."

"Be careful," Chambers said. "I'll dress and be ready."

McMahon nodded and stepped quietly into the hall and turned to the back stairs. A door opened suddenly and room light made its rectangular yellow shape across the hall, placing his body from the waist down in full view. He stepped into the wall shadow and saw Alice Trumbell in the doorway, dressed in a long blue quilted robe, her hair undone and falling thickly about her shoulders, her face touched with that odd, deeply hidden laughter he had noticed the night before.

"Good evening, Mr. McMahon," she said. "You're up late."

"You are, Miss Trumbell," McMahon said.

"I'm bored," Alice Trumbell said. "This town is sickening. Are you about your business?"

McMahon said, "Yes," and glanced toward the front stairs, wondering how many people were standing behind doors, listening to the woman talk. Faintly, across the hall, came the scent of her perfume mingled with the odor of brandy. He formed a clearer picture of her life and past.

"Your own?" she said. "Or my father's?"

"You'd better go to bed," McMahon said quietly. "It's drafty in the hall."

"Wait," she said. "You don't like Mr. Mason, do you?"

"I have no feeling for men I don't know," McMahon said.

She laughed softly. "He dislikes you quite heartily. For the oddest reason."

"Very well," McMahon said. "You want me to ask. What reason, Miss Trumbell?"

"That you are interested in me."

"I've seen you twice," McMahon said. "The man's a fool."

"Three times," Alice Trumbell said. "And don't call Paul a fool. He isn't, really. I may marry him."

"My apologies," McMahon said stiffly, "but marriage doesn't make a man less the fool he was before. Good night."

"I may," she called after him. "And I may not."

"Your business," McMahon said.

Her voice followed him. "I told him you were not interested, Mr. McMahon. Perhaps I was correct."

Alice Trumbell watched him dip from sight down the back stairs and wanted to swear aloud in a fashion unbefitting any lady. She regretted coming with her father and Paul Mason on this trip into the virtual heart of nowhere. She had grown weary of Paul's attention in the past three months, knowing the man much too well for marriage and equally well in other respects. In his own way, Paul was an excellent partner for her. He enjoyed the benefits of wealth but hated the thought of working for those innumerable assets. Like herself, he drank too much. A pretty face pulled him away from her at intervals, just as a handsome face drew her attention; and McMahon, in her judgment, was the strongest man she had met in years. Unable to sleep tonight, she remembered the room clerk, Will Overton, and her memory of his thin, composed face turned her to the front stairs. Lacking other companionship, she thought, a little fun with Overton would pass an otherwise dull stay. She took the stairs carefully, came to the foot and smiled at Overton. "You must be lonely at night, Mr. Overton. Are you?"

Will Overton looked up and flushed. "No, Miss Trumbell. I read. I can always find enjoyment in a good book."

"You amuse me," she said. "Would you rather read a book than talk with me?"

"You're very kind," Will Overton said. "Of course I'd rather talk with you, Miss Trumbell."

She moved into the alcove behind the stove and sat on the padded seat. She said, "Then talk. I'm going crazy in this miserable town. Nothing to do, no one to talk with."

"Your father," Will Overton said awkwardly. "And Mr. Mason . . ."

"Sit down," she said curtly. "Tell me about yourself."

"Now you're joking," Will Overton said. "What could a hotel clerk tell you, Miss Trumbell?"

"Certainly I'm joking," she said. "But I know nothing about hotel clerks. Perhaps I want to know. Tell me, do you intend being a clerk all your life?"

"No," Will Overton said. "I . . ."

"Then you do want something else," she said. "Don't we all? Come sit down. What's your first name? Will, isn't it? I like you, Will, especially now when you blush. I can't seem to blush. Tell me about your girl, Will. Perhaps that will make me blush."

Sitting beside her, Will Overton smelled the brandy and did not want to talk with her. This kind of talk and the insinuation behind her words gave him a feeling of threadbare cheapness, but an awareness of his own duty as a clerk toward a guest turned him from the desk to the alcove. He wondered if she had set her cap for anyone else in town. McMahon would be a good-looking man if he cleaned up and stopped drinking. Thinking in this way and glancing at the clock, Will Overton began talking easily about the life of a hotel clerk.

Stepping into the alley, McMahon had a clearer picture of Trumbell's daughter. She was bored and she looked for amusement in this town, in the hotel, but most of all in a man like himself. He thought of her briefly as he ran through the alley and away from the town into the bare trees bordering the river. He passed a row of nine identical shacks thrown up by the railroad for construction workers three years ago and stopped behind a tree some twenty paces from the last shack in line. The wind was loud and wild, covering all natural sound. McMahon walked boldly to the back door and lifted the latch. McMahon drew his gun and entered the shack, found the faint outline of the bunk against the south wall, and crossed the room in two long steps. His closed fist struck the pillow. The bed was empty and cold. McMahon lit a match and found the lantern, lit it, and closed the door.

The shack's interior was one rough, unfinished room filled with chairs, boxes, the bunk, stove, cupboard and a dirty rug beside the table. The fire was cold and the cupboard shelf littered with unwashed dishes and scraps of food. A tobacco jar, lid half off, stood in the center of the table. McMahon studied this dusty, stale-smelling room, forming additional facts about Mathews, filling out the mean, sharp character of the man, and then began his search for the object he hoped to find. He covered the room completely in five minutes, finding nothing of value.

In building these shacks the railroad had used flat rock for foundation piers and upon these rocks placed defective ties as sills. But the floors were badly fitted and wind swept beneath the raised sills and into the room; against this construction McMahon remembered that the men had banked earth around the outside foundation to cut off the wind. This shack was no exception; the floor was cracked and pocked with knotholes, but not drafty. That meant the earth had set and possibly grassed over, forming a quasi-cellar some two feet deep below the floor.

McMahon pulled the bunk from the wall and saw the floor boards cut neatly, fitted tightly in place, but loose to the touch. He lifted six and, lowering the lantern, he saw the valuable property of a man who believed in nothing and trusted no one. Stacked along the inner wall of banked earth, McMahon saw cases of whisky, canoe paddles, fish spears, nets, empty bottles, stone crocks and jugs, bundles of clothing, rifles and shotguns sealed in leather cases. He dropped through the hole and crawled along the south sill, looking for a square object that would certainly be wrapped carefully in a protective covering. In the southwest corner, hidden behind a stack of whisky cases, was the oilcloth-wrapped bundle, the key to a puzzle he had sought through long, unlucky weeks. When he removed the oilcloth and looked down on the little trunk, he wanted to dance a jig.

McMahon selected a small box, wrapped it carefully in the oilcloth, and replaced this behind the whisky cases. He backed toward the hole, erasing his knee and hand prints with a sack, and lifted himself through the hole into the room, sweating lightly despite the cold. He moved swiftly now, replacing the boards, pushing the bunk against the wall, smoothing the pillow and smothering the lantern flame. He stepped outside and closed the door and ran for town, the trunk a comfortable weight under his right arm. When he knocked on Chambers' door and entered the room, Chambers smiled broadly.

"Trumbell's trunk!"

"Mathews is vain," McMahon said. "He's vicious and dangerous, but one small part of him is a fool, a vain fool. He saves everything he can steal, beg, or borrow. He's got a trap door in the floor under his bunk—you know how those shacks are built—and underneath you can't move for hitting something. We know why he kept the trunk now. Mathews is our man, but someone is giving him orders. Trumbell's bookkeeper was killed with a knife. Red Egan got a fish spear in the back. Mathews is good with a knife. I saw a dozen spears under the floor in his shack. And the trunk, which proves everything. Mathews went to St. Louis, did his job, but he couldn't part with this trunk. He did a foolish thing. He brought it home, hid it, gave the papers to his boss and said nothing about the trunk. If his boss, whoever the man is, knew this, we would have the pleasure of seeing Mathews lying in the snow within minutes after the fact was told."

"What about this trunk?" Chambers asked.

"Take it to Abe Bloom's house tonight," McMahon said.

"And Trumbell? Do we tell him?"

"Not yet," McMahon said. "I'm riding north in twenty minutes. Red Egan is dead and Casey too frightened to give me away for a week. I'll take a chance on finding Mathews while I have the time. Our man, in town, will think I'm done for. He won't know for a few days. That gives us time to get Mathews. Now listen carefully. I want Abe to dig up some information for us. Tell him to get everything known about Mathews and Timberlake, and anyone who hangs around them."

"Very well," Chambers said. "If you get Mathews, where will you take him?"

"I'll bring him to town," McMahon said. "Abe will have to provide the house until I fill out the warrant and wire the United States marshal. No use asking this town marshal or county sheriff. We'll play it safe."

"I don't like the smell of this case," Chambers said softly. "Trumbell lied to us, John. Those papers mean a great deal more than he admitted. Someone in this town has them. Trumbell needs them to complete a deal here or nearby. We can assume that now, having found the trunk. That person is waiting for Trumbell to tip his hand. We're in the middle. I'm wiring the Colonel tomorrow morning. Whatever Trumbell paid the Colonel, it's far too little for the risk involved. That brings us to the most important point: when do we have our showdown with Trumbell?"

"After I get Mathews," McMahon said. "We'll know what this is about then. Now I'm on my way. Get out to Abe's within an hour with the trunk. Keep things moving here."

"Certain you don't need me?" Chambers asked hopefully.

"In this weather?" McMahon smiled. "One man is bad enough; two would leave a plain trail. Expect me back within five days."

"If not?"

"I'll send a message. If you hear nothing, take over."

"Very well," Chambers said quietly. "Good luck."

McMahon went to his room and stripped to the skin, sponged himself hurriedly, and dressed in clean clothing from long underwear out to a heavy scarf and his spare mackinaw. Stuffing tobacco and cigarette papers in one pocket, he heard the tiny sound of Chambers moving to the back stairs. McMahon snuffed the lamp and followed Chambers after a five-minute wait. He walked to the livery barn in a roundabout way and woke Tom from a noisy sleep. McMahon said, "Listen, Tom. I'm going after that rat tonight. I'll take a horse from the barn, pay on return. If anyone asks about me, you haven't seen me. I'm dead so far as you know. Understand?"

"You bet," Tom said. "I never saw you tonight, Johnny."

"I'll make it right when I get back," McMahon said. "Lie still, Tom. I'll pick my horse."

Mason woke and lay five minutes, staring narrowly across the room, remembering the previous afternoon in Buchanan's private office. That meeting had been the exact duplicate of a hundred others in which Trumbell did all the talking and made it painfully apparent that Mason was his lawyer, a good man in his place, but lacking Trumbell's ability. Mason dressed quickly and hurried downstairs to the lobby's dubious warmth. Will Overton was just off duty and smoking an after-breakfast cigar when he passed the alcove.

"If Mr. Trumbell asks for me," Mason said, "will you tell him I ate early breakfast and went for a walk?"

"Glad to," Will Overton said. "The ham is excellent this morning, Mr. Mason."

"Thank you," Mason said, and moved directly into the

dining room, ate a hurried breakfast, and stepped onto Front Street, shivering beneath his heavy overcoat. His feeling this morning was sharply divided between a long-nurtured hatred for Trumbell and an equally sharp desire for Alice Trumbell. He had worked like a dog four years ago building an entirely new personality and past for himself to secure his position with Trumbell after meeting the daughter at a party. Through the girl would come the power and wealth of the father, but thus far he had seemingly wasted four years. Alice would not promise or set a date. His patience had finally ended on this trip and then, nearly ready to call the game quits, good luck had happened with unexpected suddenness. Today he would do something about his immediate future. Marshaling his courage and reviewing certain past events in New Orleans, Mason walked firmly along the sidewalk to the bank. Stepping into the main room he saw Ferris Buchanan talking with the cashier. Buchanan smiled broadly and called, "Good morning, Mr. Mason. What can I do for you?"

"Busy?" Mason asked.

"Never too busy," Buchanan said. "Come inside."

Mason followed him into the private office, a large room furnished in surprisingly good taste for this wild frontier country. Buchanan settled his bulk behind a walnut desk, passed the cigar humidor, and supplied the match. Mason smoked in pleasant silence for a moment and then leaned forward in his chair.

"We had little chance to talk yesterday," he said.

"True enough," Buchanan smiled. "Mr. Trumbell is a forceful man when he takes the bit in his teeth."

"Yes," Mason said dryly. "He enjoys talking."

Buchanan rested fleshy elbows on the desk and built an arch of pink, fat fingers, the cigar glowing brightly between them. "And what brought you here this morning, Mr. Mason?"

"Pure chance," Mason said. "Call it luck."

"I don't follow you, sir," Buchanan smiled.

Mason took the final step. "A little talk, Mr. Buchanan, is what I came for. I feel that I've known you before."

"Entirely possible," Buchanan said cheerfully. "I've been here five years. Perhaps you saw me in Chicago?"

"No," Mason said. "It was in New Orleans. Six years ago."

Buchanan's round, fat face did not move or change; it remained pleasant and half-sleepy with comfortable warmth. Only the eyes studied Mason with new interest. Buchanan said, "Quite possible. Were you engaged in business there?"

"Of a sort," Mason said evenly.

"And since then?"

"I've been with Mr. Trumbell three years," Mason said. "I'm his right-hand man, so to speak."

"A responsible position," Buchanan said. "I guessed as much yesterday"—the eyes twinkled with humor—"although Mr. Trumbell neglected to say so."

"You remember his conversation of yesterday?" Mason said.

"Indeed I do," Buchanan said. "He seems eager to purchase farm land in the valley north of here. As I told him, I'll be delighted to act as agent. I can purchase some rich ground for him, ideally suited to his purpose."

"Did you actually believe his story?" Mason asked.

Buchanan laughed soundlessly. "Confidentially, Mr. Mason, I did not."

"We're alone here?"

"Completely. The walls are a foot thick."

"Then I'll talk frankly," Mason said. "Are you interested in making a great deal of money?"

"Money is always a great help, Mr. Mason. However, its making depends on the method."

"Strange to hear you say that," Mason said softly. "So . . ."

"I was thinking of a river steamer," Mason said. "The *Frankfort Belle*. And a stock company formed to sell shares in a Texas land deal. The method did not matter then, as I recall."

Buchanan dropped his hands and the cigar ashes spilled unnoticed across the polished desk top. "We will assume I heard nothing just now. It would be much better for all concerned. Now, what is this about a great deal of money?"

"Then we understand each other?"

"Quite thoroughly, Mr. Mason."

Mason found himself sweating beneath his coat. He spoke quickly. "What happened six years ago is of no importance to me, Mr. Buchanan. What can happen three months from now is vitally important. What would it be worth to know the real reason for Mr. Trumbell's visit to this charming town in the dead of winter?"

Buchanan spoke without changing his voice. "You're a faithful rascal, Mr. Mason. It depends on Mr. Trumbell's real reason, of course. I take it you are willing to sell out your employer for a price?"

"You take it correctly," Mason said. "Are you interested?"

"In a legitimate business deal? Indeed I am."

"This is legitimate," Mason said. "I imagine you'd like to know why I'm here, offering to sell Mr. Trumbell out?"

"I can guess," Buchanan said. "You're tired of playing second fiddle. Then too, his daughter must enter into this."

"We'll not discuss her," Mason said curtly.

"Very well. Could you give me a clue to this business?"

Mason smiled. "Come now, Mr. Buchanan. Does a man let a million slip out for all the world to hear and profit from? Shall we come to an understanding, then talk?"

Buchanan seemed to be enjoying himself immensely. The fat hands toyed with the cigar, and the bald head nodded affably. "How do I know Trumbell hasn't sent you here to trick me?"

"You don't. That's the chance you take. How do I know you won't tell him about my visit? I take that chance. Cards up, Buchanan. I know you. The name is different but the face is the same. Let's get down to brass tacks. We can make a million apiece, with little risk, if you'll agree to the split."

"Fifty-fifty, Mr. Mason."

"Exactly."

"I furnish the capital," Buchanan said dryly. "You furnish the tip. My capital does the necessary work, takes the chances. And you want a fifty-fifty split? I can't hear you, Mr. Mason."

"What can you hear?"

Buchanan opened a desk drawer and riffled bills between his fingers. "Here is five thousand dollars, Mr. Mason. A considerable sum of money. I can hear five thousand now and thirty per cent of all net profits. Can you hear me?"

Mason saw the money and remembered his own salary of five thousand a year. He thought of the months ahead, the money waiting to be made, and most of all, the freedom from a position he hated with a man he hated even more. He said, "I hear you."

Buchanan tossed the bundle of bills across the desk and said tonelessly, "Talk, Mason. You've made a deal."

Mason placed the bills carefully in an inner coat pocket, puffed his cigar slowly, and leaned forward on the desk. "Go back several years," Mason said. "The railroad built the branch line north to Warbonnet. There was some talk about continuing the branch north through the valley to the Gap and beyond into that plateau country. But nothing came of this."

"True," Buchanan said gently.

"Trumbell was a majority stockholder in the railroad at that time. As such, he voted to build the branch to Warbonnet. He also made an unpublicized trip here and examined the valley and the Gap and the plateau country.

What he saw made him go home like a cat running on a hot stove and immediately veto all plans for continuing the branch. Now why should he do so?"

"You are asking me?" Buchanan said.

"I wonder if you've had your eyes open?" Mason asked.

"Perhaps," Buchanan said. "Go on."

"Very well. Trumbell then sold his stock in the company. He did this two years ago. Since then he has planned toward a project which will be the climax of his business career to date. And let me warn you, Buchanan, don't underestimate him. He's filthy rich. He's smart and tough and ruthless. He planned for this deal and has taken his time. That alone shows his caliber. Other men would rush in, try to do everything in a hurry, fearing that someone else would spot the opportunity and beat them to the draw. Not Trumbell. Everything was going smoothly until three months ago."

"The best plans go awry," Buchanan said. "Don't tell me he went broke."

"Certainly not," Mason said impatiently. "A sneak thief murdered his bookkeeper, robbed his offices, and took valuable papers pertaining to this deal." Mason paused and studied Buchanan thoughtfully. "It has puzzled me ever since, the theft of those papers."

"Get to the point!"

"So you're interested," Mason said. "I thought you would be. The point is a continuing of the branch through the valley, over the Gap, into the plateau country. Not a continuation in the sense of the word, but a privately owned railroad serving an entirely untapped, fertile section of rich farm land."

"Five thousand for this," Buchanan said. "What can I do about it, Mason? Ask Trumbell to cut me in? You're a fool."

"Wait. To build his road Trumbell must buy right of way north from this town."

"I imagine," Buchanan said dryly, "he can afford to do so."

"If he can buy it," Mason said eagerly. "Don't you get it, man? He can buy right of way from here to the north pole, but what happens if he cannot buy just one small piece somewhere along the projected line?"

Buchanan said, "You have a point. When does he plan to start construction?"

"This spring. But there's the catch. Those papers must be found. And listen, Buchanan. Trumbell has detectives trailing that thief. They've traced him here to Warbonnet. They . . ."

"Detectives?" Buchanan asked mildly.

"Yes. Sloane's agency. Sloane's best man-hunter, Mc-Mahon, and now another one, Chambers."

"Sit back," Buchanan said evenly. "We can strike a deal, Mason. Now I want to know everything about this, from the beginning. How much time can you spare?"

"Half an hour more," Mason said, glancing at the wall clock. "They'll be up then. I can tell you everything in half an hour. We can get together later to elaborate. Now, about those papers . . ."

Four

McMAHON PICKED a bay gelding from Jensen's stock and rode north into the storm. He followed the wagon road that paralleled the river's gently winding course, riding through a completely white and horizonless world bounded by the high bluffs and frozen river on the east and the rolling, drift-blocked valley that lifted upward slowly to the west. He passed farms at regular intervals, and in first dawn exchanged a few words with a farmer coming from his house to the river who gave him directions to Fletcher's place which, at that point, was some six miles north. Two hours later, the bay blowing hard against the steady, insistent rise of the land, McMahon topped a low hill and looked across a mile of uneven ground at the rough and snowy bluffs of the Willow Ridge, with the Gap a triangular-shaped opening from south to north, beckoning silently toward the infinite, vast unknown of the plateau land and great river beyond. Fletcher's farmyard lay on the first steep slope west of the wagon road, laid out with skill and forming a warm shelter against the elements. McMahon turned the bay up a wide lane defined only by the tops of cottonwood fence posts pushing through the drifts. He stopped between the house and barn, wondering if he should call out or get down and go inside. His hands were cupping around his mouth when the kitchen door opened and Fletcher shouted, "Don't stand there, man. Put up your horse and come inside."

"Thanks," McMahon said.

"McMahon?" Fletcher said, squinting against the snow glare.

"Yes," McMahon said. "With you in a minute, Fletcher."

He dismounted and led the horse to the barn, flipped the latch and pulled the double doors back, smelling the fresh, clover-scented odor of a clean barn. He led the bay into a wide, long alleyway and saw the rumps and twitching tails of three work teams in double-sized stalls. He found a small, empty stall at the far end, pulled the bay between the walls and unsaddled. Looking for a dry grain sack to rub the bay down, he saw the equipment hung in neat, straight rows, the floor bedded with fresh hay, the feed boxes filled with oats, the hay pressed down thickly in the mangers. This was the place to find the true worth of a good farmer, and Fletcher, without doubt, was far above the average. McMahon pulled two grain sacks, already split at the seams and shaken out, from a pile in the bin, rubbed the bay thoroughly, brought oats and pulled hay down, saw the small water tank inside the barn, guarded by a swinging gate, and ran for the house, cold and tired and eager for coffee and food.

Fletcher led him into the kitchen and pointed to the table. McMahon saw hot coffee, already poured, and smelled the sharp, hunger-biting odor of frying ham and eggs; and turning to the table, he saw Mary Fletcher standing beside the cookstove, regarding him soberly. She wore a gingham housedress today and her hair was divided in two thick braids that hung girlishly behind her shoulders and far down her back. Seeing her in woman's clothing for the first time McMahon was surprised and then pleased. She was older than he had judged and her body, so boyish beneath the overalls, was completely feminine in the gingham dress.

"Bad weather," Fletcher said. "You want the job?"

"Not yet," McMahon said. "I'm looking for a place west of here. I hoped you could tell me the trail."

"What place?" Fletcher asked.

"Timberlake's," McMahon said.

Mary Fletcher turned abruptly over the stove. Fletcher coughed softly and sat at the table and filled a stubby pipe and scratched a match along his pants leg before answering.

"Timberlake's is twenty miles west," Fletcher said, "and three miles north. Ride south from this yard and you'll hit a trail in a quarter mile. Keep the ridge on your right. When you see a gap in the ridge, not as deep as the Willow here, turn north. Timberlake's is back in the ridge."

McMahon felt their distrust and antagonism, a real and heavy weight in the kitchen. He took a chair and spooned sugar into his cup and stirred it slowly, wondering why these people disliked Timberlake. He drank the coffee and immediately burned his tongue and said, "Damn!" The girl turned and frowned, and brought a plate covered with ham and four eggs. McMahon smiled and said, "This is good of you. I'll admit I'm hungry."

"Bound to be," Fletcher said. "Riding all night to get this far."

"About all night," McMahon said.

"Eat," Fletcher said. "You're starved."

Fletcher went to the stove and selected a sugar cookie from the crock, wrapped a gray muffler inside his sheepskin coat, and left the house without speaking. McMahon ate rapidly, feeling acutely the girl's presence and ashamed of himself for the second time. Mary Fletcher became extremely busy over the stove with a bowl, mixing dough and paying no more attention to McMahon until he finished and rolled a cigarette. Then she turned and said, "More coffee?" and brought the pot without an answer.

"Do you know Timberlake?" McMahon asked.

"Yes, we know him."

"Tell me," McMahon said quietly, "does he live alone?"

"No," Mary Fletcher said. "I can't tell you how many men he has"—her eyes clouded with secret anger—"it might be one, it could be ten."

"You don't like Timberlake, do you?" McMahon said.

She regarded him passively, arms folded across her breast, face sober and unresponsive. "We do not, Mr. McMahon."

"Would you do one favor more?" McMahon asked. "Did you see anyone riding toward Timberlake's early this morning?"

"No."

"Wind and snow is bad," McMahon said agreeably. "My thanks for a wonderful breakfast, Miss Fletcher. I'll be happy to return the favor next time you visit town."

"It isn't necessary," Mary Fletcher said. "We feed all visitors in this house."

McMahon drew deeply on the cigarette and walked to the door. He said, "I understand that, Miss Fletcher. Thanks again."

Outside, plowing through drifts to the barn and saddling the bay, McMahon found himself bitterly resentful of Will

Overton, not because this girl liked Will and seemingly disliked McMahon, but for the ever-present, unshakable specter of the case that made him worse than he could ever be in a good woman's eye. Fletcher came around the barn and nodded curtly as McMahon urged the bay south.

"Many thanks," McMahon called.

"A long ride to Timberlake's," Fletcher said. "Take your time."

McMahon rode south. A quarter mile from the farmyard he turned along a line fence running westward and saw the faint depression of the old trail moving along the base of the Willow Ridge. McMahon murmured, "Full of beans again, boy?" patted the bay's cold shoulder and rode on.

Buchanan remained in his private office for an hour after Mason went away, smoking a second cigar and smiling enigmatically at the tips of his blunt fingers. Mason's knowledge of New Orleans was something to consider; it was unfortunate that Mason happened to be in New Orleans while he was concluding two profitable deals. That alone had made him string along with the man; it would be utter foolishness to endanger this deal for the sake of a few dollars. And Mason had sold out cheaply. Five thousand was nothing for an advance payment; but then, Mason was undoubtedly estimating future profits. Buchanan snapped his fingers sharply; there would be no future profits for Mason after a certain time. In fact, there would be no Mason. Remembering Alice Trumbell, Buchanan decided he was doing the girl a favor.

He had known what Mason would say before he spoke, but the five thousand had been worth paying to learn those few facts he had failed to gather previously. McMahon was out of the picture, but Chambers was here and must be finished. For a moment, considering the best method, Buchanan was haunted by the specter of other detectives following Chambers in a never-ending stream.

Then he shrugged philosophically and rose from the desk and waddled to the outer door.

Buchanan stepped into the banking rooms and observed the smooth-running machinery of his first legitimate business venture. This fact was a pleasant and satisfying glow when he remembered the past; coming to Warbonnet five years ago, he had been on the trail of certain contracts with the railroad. Someone mentioned the need for a bank in the rapidly growing community and he had added up his capital, which was considerable, considered the future, and taken the plunge. Since that day the bank had made a profit. A year later he had sent for Timberlake and Mathews, and through them had carried on the other side of his business while planning for this, his biggest coup. Judging himself, Buchanan decided he was a thorough rogue but nonetheless an able one; and most important of all, he recognized himself as such and had no illusions about his life.

Thinking in this satisfactory manner, Buchanan walked to the cashier's desk. "That Timberlake is overdue on his loan, isn't he?"

"Two weeks," the cashier said. "I was going to call your attention to it, Mr. Buchanan, but the weather has been miserable. Timberlake probably can't get in."

"Nonsense," Buchanan said shortly. "Other people do. The man is slippery, Henry. We'll do well to watch him more closely on loans in the future. Will you find someone to ride out there and take Timberlake a note from us?"

"Yes, sir," the cashier said. "After this storm blows over."

"Very well," Buchanan said. "Get a man and let me know. I'll write Timberlake a letter that will shake him up, believe me. If anyone wants me, Henry, I'll be at the hotel."

Leaving the bank and walking slowly toward the hotel for his mid-morning coffee, Buchanan was satisfied. There

was no real hurry in taking care of Chambers. Roy Timberlake would understand the note and come to town immediately to take care of Chambers, and after that things should
happen on schedule. Buchanan already anticipated the
showdown scene with Trumbell; that would be a soul-fill-
ing day.

In the late afternoon McMahon noticed a change in the
land. The trail had followed along the base of the ridge
and given McMahon his first clear picture of the valley to
the south. The ridge was not a single humping of the earth
running from west to east, but rather a broad, rough rise of
land that began in the mountains and flowed like uneven
water many hundred miles to the east before dissolving
into prairie. The Willow Valley began where he had ridden during the afternoon and stretched for twenty miles
south to Warbonnet. The valley from Warbonnet to this
ridge was some twenty miles wide, a slowly rising layer of
rich black earth that edged into the hills and disappeared
among clay banks and graveled washes and plump brush
thickets covering the hillsides and spreading unchecked
through the canyons and draws. McMahon rode between
small, round hills and saw the Gap on his left, a V-shaped
cut in the ridge that wound inward and disappeared almost
at once in sharp bends and high, rough canyon walls fes-
tooned with a thin growth of pines.

He urged the bay into the Gap, loosening his new mackinaw and pulling his gun butt near his right hand. He
made the first bend and looked back for one quick, vanishing glimpse of the valley; and then moved in a white-walled
world that took the bay's careful hoofs around sharp bends
and through silent, narrow stretches of canyon trail. Three
miles in, with no lessening of the ridge in depth, he saw
the narrow canyon trail to the west. Hoof marks were still
readable beneath covering snow leading from this main
trail up the side canyon. McMahon listened to the wind

toss feathers of snow from the canyon walls and moan softly through the jack pines. He murmured, "Here we go,"
and turned the bay up the side canyon trail. A mile west an
inner caution stopped him ten feet from a sharp north
turn. He dismounted and walked slowly to the turn and
looked north. Appearing suddenly, no more than a hundred feet ahead, was a natural cup in the hills, dipping
sharply from the trail into a hollow some five hundred
yards in diameter. Against the north wall of this cup he saw
the log house and outbuildings of Timberlake's place.

Smoke rose in a straight gray column from the chimney
and disappeared into nothingness when the wind caught
and blew it away. Night was very close, and as McMahon
watched the house, a lamp came on and turned the two
south windows to dull yellow gold. In the barn to the east
of the house, visible through the open south side, Mc-
Mahon counted eight horses tied to the mangers, eating
hay and stamping their feet against the cold. The barn was
a rough shed with a log roof covered thickly with dirt and
hay, giving the horses protection from wind and snow, and
open on the long, south side. McMahon led the bay down
the trail, around two turns, before he found the small crevice in the north wall of the cup.

He broke a path into this crevice and smiled with grim
satisfaction when the crevice enlarged and became a topless cave shaped like a jug, the entrance small, the body of
the jug round and protected. He tied the bay to a stunted
pine, loosened the girth and slipped the bit. He rubbed
the bay's smooth, wet nose, slipped from the crevice into
black night, and moved slowly toward Timberlake's. Six
weeks of inactivity and forced drinking took their toll from
his lungs and legs. He was breathing gustily when he came
down into the cup and walked around its eastern flank toward the barn and house. He slipped between the barn
and the end wall, and moved with infinite caution toward
the house. He could hear voices and sounds within the

cabin, faint and jumbled, and smell chimney smoke and the sharp, fresh odor of a drying beef hung behind the cabin. Then he touched the logs in the east wall and flattened himself gently against their rough, unpeeled curves.

Voices were clear now from within; he distinguished six, ranging from a deep, hoarse bass to a squeaky, high-pitched treble. "I bet ten," the deep voice said confidently, and the other voices answered in the various ways. "Call you," and "I drop," and "I'll just see that and raise you ten, Roy." McMahon felt better suddenly; men in a poker game were confident men, expecting no one up here in the wilds. He heard a chair creak and a seventh man come from deep across the room and say angrily, "Come on, Roy. Loan me a hundred and let me back in the game." McMahon grinned with satisfaction. Mathews had gone broke, left the table to curse his bad luck, and was back again, wheedling Timberlake for a loan. It gave McMahon grim pleasure to know that Mathews had lost the sixty dollars he had won two nights before; and a grimmer satisfaction that Mathews was unafraid and no longer concerned about a drunk named McMahon. Thinking thus, the danger of his own position gradually seeped, with the night's increasing cold, into his mind. He couldn't stay here, against the cabin wall, and get Mathews, or remain in this area longer than two hours before dawn.

He was turning from the cabin toward the barn when Timberlake slapped one hand on the table and called, "Who's feedin' the fire? George, get some wood."

Mathews said petulantly, "I'm the sucker tonight."

"Get the wood," Roy said shortly. "I raise ten."

McMahon faded back from the cabin wall and stood against the barn. The door creaked open, closed with a sharp thud, and lantern light danced from the cabin toward the barn. McMahon slipped behind the barn and heard Mathews cursing softly to himself as he walked past the horses in front of the barn. McMahon moved slowly to the other end, in step with Mathews, and paused at the corner. He saw the lantern light wobble across the packed, dirty snow and stop before a small lean-to. Mathews set his lantern on the chopping block, the glow showing a three-sided lean-to, filled with kindling and two-foot sections of log. Mathews fumbled in the darkness behind the lean-to, and pulled a woodbox attached to sled runners into the open space. Mathews cursed steadily as he began loading the woodbox. Each time he tossed a heavy piece of cut pine log into the box, McMahon moved forward two steps in the shadows just beyond the lantern light. He was six steps from the man's back when Mathews tossed a log and said, "Enough for me, damn you, Timberlake," and walked to the sled and stooped for the pull rope. McMahon came around the lean-to, made his leap in one stride, and smashed Mathews behind the ear with his gun butt. Mathews made no sound falling on his face across the rope.

McMahon straddled the limp body for a breathless moment, watching the cabin door and the window, before bending over Mathews and lifting him up and behind the sled. He swung the lantern away from the lean-to front and placed it in deeper snow, the light cut off and suffused, throwing long, indistinct shadows into the night. McMahon unloaded the wood from the sled box, and lifted Mathews into the empty box. It was a never-ending source of wonder to him how luck stepped in when a man had made no plans beyond a certain point. He wanted Mathews, had gotten the man through the turn of the cards, and now, unable to carry him to the horse this sled appeared by magic or luck. He tightened the pull rope and stepped within its circumference, pushed his body against the taut strand, and moved south in a quick circle, heading for the canyon. He had fifteen minutes, he judged, before someone in that game checked the passage of time and yelled for Mathews. Fifteen minutes, perhaps ten, to reach his horse and get away into the night. Running doggedly, legs already turning to lumps beneath him, he wondered at the tenacity of a man who risked his life for a few dollars; or was it more than the risk, the game, the satisfaction at the end? Perhaps it was pride, as Bloom spoke the word, a nebulous inner concentration of honor and pride and no small amount of stubborn foolishness. Whatever drove him on, it was a powerful medicine as strong tonight as it had been ten years ago when he began this work.

He reached the canyon floor and felt the wind take its full grasp of his body; in the sled Mathews groaned and moved an arm. Below, in the sheltered cup, the cabin window now a tiny rectangle of diminishing yellow light, someone opened the door and called, "Mathews, where the hell are you?" McMahon rounded the bend and broke into a high-kneed run, pulling the sled through soft, drifting snow by brute force. McMahon stumbled over a rock, fell and swallowed pain as his trouser leg was ripped and the rock gashed into his knee. He counted his steps and saw the darker shadow of the crevice, and heard the bay snorting with cold and stamping about in the snow. It took precious seconds to untie the bay and lead it into the canyon, lift Mathews across the bay's shoulders and climb into the saddle. Mathews hung inertly, arms dangling on one side, legs flopping on the other. McMahon murmured, "Stay with me, boy," and urged the bay down the trail. The sled might become the small margin of time he needed if Timberlake and his men came riding around the bend and down the canyon; one rider, falling over the sled box, could pile them all in the snow.

He cleared the side canyon and was pushing the bay hard through the Gap's winding trail when the dull hoof beats rose behind him and grew louder. He slapped the bay and called encouragement, and the horse responded courageously. For several minutes the following sound dropped back and grew faint, and then the bay faltered beneath him and again the sound closed in. Mathews moved convulsively and cried out, "Where . . . ?" and tried to straighten his body. McMahon hit his buttocks a solid blow with one fist and said, "Lie still." Even then, feeling the ridge drop away, knowing the east-west trail was a matter of yards, he pulled the bay off the trail to the west, moving up a sharp slope and stopping behind a scraggling row of pines.

Mathews was regaining consciousness, still groggy but showing fight. When it happened, McMahon was helpless to stop the move. A rider, quirting his horse, passed below them on the trail; and then the others came on in a widely extended line, calling hoarsely and evidently guiding on the lead man. McMahon leaned over Mathews' body and rubbed the bay's quivering neck. Mathews squirmed convulsively, kicked the bay's tender belly, and threw himself forward and out, legs coming up in a back kick and striking McMahon's arms. The bay snorted and whirled and Mathews shouted, "Roy—Roy—Roy!" and fell to the ground. He rolled and came to his feet and ran with a ferret's frantic anger into the darkness. A rider called, "Where?" and Mathews shouted his answer from somewhere down the slope, "Up here, Roy. He's up here!"

McMahon could wait no longer. He reined the bay around and rode quietly down the west slope of this small hill, then south and west again, losing himself in the night. They would not find him in this night with the storm rising across the entire ridge, no more than he could locate Mathews a second time. He slipped from the saddle a mile west and led the bay in a gradual swing to the south until they left the ridge and felt the flattening of the valley's northern edge. Only then did he mount and head east. He was vaguely aware of a sudden shift in the wind, and falling snow that blew with the wind against his left cheek, rocking him unsteadily in the saddle, but he had one fact to warm his mind. He knew where Mathews would be tomorrow, and the next day, and the next. It was doubtful if Mathews had recognized him, possible that Mathews believed he was Red Egan, out for quick, drunken revenge. Another day, he thought, another time.

He was approximately south of the Gap trail when the bay nickered. McMahon saw the rider huddled in his mackinaw beneath a tree as the man called, "Any sign?"

McMahon called, "Nothing back there," and tightened his knees.

"Nothing here," the man called, and then shouted, "You're not Ed."

McMahon kicked the bay solidly and rammed forward into the standing horse, swinging his gun for the rider's head. The man cried out loudly and swung a short-barreled carbine. The octagonal barrel struck McMahon's shoulder and then the bay was into the other horse and he had the man under his gun. He took another blow and made his own good. The rider went over and down, and the horse bolted into the night. McMahon's left shoulder was numb and blood was a fresh, hot streak on his face where the carbine sight had struck and raked from ear to jaw. He turned the bay and rode east, wondering if another man might be out ahead in the darkness, blocking the trail. One more time and he would shoot his way out of this trap; a man could stand so much and then his common sense evaporated completely. He came into the valley, swaying in the saddle, aware of the storm's violence and unable to think with a clear head. He felt the bay trembling and wanted to cry. This was the penalty for loving all horses and feeling one giving its last strength beneath his legs, game to the finish.

He was conscious of riding forever into the storm that was almost a blizzard, remembering other years and blizzards in this land, knowing what would happen if he did not find shelter before it reached its peak. Somewhere in that endless period of time he lost his sense of feel and touch; the blood had long since caked and frozen across his face. He hunched over the bay, face turned from the driving snow, only his knees holding him. The bay was moving, trotting brokenly through the piling snow, then walking, then trotting again, and suddenly stopping behind some object that broke the wind's force and threw McMahon from the saddle. He was falling, helpless to roll and land on his hands and knees. He struck a solid wall of something hard, turned on his back, and hit the snow. The bay cried in an almost human voice, and McMahon's last thought was, "All right, I'll just rest a minute and then get out of here."

He was being pulled to his feet then, arms were sliding around his body, and someone said, "Great God! McMahon!"

"Go to hell," McMahon said. He tried to fight, reach his gun, and then he was done, all through, and knew it.

The voice said, "Take it easy, McMahon. You're all right."

McMahon had confidence in that voice. No reason for it, he thought, but he liked the sound. He tried to speak and the words died in his throat and he fell forward into the snow on his face.

Five

McMAHON WAS certain of only one fact when he woke; he was warm. He looked up and around and saw the room and the faces. Mary Fletcher stood in the doorway and her father sat in a rocking chair beyond the foot of the bed, smoking his corncob pipe and reading a book. McMahon said, "I hit your barn."

Fletcher said, "You're the damndest man, McMahon, not to mention being the most perverse sonofagun we've ever met."

"What do you mean?" McMahon asked.

He felt a pleasant lethargy and wanted to close his eyes and sleep for another day, but time was running short. He pulled himself up in bed and instinctively rubbed one hand against his stomach, knowing before the fingers touched skin that the money belt was gone. He looked at Mary Fletcher and suddenly didn't care about concealing his identity. Her face was pleasant and smiling, entirely different from the last view of her, bending angrily over her cookstove with a bowl of dough in her hands.

"Is my horse all right?" McMahon asked. "And what about me being perverse?"

Fletcher closed the book and rose to face the bed, grinning broadly. "The horse is tired but sound, McMahon. As to your being perverse, why didn't you tell us the truth?"

"About what?" McMahon said.

"Come now," Fletcher chuckled. "We found you outside the barn, more a snowball than a man. We dragged you into the house, undressed you and got a little whisky down your stubborn neck and put you to bed. I found your money belt and took the privilege of examining its contents"—Fletcher grinned—"just in case you died and we were forced to notify your relatives. Just a bum in Warbonnet for the winter, eh? Don't look so damned put out. We won't give you away."

McMahon said, "I'm sorry you had to learn the truth. I know you won't tell, but it puts me in your debt."

"What is wrong with that?" Mary Fletcher said. "It's an honest debt."

"You misunderstand," McMahon said thinly. "I'm in your house, people may hear about it. I don't want to cause you trouble."

"I see," Fletcher murmured. "Meaning that certain people might put two and two together, McMahon?"

"Yes," McMahon said. "I'll leave as soon as possible, at night."

"Look outside," Mary Fletcher said.

She pulled the curtains from the bedroom window and McMahon saw the whiteness of a snowbank completely covering the window; and heard then, as he came fully awake, the rough, angry howl of the wind. Mary said, "We put you to bed at six this morning. It's eight in the evening now and the storm is just getting a good start. You can't leave for at least two days."

"And no one will be riding around willy-nilly looking for you," Fletcher smiled. "So lie down there and be sensible."

McMahon thought of the night passed and Mathews slipping from his horse and rushing away to freedom. The memory was a harsh, bitter astringent that rankled in his mind. Mary Fletcher said, "You'll be hungry," and went to the kitchen. Fletcher came to the bedside and extended his right hand.

"Time we made a fresh start," Fletcher said. "Glad to know you, John."

McMahon took the hand and shook it firmly. "Mighty glad to know you, Sam," he said, and added immediately, "I hope you understand my position. I cannot trust anyone on a case."

"But once they get to know you?" Fletcher said.

"That's different," McMahon said. He smelled hot coffee, and was immediately hungry. "How bad was I when you found me?"

"Tuckered out," Fletcher said. "You were lucky, John. It hadn't got cold enough to freeze you, dressed warm like you were. But you had a bad cut on your face, and you were so tired you couldn't lift an arm. A couple days' rest and Mary's cooking, and you'll be good as new."

McMahon said, "I'll get up to eat. No sense babying me."

"Lie back," Fletcher said sternly. "Don't start giving orders. You eat right here and smoke a cigar, and then you sleep the clock around again. Tomorrow morning you can get up for breakfast. Say, you play cribbage?"

"Yes," McMahon said.

"Fine," Fletcher smiled. "We need new blood up here. She takes me four out of five and I'm tired of being licked by a girl. Maybe you can take her down a peg."

Mary Fletcher came from the kitchen with a bowl of soup and a plate of soda crackers, buttered and browned slightly from oven heat. She placed the bowl carefully on McMahon's lap and said, "It's hot. Don't burn your fingers."

McMahon said, "Chicken soup. Nothing better," and began eating with unashamed hunger. He finished the bowl in record time and was demolishing the plate of crackers when Mary brought a wooden tray filled with plates. McMahon looked down on the steak and baked potato, the home-canned corn and peas, and the basket of white bread with a half-pound pat of yellow butter on the side, indented with a lacy mint leaf design that brought back memories of his own childhood. He looked up to thank her once more and saw her eyes, smiling with understanding, and thought better of using foolish words.

"You'd starve a man to death in a hurry," McMahon said.

She laughed and placed salt and pepper shakers beside the tray, and Fletcher, sitting again in the rocker with his pipe and book, said forcefully, "She sure would. Last hired man we had here gained twenty pounds in six months, took his full salary, and couldn't give me value received because he was too full after meals to work for an hour. Eat up, John. You're hollow under the eyes."

McMahon was afraid he could never eat the full meal, but fifteen minutes later he wolfed the last piece of steak and sopped up the juices with the last slice of bread. Mary brought hot coffee with thick yellow cream and a small bowl of sugar cubes; and stood quietly until he poured the cream and dropped three lumps into the steaming cup. Then she said, "Would you like a drink?"

McMahon smiled and remembered his torn cheek, feeling the sharp pain as the cut wrinkled with his grin. He said, "A small one, Mary. But only because I need it. I've downed enough rotgut liquor in the past six weeks to last a lifetime."

She nodded soberly and went for the whisky, and Fletcher said, "That kind of a job, John?"

"The worst kind," McMahon said. "Playing the part of a loafer, a drifter. You saw me in the hotel that afternoon. Will Overton was stepping over the social line to introduce us."

"No, he wasn't," Fletcher said. "I made him. We saw you come through the door and I figured you'd be a good man to know."

"Now you're spreading the blarney," McMahon said. "I looked the part and what's more, I felt it. And I felt worse when Will introduced us and you offered me a job."

"Say when," Mary said, holding bottle and glass.

McMahon said, "When," and took the glass and felt her fingers against his own for a moment, warm and strong. He said, "To your good health, with my thanks," and downed the drink in one swallow.

"Now you lie back and get some more sleep," Fletcher said. "And don't worry about anything, you hear? Just sleep."

McMahon slipped under the blankets and felt the bed's softness hold and loosen his body. He looked up at them and smiled, and murmured, "Tomorrow morning we'll have a good talk."

"You bet," Fletcher said. "Good night, John."

McMahon said, "Good night," and saw her face and eyes and full, sweet mouth. He said, "Good night, Mary," and closed his eyes and felt sleep coming, but not before she said, "Good night, John," and made him feel like a boy holding his first girl's hand on the front porch late at night.

McMahon opened his eyes and saw the dark ceiling, then the whiteness of the window, and the small hard-coal heater. He was wide awake and alert again; his body had fresh strength and resiliency. The least he could do, he thought, listening for sound in the quiet house and hearing none, was get up quietly and start the kitchen fire and make breakfast for the Fletchers.

He slipped from bed and stood on a rag rug. His clothing was laid out neatly across a chair, his boots, dried and saddle-soaped on the floor beside the bed. He dressed quickly and walked on tiptoe to the kitchen. McMahon started the fire, checked the water reservoir, and began looking for food. He found the ham and bacon in the pantry, brought the dripping can from its place on the stove's warming shelf, and lifted the biggest frying pan from its hook. The fire was burning with a snap and tiny roar when he added larger pieces of wood through the front door. He ground fresh coffee from the bell-topped wooden mill and sliced the ham and bacon, and turned to set the table under the two big windows on the south side of the room. He was laying the last blue-bordered plate and listening professionally to the ham's first crackle in the hot pan when Mary Fletcher came from the parlor, surprise and then laughter shining in her face.

"Bless my heart," she said. "Don't tell me you cook?"

"I'm the best," McMahon said. "Have a cup of coffee and watch me get breakfast."

They stood beside the cookstove, watching the fire curl and show growing red strength between the lid cracks. McMahon lifted the front lid and dropped a handful of corncobs and dry husks; the fire leaped upward, shining on their faces until the lid slapped back in place, leaving them no nearer in one sense, but much closer with another feeling of mutual understanding. She said, "I'd better fill the reservoir," and went into the pantry.

"Cookstove heats up a room faster than anything else," he said.

"On a cold morning," she said, "nothing heats fast enough."

"Be reasonable," McMahon said. "Nothing goes fast enough for us. Only time, and that's gone before we set the brake, if we had the sense to do so."

"Let me get breakfast, John," she said.

"Sit down," McMahon answered. "You've done everything for two days. I'm on my feet. I'll cook a breakfast you can eat."

She said, "All right," and poured coffee and sat at the table while McMahon fussed over the stove, conscious of her stare, turning the ham and cracking eggs in a bowl.

Her soft laughter was a pleasant sound above the fire sputter and the eggs sliding into the hot pan and turning white around the yellow yolks as they fried with a small, steady sizzle. McMahon heard Sam Fletcher enter the kitchen, stop and stare, then say, "Well, I'll be damned." McMahon turned and said, "Good morning, Sam."

"You'll make a good wife," Sam said. "I'll have my eggs over lightly."

McMahon brought the frying pan to the table and filled the plates. Mary got the coffee and bread, and they sat together in the warming kitchen over the hot food. Sam grinned and said, "You got well fast, John. Pass the butter."

They talked of the storm now past its peak and easing off, and Sam drank his fourth cup of coffee before dressing to check his buildings and stock. McMahon said, "Let me help out, Sam," but Fletcher shook his head and said, "I know where things are. Sit there and talk to my daughter.

She gets tired of listening to the old man babble." Fletcher wound a scarf about his neck and chin, and plunged outside with a bellow of defiance at the wind.

"More coffee?" Mary asked.

"One more," McMahon said. He rolled a cigarette and looked at the fumes rising from the hot coffee. "Your father's a good man," he said thoughtfully. "Remember what I told you last night. I don't want to get you people in my trouble."

"You won't," she said. "No one is out today. Tomorrow will be bad too. As for trouble, we know how to handle it."

"Not my kind," McMahon said. "That's why I'm serious about leaving at night. You've been wonderful to me and I won't take advantage of your kindness."

She said. "It's funny. I remember meeting you in the hotel and wondering what you did." She smiled faintly. "Will hated to say anything bad about you. He seems to like you a lot."

"What did you think?" McMahon asked. "If you believed me a drifter, I'll be flattered."

"No," she said seriously. "I tried to, but it didn't seem right. I guess it was a feeling, not a fact."

"Don't let your heart rule your mind," McMahon said. "I was a drifter, nothing more. But that's done now. How long have you and your father lived here?"

"Three years," she said. "We came in '84. Father bought this farm and then bought the one on the south the next summer." She looked up and McMahon saw the touch of old sadness in her mouth. "You're wondering about my mother. She died a long time ago. I was six. Father has been both parents since then."

"You have a good farm," McMahon said quickly. "It will be better every year you work it. I've thought many times about getting a place in good country and settling down."

"Father says this will be a garden spot in ten years," she said. "You couldn't do better than come here."

"Habit is an evil," McMahon said. "I'm always talking like this, to myself mostly, about buying a farm. I've been with the Colonel five years, before that with other agencies for six. It gets in your blood and you can't stop. Each job, I tell myself it'll be the last one. Each time the Colonel dangles something tricky and I take just one more job."

"And this one?"

"The worst," McMahon said. "I ought to help your father."

"He'll be in," she said. "We have three teams and the saddle horses, chickens, ducks and the cow. It doesn't take long to water and feed them. They won't eat too much during the storm."

McMahon said, "Very well," and helped her clear the table and wash the dishes. Fletcher came back from the outbuildings, blowing on his fingers, stamping snow from his boots, and grinning broadly.

"Didn't lose an animal," he said. "And it's cold outside, believe me. What's she got you doin' now, John? Drying dishes?"

"Got to earn my board," McMahon said. "When will this clear up, Sam?"

Fletcher scowled in thought. "Tomorrow morning. Why? You got urgent business?"

McMahon had not intended to tell them, but their kindness and complete honesty broke his resolve. They deserved that much in case Mathews and Timberlake came onto the place, asking questions and looking for him.

"Urgent," McMahon repeated. "I'm after a killer. I had him earlier in the night, before you found me . . ." He explained quickly about Mathews and the St. Louis killing, the murder of Red Egan, and the subsequent developments, leaving out all reference to Trumbell and the reasons behind the case. The killings were sufficient information to alert these people, make them realize he had placed their safety in jeopardy. In conclusion he said, "I've got to tell Chambers about this soon. He has work to do in town. Mathews can't go too far. I don't think he recognized me the other night. I'm hoping he thought I was Red Egan. That'll make it easier. Now you know."

"Would you like to stay here?" Fletcher asked.

"After I ride to town," McMahon said, "I'll have to come back."

"Let me go in for you," Fletcher said quickly. "I can carry a message to Chambers. You can operate out of here. It's close to Timberlake's and nobody will see you if you're careful."

"No," McMahon said. "That's too dangerous."

"Bosh!" Fletcher said. "I know this Mathews. A little rat if ever there was one. And Timberlake is my idea of a first-class thug."

"We'll see," McMahon said. "Wait for morning. If the storm blows over, we'll talk about it then."

Fletcher regarded him curiously. "You're a stubborn man, John. I still say let me go to town." Fletcher grinned. "If you're not afraid to stay here with Mary."

"No," McMahon said solemnly, "but don't tell Will Overton."

Mary colored and clattered pots loudly behind the stove. Fletcher winked at McMahon and made shuffling motions with his fingers, and went immediately to the parlor for cards and the cribbage board. McMahon said, "He likes to tease, doesn't he?" and saw her quick, warm smile as she turned from the stove and rubbed one long finger across her cheek. Fletcher returned with the board and cards, sat opposite McMahon, and said, "Cut for deal. And you'd better be good, because I'm tough at this game."

Hours later McMahon had lost twelve and won five games from Fletcher. Mary sat beside the stove and read and occasionally stood over them and watched the play. McMahon was lulled by the kitchen's fragrant warmth and their feeling of strength and family unity, something he had lost long ago on the trip through years of loneliness. In late afternoon, board and cards pushed aside, drinking coffee and eating the cinnamon buns Mary had baked, he could not remember a moment in the past ten years that compared with this day. He wanted badly to tell the Fletchers what it meant to sit in a home made solid and lasting by two people he already admired more than his usual taciturn suspicion allowed under such short acquaintance. The wind had dropped away to a steady moan and snow no longer pelted the north wall with a slapping sound. Fletcher sipped coffee and cocked his head, eyes gleaming brightly with understanding of the weather.

"She'll clear by morning," he said. "You decided to be sensible and let me go to town?"

"All right," McMahon said. "But under no circumstance are you to involve yourself in my business, other than giving Chambers a message. You promise that or I'll ride myself."

"I promise," Fletcher said. "What's the message?"

McMahon said, "Chambers is posing as a drummer, ladies' and gents' ready-to-wear. Can we trust Will Overton?"

"All the way," Fletcher said. "Will's four square."

"Good. Now you've got to have a reason for going to town. Supplies, medicine, something legitimate. You buy that first, then go to the hotel, tell Will the situation. He can go upstairs without comment. You can't. Will can relay the message to Chambers and give you Chambers' answer. Can you do that?"

"Yes."

"That's the hard part," McMahon said. "Tell Chambers I located Mathews' hideout at Timberlake's ranch, had him once and lost him in the storm. They saw me, but I don't think identified me. I'm going to stay here for the time being and work out when the weather clears. He is not to tell our client as yet. And last, he is to be doubly careful. I feel pretty certain they know his real identity. That's all. Got it?"

Fletcher repeated his message verbatim and rose immediately, going to the stove and warming his hands, then walking to the clothes hook and picking up his mackinaw. Over his wool pants he pulled on warm chaps.

"I'm starting now," Fletcher said. "It's almost dark. I can be in town by early morning, with luck. Mary's got a bad cough in her throat. We need medicine." Fletcher grinned. "Will is alone during the night. It'll be easier to tell him then. I can start back about noon."

The storm was blowing itself out to the south and Fletcher knew the wagon road from Gap to town as he knew the farmyard. McMahon nodded reluctant approval and watched Fletcher slip a short-barreled colt revolver into one mackinaw pocket, and pack a lunch in the lard pail. Mary filled a burlap-covered bottle with hot coffee and kissed him gently.

"Be careful," she said.

"Always am," Fletcher said gruffly.

"You want help in the barn?" McMahon asked.

"You stay inside," Fletcher said. "I don't want some jaybird catching sight of you from the ridge. There's still an hour of light. Expect me late tomorrow."

Six

McMAHON STOOD beside the big kitchen window and did not relax until Fletcher led a stocky black horse from the barn and rode down the lane toward the wagon road. Then he turned away and smiled at Mary. "He'll make it."

"It isn't too bad," Mary said. "He'll make good time."

McMahon said, "I hope he forecast the weather."

"Don't worry about him," she said. "Now, do you still think you're a good cribbage player?"

"When a woman beats me," McMahon said, "I'll quit."

They played three games and McMahon said, "All right, I'll quit," and watched her start supper. McMahon had fancied himself the best cribbage man west of the river, but now, wondering how a woman could be so competent, beautiful, and smart, all in one slender body, he no longer wanted to play cribbage with anyone. They ate late supper and washed the dishes, and then the night stretched before him, endlessly, for he was not sleepy and he had to talk with her until he was. He was never certain how it began, but sometimes before midnight, sitting in the kitchen beside the stove, eating sugar cookies and drinking coffee, he was telling her of his past and how he began in the only business he knew and understood.

He told her of his childhood in Illinois, along the great river, and going west at the age of fifteen to work and roam at random from border to border until he became a jack-of-all-trades rapidly approaching the dubious title of the thorough and incurable drifter. He was good with a gun, he had killed three men, and the difference between honesty and going down the long-rider trail had become a narrow gap, easily bridged in whichever direction the wind blew. It was then he met a deputy sheriff in southwestern Colorado and helped that man chase and bring in two horse thieves. The sheriff made side money working for the Pinkerton Detective Agency and recommended strongly that McMahon take a job with that organization. He took the train to Denver, was hired, and began the work he had followed ever since.

He entered a new world when he took that job. He rode the trains, for the agency protected all railroads in many ways. He was always on the lookout for a catch. He watched for conductors accepting cash instead of tickets;

he kept alert for other Pinkerton men dodging their duty. He became intimate with saloonkeepers and gambling-house crowds. He became an expert with dice and a tin cup, or a horn, and was known in many places as a tin-horn gambler. Between serious jobs he marked time at the hobo act, which consisted of traveling the railroads as a tramp in an effort to discover fraud among the trainmen.

He told of the time he turned in a conductor for taking side money, and when the conductor was called on the carpet and denied he had ever seen McMahon, the officials wired the home office to send McMahon to the division point to identify the conductor. He took the next train and on arrival was shown into a room filled with con-ductors and brakemen. He walked along the line of grim faces, spotted his man, said, "Hello, James," and reached for the angry hand. The trainmen shouted with laughter and everyone went to the corner saloon for a drink, but he had never felt the same after that incident. He liked the railroad men and hated to think that James had lost his job because of McMahon's snooping. It was shortly after that, five years before, that Colonel Sloane ap-proached him with a better offer and he resigned from Pinkerton's and went with the Colonel. It was the begin-ning of a new career that sent him after new game.

Colonel Sloane took cases that offered more reward and a great deal of personal danger to his agents. Sloane's did the routine jobs for their steady money—the guarding and sneak-thief chases, the usual run-of-the-mill cases—but since the Colonel had the reputation of never giving up on a killer's trail, and having a dozen men in his employ who were, for all purposes, killers themselves, his success was understandable. McMahon had never failed on a case. He had chased killers, embezzlers, jewel thiefs, with equal suc-cess, and during this time his life had set and hardened into a distinctive mold. His home was under his hat. He took his rest between cases, reading and going away on fishing and hunting trips, and once, traveling to Mexico City for a two months' stay to see if that lovely place was as beautiful as it had been when he first saw it, trailing a killer.

McMahon stopped talking and looked at the Seth Thomas clock; it was almost midnight. Mary sat motionless, watching his face, her fingers clasped tightly, her mouth touched with a secret longing and faint envy, as if she had wished to be a man. McMahon laughed softly and rattled his cup, now cold to the touch and filled with a faint, hardening scum of coffee.

"Stop me," he said, "when I ramble on."

"Why?" she said. "How can we know people unless we hear them talk honestly?"

"And was I?" he asked.

"You can't talk any other way," she said soberly.

"No," McMahon said. "But it was true, all of it, and I'm ashamed of parts. Sometimes I think the joy is gone from the work. When I meet people like you, like your father, I want to change."

"If you want something," she said, "you can always change."

Her face was the color of soft ivory in the lamplight, her eyes round with wonder at the pictures of another world she would never see. But watching her, feeling her nearness impinge on his inner loneliness, he had the bitter feeling that she was stronger in many ways than he could ever be; and this strength came from her life, a whole and satisfying living that held her closely through the good and bad days. He felt this keenly, more a hunger than envy, sitting in the kitchen with the tools of that life buttressing the walls of her home. With this thought he remembered Will Overton and experienced a sharp, completely foolish pang of jealousy.

"Yes," he said. "You can change if you turn in time. Tell me, do you like Will Overton?"

He saw the color touch her face and draw her mouth

upward in a little smile that could mean many things. "We've been friends for two years. He comes from our old home back east."

"Where is east?" McMahon asked.

"Ohio," she said. "Will lived in town. He came out here and took the hotel job. He's saving to buy the farm south of us."

"He's a good man," McMahon said. "He knows what he wants. He'll get it."

"I hope he does," she said softly.

He was cheered by her words without knowing why. She had promised Will Overton nothing, only friendship, which could remain just that for life. He said, "How old are you, Mary?"

"Twenty-three," she said. "A hopeless old maid out here."

"No," McMahon said. "A sensible woman who hasn't taken the first young man that came along."

"Or the second," she said, "or the third or fifth."

"He'll come along," McMahon said. "When he does, you'll know. He's worth waiting for, whoever he is, wherever he comes from."

"Father says the same," she murmured. "I can wait."

"Look at the time," McMahon said. "One in the morning. You go to bed, Mary. I'll bank the fires and put out the lamp."

"Sleepy?" she asked.

McMahon smiled. "Not now. I'll sit a while. Good night, Mary."

She moved from the table to the parlor archway and paused there, one hand touching the beaded drapes, her eyes smiling. She said, "This has been a wonderful evening, John. Good night."

She was gone then, the kitchen silent and suddenly colder although the fire was bright and strong through the stove door grates. McMahon poured hot coffee and rolled a cigarette and sat heavily at the table. He wished that this case could have concluded before he met the Fletchers; it would be impossible to leave without taking a part of them in his memory. He sat at the table until the fire burned low, reminding him of nights in the depot waiting room, and then he banked the fire and snuffed the lamp and went through the silent house to his room. The wind had dropped to a low whine when he got in bed and closed his eyes. Tomorrow would be clear and cold, and the game would start again.

Roy Timberlake saddled, muffled himself in furs, including bear-skin chaps and rode south at the first slacking of wind that night. He rode straight and top-heavy on his big horse, a fully bearded man with a stomach that threatened to pop the belt on his mole-skin trousers, which were pushed far down in heavy five-buckle overshoes. He did not make a pretty picture atop the fine horse that trotted easily beneath his weight, but then, Timberlake had never concerned himself with how he looked. He was forty-two years old and two hundred and forty pounds, a loose-cheeked but thoroughly capable man at his own brand of work. He came from the Gap trail and cut cross-country toward Warbonnet, thinking of Mathews, as he rode, wondering where Red Egan had found the guts to ride north in a storm and half kill Mathews before he got away. Mathews could not ride for a week, but Timberlake could. He wanted to see Buchanan and pay Red Egan a visit.

He rode into Warbonnet at dawn the following morning, stabled his horse at Jensen's and stamped into the hotel just as Fletcher turned from the alcove with Will Overton. Timberlake walked to the stove and beat the snow from his clothing with huge arm sweeps and regarded them incuriously.

"You ride in, too?" he asked.

"Yes," Fletcher said wearily. "The girl has a sore throat.

Figured I better get some medicine. Will, you get it quick as possible. I'll grab a few winks."

"Something for you, Roy?" Will Overton asked.

Timberlake said, "A room."

"Number ten," Will Overton said. "Go on up, Roy."

Timberlake said, "Call me at seven," took the number ten key from the hook, nodded to Fletcher, and went upstairs with noisy feet, disappearing into the hotel's upper blackness, a big saddle-galled man, surly and short-tempered after his ride. Fletcher murmured, "Something up, Will. Get that medicine fast."

Fletcher stretched himself on the cot behind the stove and slept until Will Overton returned from Dr. Teboe's with a bottle of cough medicine and detailed instructions for its use. Will Overton said softly, "I'll remember what I hear, Sam. Be careful."

Fletcher hurried down Front to the livery barn, saddled the gelding, and swung north toward home. McMahon needed to hear about Timberlake.

The day clerk called Timberlake at seven o'clock and scurried downstairs. He wanted no part of Timberlake, who was known to tear up saloons with both hands when crossed, or drunk. Behind him, in the small room, Timberlake washed his face and hands, lit a hastily rolled cigarette, and went downstairs. He walked directly to the bank and slapped one meaty hand on the cashier's marble counter. "Buchanan," he said.

Buchanan appeared in the private office doorway, face impassive. "Want to see you, Timberlake. Come inside."

"Want to see you," Timberlake said.

He bumped an early depositor rudely, followed Buchanan into the private office and stood beside the desk while Buchanan locked the door and then grinned. Timberlake chuckled and reached across the desk for a cigar in the ebony box.

"Good act, Ferris?" he said.

"Never better," Buchanan said appreciatively. "You should be treading the boards, Roy. What's the trouble?"

Timberlake spoke rapidly for three minutes, outlining events of that past night. "I figured you should know right now, Ferris. George couldn't tell who it was, but Egan has to be our man. Casey never had the guts to ride a mile in the rain. With this McMahon out of the way, George said we'd better close all the mouths."

"I'll leave Egan to you," Buchanan said. "Now then, there's another one in town, at the hotel, posing as a drummer. A man named Chambers, short, fat and red-cheeked. He may be harmless, depending on how much McMahon told him. In the meantime, take care of Egan and Casey. Keep Mathews out there for another week. I'll send a message if anything happens. Otherwise, tell Mathews to stop by the house a week from tonight."

"What about Egan and Casey?" Timberlake asked. "You want them run out of the country or . . ." he snapped two fingers, the sound sharp and full in the room.

"Take Egan with you," Buchanan said. "Keep him there. Throw the fear of God into Casey. He'll keep still."

Timberlake nodded and started for the door, then stopped and patted his stomach, with both flat hands. "That note is due," he said. "Did I come in to pay up?"

"Yes," Buchanan said. "You paid in here. Go out breathing fire. It will look good."

Timberlake grinned and opened the door and paused in full view of the bank to shout, "Take your money and eat it!" and then plunged through the aisle to the street. He turned north and crossed the street to Casey's saloon, empty at this early hour, and slammed one clenched fist on the bar. Casey came from the stove, smiling with ingratiating falseness, rubbing the bar with a dirty gray towel.

"Hello, Roy," Casey said. "What'll it be?"

"We alone?" Timberlake asked.

"Yes."

"Listen," Timberlake said softly. "Where's Egan?"

Casey hesitated, mopped the bar vigorously, and said, "I don't know, Roy. Ain't seen him for three-four days."

"I guess you didn't hear me," Timberlake said. "I don't give a damn when you saw him last. I want him. Get him."

"I tell you I don't . . ."

Timberlake leaned over the bar and lowered his voice to a gentle whisper that came softly from the full beard. "I want Red Egan right now, or I'll break your greasy neck."

Watching Casey's face, Timberlake felt the change in the man, saw the fear of something greater than hiding Red Egan cross and then remain constant in the frightened eyes. Casey said, "Listen, Roy. I can't get him. Believe me, I can't."

"He pull out?" Timberlake asked. "I'm not telling you again, Casey. Either get him or lock up and we'll start riding."

That was a real threat and Casey accepted it as such. His promise to McMahon withered before the presence of Timberlake, not so much the fact that Timberlake stood across the bar, but guessing what would happen when he rode north. Casey said, "Listen, Roy. It wasn't my fault. It happened. They changed coats and hats. I told Red he . . ."

"Stop blabbering," Timberlake said harshly. "Talk sense."

"Mathews done it by accident," Casey whispered. "We tipped Bloom's cash box last Saturday night. McMahon beat Mathews up the night before. I guess George figured he owed McMahon something. But he got Red with the fish spear by mistake. I ain't told a soul, Roy. I've got nothing against George."

Timberlake absorbed this silently, accepting the fact and thinking ahead instantly. He said, "Where's Egan?"

"In the ice house," Casey said. "You want to . . . ?"

"Leave him there," Timberlake said sharply. "Close up. Start north for my place. Be there by supper time."

"But . . ."

"Close up!" Timberlake said. "Take the short cut. You want me to write it for you? Close up and ride!"

He turned from the saloon; Buchanan had to know this immediately. Now events of the past night were coming clear. McMahon had ridden into the cup, slugged Mathews, and was either in town or hiding out in the hills near the cup. Timberlake went into the bank and exchanged some bills for larger denominations at the cashier's window, saw Buchanan talking with an elderly lady in the rear, and spoke for the cashier's benefit.

"The note's paid. You reckon I can get some more credit?"

"See Mr. Buchanan," the cashier said primly.

Timberlake removed his hat and said, "Excuse me, ma'am," and turned to Buchanan.

"I need another loan," he said bluntly. "I got to head home and take care of my stock. Have you got a minute?"

Buchanan bowed his head to the woman and said, "See Henry about that, Mrs. Wimdon. Mr. Timberlake is in a hurry and has a long way to ride. Come in, Timberlake."

Inside, the door closed, Timberlake said, "McMahon's alive. Evan got it by mistake. They switched hats and coats that night, Mathews threw in the dark, I figure, and got Red. McMahon's up there somewhere right now. What do we do, Ferris?"

Buchanan swore softly and viciously for half a minute, then regained his composure. "Casey?"

"Riding back ahead of me," Timberlake said. "I'll put him away for the time being. Egan's in the ice house. He'll keep."

"Fine. I'll check on McMahon in town. I don't think he could have come back before you rode in. He's got to be up there someplace. How many men have you at present, Roy?"

"Eight, counting Mathews."

"Get him!" Buchanan said. "Get McMahon fast and let me know the minute you do. If you don't find him within two days, move Mathews away from your place. McMahon wants him, we know that, and now I'm wondering how much McMahon really knows about George. If you get him, send George in here on whatever night it happens. Chambers comes next. Understand?"

Timberlake said, "We'll get him. I'll send word in if anything else comes up."

"Good luck," Buchanan said. "And don't fail me, Roy."

For a moment they stared and Timberlake dropped his glance, feeling once more Buchanan's cold, implacable will. He was physically able to kill Buchanan with one hand, but the man had brains and guts and some other quality Timberlake could never fathom; whatever it was, it made Buchanan the boss. Timberlake hurried from the office; riding from town, preparing to head northwest off the wagon road, he saw the fresh track of Fletcher's gelding in the snow. On impulse, he reined back and continued north on the wagon road.

McMahon slept later than he intended that morning and woke to the smell of breakfast. Mary had beaten him up by a good hour. It was past noon and outside the day was clear and almost bright. They ate together in a companionable covering of small talk and pleasant warmth from the fire, and, rising to do the chores against her wishes, McMahon saw her father coming from the wagon road. John bucked across the drifted yard to the barn and waited beside the south door, watching Fletcher top the last gentle rise and turn the weary gelding into the yard.

"Up and about," Fletcher said. "You look good, John."

McMahon opened the double door and followed Fletcher and the horse into the barn. "Sit," he said. "I'll do this."

He stripped the gelding, rubbed it down, and turned it into the big stall beside Mary's horse. Fletcher lit his pipe and rubbed stiff hands together. McMahon carried oats to the horses, patted the bay and smiled when the horse turned and nuzzled his shoulder. "Ready to go, eh?" he said and then stood across the alleyway and asked, "Everything run all right?"

"Yes," Fletcher said. "Will took your message up to Chambers. Good thing, too. Will just came down and gave me the return when Timberlake came in. Will gave him a room key and went for my medicine. Timberlake growled a few words and went upstairs to bed. Will was to call him at seven o'clock. That was at five. I wanted to stay longer but I couldn't after he heard Mary had a sore throat and I was heading back with medicine. Anyway, Chambers said everything was going all right in town. He wants to know if he should come up here, or wait for word from you."

"Thanks, Sam," McMahon said. "You know damned well words are a poor substitute for what you've done. So Timberlake came to town. I like this better all the time. Mathews didn't come in. That means he's scared, or has orders to stay out there."

"What will you do next?" Fletcher asked.

"Wait for darkness," McMahon said. "Then take a ride west."

"That's sticking your head in the lion's mouth," Fletcher said. "What can you do when you get there?"

"Nothing tonight," McMahon said. "I want to study the country, Sam. A good soldier maps the enemy terrain if possible. Don't worry. I'm not going down there alone, not tonight. I'll be back before dawn. If I can impose on you for another day, I'll wait and ride to town tomorrow night."

Fletcher said, "That's sensible," and was lighting his

pipe when the knock sounded on the south door and Timberlake's deep voice called, "Fletcher, you in there?"

McMahon drew his gun and stepped back into the darkness of the stall beside the bay. Fletcher nodded and answered immediately, "What do you want, Timberlake?" and watched McMahon swing himself up the ladder into the hayloft.

"Wondered if you got home," Timberlake said. "Open up and let a man warm his hands."

"Coming," Fletcher said. "Wait till I hang this saddle."

Fletcher walked heavily across the alley, lifted his saddle easily from the wall hook, then dropped it back in place with a loud thud. He turned and went to the south door and pushed it open. Timberlake stood beside his horse, slapping both arms, trying to smile and failing by virtue of his beard now caked with breath ice and matted wildly over his lower face, a huge figure in his sheepskin coat and bear-hide chaps.

"You must have started soon after me," Fletcher said.

"About nine," Timberlake said. "The girl's throat better?"

"Some," Fletcher said. "It's a bad chest cold."

Timberlake was rolling a cigarette and glancing idly around the barn. The bay, hidden from view in the last stall, was eating quietly. "Say," he asked. "Anybody stop here during the storm?"

"You crazy?" Fletcher exclaimed. "Nobody was out in that weather."

"Just wondered," Timberlake said. "Fellow was supposed to come up to my place couple of days ago. I figured he might of left town and had to hole up somewhere on the road."

"Most likely he's south of here," Fletcher said. "Well, I've got work to do, Timberlake."

Timberlake nodded and walked to the south door and threw his cigarette into the snow before mounting the

Morgan. Looking down on Fletcher, he said, "If anybody does stop, tell 'em the trail west is hard going."

"Very well," Fletcher said. 'So long."

Timerlake smiled in his beard and said, "If you can't be good, be careful," and swung south toward the trail.

Fletcher closed the doors and stood inside, peering through a knothole, watching Timberlake ride steadily away. Behind him boots scraped faintly and McMahon dropped lightly from the loft. Fletcher spoke without turning, "A close one for you, John."

"Not for me," McMahon said. "For you. I told you what to expect. They'll give you no peace if they ever see me."

"A small worry," Fletcher said. "He's over the rise. Let's go up and have some coffee. I'm half froze."

McMahon followed him across the yard to the house and saw the tracks below the back porch. Mary opened the door and said sharply, "Hurry up," and closed it quickly after them. Fletcher said, "Did you see him?"

"See him?" Mary said. "He rode up and I had to talk with him before he went to the barn."

Fletcher sat heavily in the nearest chair and murmured, "Did you talk like you had a sore throat?"

"No," she said. "Why?"

Fletcher said, "Heat the coffee, Mary. We need it. You tell her, McMahon. I don't feel so good."

"Timberlake came from town," McMahon said quietly. "He heard your father telling Will Overton about your sore throat."

Her face twisted with shame. "I'm a fool. Now he'll know something is wrong."

"Nothing is hurt," McMahon said. "You may have helped this business along, Mary. I'll ride to town tonight. If Timberlake comes back, he'll find nothing."

Seven

McMAHON STABLED the bay horse at Jensen's shortly past midnight after a fast ride on the wagon road. Tom, the hostler, led the bay to a corner stall and eyed McMahon's cut face inquisitively. McMahon said, "I'll want a fresh horse in two hours, Tom. Pick your best and keep the news to yourself. Understand?"

Tom nodded importantly and began rubbing the bay with a burlap sack, proud to be included in something big and exciting. McMahon stepped from the barn's side door, crossed Front in the middle block darkness, and entered the hotel by the back hallway. He passed the kitchen, silent and deserted, and stood in the shadows behind the lobby archway. He saw a man's feet stretched toward the stove and beyond the stove an empty, quiet lobby. Chairs were faded and dusty looking in the yellow lamplight of the side brackets and the man's feet twitched comfortably. McMahon spoke softly, "Will!"

The feet jerked and came to a crouched position as Will Overton laid his book aside and said, "John?"

"Sam got home in good time," McMahon said. "Timberlake followed him, almost saw me in the barn. He stopped at the house first and Mary forgot to cough. Know what that means?"

"Damn!" Will Overton said. "He heard Sam tell about her sore throat right here."

"That's why I'm in tonight," McMahon said. "Timberlake might double back on the farm and look for me. This way, Sam can let him search. Now, did you watch Timberlake yesterday?"

"Most of the time," Will Overton murmured. "He went to the bank, but that was business. Henry Slater, the cashier, is a friend of mine and he told me at supper Timberlake paid off a note, cussed Buchanan up and down, and left

84

the bank. I stood in Abe Bloom's and watched him go down to Casey's . . ."

"Ah," McMahon said softly. "The brave Casey. Go on, Will."

"He was in Casey's ten minutes, then he went back to the bank, insulted Henry, asked for another loan, evidently got it from Buchanan, and left town. Does that help, John?"

"Yes," McMahon said, "and my thanks, Will."

"You dirty dog," Will Overton laughed gently. "Fooling me for six weeks. You did a magnificent job of acting, John."

"I suffered," McMahon said. "Hard beds, lousy whisky, nosy room clerks. Don't get the yen for my job, Will. It's not what it seems on the surface. Where's Chambers?"

"Abe Bloom's," Will Overton said. "He came down and left the message. They hoped you'd ride in tonight."

"I'll go out," McMahon said. "My thanks again, Will. I'll see you don't lose by this help."

"Don't worry about that," Will Overton said. "Any friend of Sam and Mary is my friend, John. Please call on me from now on if you need help."

"Only if it's necessary," McMahon said. "Go back to your book, Will. You didn't see me tonight."

McMahon walked through the dark hallway to the alley and turned north toward the edge of town. Five minutes later he tapped on Abe Bloom's bedroom window and heard feet shuffle on the floor. "John," McMahon said clearly. "Open up, Abe."

Abe Bloom lifted the sash and assisted McMahon through the window, holding his arm and guiding him into the kitchen where Chambers stood before the stove. Abe Bloom saw the cut and asked, "Who hit you, John?" and Chambers grinned sourly, waiting for McMahon to guide the conversation.

McMahon told them about Timberlake and then said, "I had Mathews. Had him and lost him."

"Luck of the game," Chambers said. "He can't run far. What comes next?"

McMahon said, "We can get Mathews if we want him. But there's the problem—do we want the little rat now? Let's review everything that happened. I beat Mathews up. Red Egan is killed. Mathews rides north to Timberlake's place. I find Timberlake's, get Mathews out by sheer luck, then lose him in the storm. The Fletchers took me in. Timberlake comes to town, sees Fletcher and makes Sam offer a reason for being in town. Timberlake pays a visit to Casey —and Casey is next on my list tonight—and then rides north to Fletcher's. Mary made an innocent mistake. Now Timberlake knows damned well I was there, or might still be there. If he knows, Mathews does. But most important, someone in this town will know soon, if not already. We've got Trumbell's trunk. Mathews is our killer. We can get him. But that doesn't find those papers for us, and there's the entire case. What's your opinion, Abe?"

Abe Bloom spread his hands in an ancient gesture. "You ask me, John? Please, I wouldn't know what to do. I can help you. I have a few friends who stand ready to help. But we need orders. You do what you think, John. We're all with you."

"All right," McMahon said. "Thanks, Abe."

Chambers puffed deeply on his cigar and said, "I'd like to take him in, and we can do it if we have to bring the local law into the game, but that's playing it dumb, John. I think I know what you're planning—let Mathews and Timberlake run—and hope they lead us to the big boss here in town. I'm satisfied he lives here. But who he is, what he does, I don't know. And Abe has failed to dig up anything pertinent. But, about letting them go for the present. Is that your idea?"

"It has to be that way," McMahon said wearily. "Did the Colonel answer your wire?"

"Yes. Whenever we're ready to talk turkey with Trumbell, the Colonel will raise the ante."

"How is Trumbell?" McMahon asked. "Has he missed me?"

"Grouchy," Chambers said. "Impatient. His lawyer Mason wanders around town, acting important and doing nothing."

"Here's something to remember, both of you," McMahon said. It's possible they have discovered your identity, Chambers. Abe, once Chambers is seen coming here, you're marked too. I'm telling both of you this to put you on your toes." McMahon scowled at the floor. "I'd give a month of my life to crawl inside that Timerlake's mind and think with him. That one worries me. Mathews is a killer, no more. But this Timberlake has a mind and uses it. When he moves, it'll be fast. He's got half a dozen men up there in the hills, maybe a dozen more within a day's ride if he needs them. I'm worried about the Fletchers. I pulled them into this deal. I've got to watch them."

"Fletcher seems capable of protecting himself," Chambers said quietly.

"One man," McMahon said, "and a girl against a dozen? Timberlake won't follow the rules when he cuts loose. Now listen carefully: I'm going from here to Casey's saloon and scare the living hell out of that rat. Then I'll ride north, stop at Fletcher's, circle farther north and come down near Timberlake's from the west. I will stay out no longer than two days. Two days from now, have Will Overton ride up to visit Mary Fletcher. They're good friends and it's entirely in order. If I'm not back, Will is to come immediately to one or both of you. That being the case, wire the Colonel for five new men. When they arrive, come north to Timberlake's and take it apart. Get Mathew and make him talk. Abe, what have you learned about Mathews and Timberlake?"

"Very little," Abe Bloom said. "Timberlake came here two years ago, perhaps a little earlier. He bought that place in the hills. He runs a few cattle, but nothing else. He has a bad reputation farther north along the river and in the reservations. Mathews came here three years ago. He neither toils nor spins, but he lives nicely. He is known to be a friend of Timberlake's—but concrete facts, not a one. You have learned more about them in a few days than the town has in three years. I'm sorry, John."

"Can't be helped," McMahon said quickly. "Now, directions clear for the next two days?"

"We'll handle our end, John," Chambers said. "Be careful with yours. One more thing. Trumbell won't wait for progress much longer. We've got to tell him the facts soon."

"In good time," McMahon said shortly. "The man will keep."

He shook hands with Chambers and walked to the back window with Abe Bloom and there, holding the sash open with one hand, took Abe's in the other and squeezed it tightly. Abe Bloom murmured, "Watch yourself, John. A man hates to lose his best friend."

"You won't," McMahon said. "The bad penny always comes back, Abe. Good night."

He stepped lightly through the window and moved east around the edge of town toward the alley that passed the rear of Casey's saloon. He walked around the saloon and stood just off the sidewalk, listening to the faint sounds of late drinkers a block down Front in the Antlers. Casey's was closed; the lamps were out, the door locked. McMahon turned and walked to the back door and tried the knob; it turned slightly and caught. Casey had locked up and gone to bed, he thought, and then he felt that Casey was not inside. McMahon lifted himself through the back window and crossed a storeroom to the back hall. The hall was cold and still, and the small back room in which McMahon had smashed Mathews against the wall was empty and even colder. Casey slept in that room, but the bed was smooth and untouched. McMahon went through the hall into the saloon proper and stood behind the bar, rubbing one hand over the smooth, worn surface, staring into the darkness and trying to think as Casey had been thinking when someone entered the saloon and gave him certain orders. Timberlake, he thought grimly, a man big enough and tough enough to scare Casey witless. There was nothing more to do here; the bird had flown. McMahon walked rapidly to the back window and dropped onto the hard-packed snow.

Tom had a chunky dun saddled and waiting in the livery barn when McMahon entered from the side door. "This one," said the hostler, "will carry you to hell and back, Johnny."

"Good," McMahon said. "I'll be gone a few days this trip. Keep your mouth shut real tight."

"Eyes and mouth," Tom said, accepting a gold piece and grinning broadly. "Hope you get that poker money back, Johnny."

McMahon said, "I will, Tom," and rode slowly toward the wagon road. He had to reach Fletcher's in early morning, pack food and blankets, and be into the Gap hills before full day. Timberlake was a man who wasted little time on a trail; his men might be watching Fletcher's from the ridge in another day.

Paul Mason ate a small breakfast and concentrated over coffee and a cigar, watching Alice Trumbell eat heartily. She looked up after a while, eyes bright, and caught him in this bold study.

"You're thinking about me," she said.

"All the time," Mason smiled. "You know that."

"I do?" she said. "But not all the time, Paul."

"Well then, most of the time."

"Much better," she said. "When are we going home?"

"Soon," Mason said. "Are you anxious to leave War-bonnet?"

"I hate this town," she said sharply. "Cold hotel rooms, lumpy food, lumpy people. That reminds me, have you seen our mysterious friend lately?"

"McMahon?"

"Yes. Is he trailing this murderer?"

"I imagine he has a lead," Mason said. "You might ask Chambers. He should know. I don't."

"I have," Alice Trumbell said. "He gave me kind words and no answers."

"This is man's business," Mason said. "Don't worry about it. Let's discuss something important."

"I'll give you an answer to that," she said immediately.

"The same one," Mason smiled. "You may marry me, but let's not set the date. Now that I've answered my own question, here's another. I want a serious answer. I've felt for some time that you doubt my ability. Also, you think I'm trying to marry you in order to feather my nest, as the boys say in the corner saloon."

She laughed softly. "Well, aren't you?"

Mason said, "Can you blame me, Alice? Money and beauty in the same package. But seriously, working for your father is very nice, the job pays excellently, but I'm not my own master. What would you say if I struck out on my own and make good? Would it change your opinion? Would you consider marriage under those circumstnces?"

Alice Trumbell said, "Paul, you surprise me!"

"I hoped to do more," Mason said dryly. "I hoped you might express violent enthusiasm and elope immediately. I have always felt you believed in that sort of a person."

"I do," she said quickly. "Father has a bad habit—we'll call it that in politeness—of brow-beating his trusted employees. I admire a man who stands on his own feet. But you aren't serious about leaving, are you?"

"I am," Mason said flatly. "Within the next month— three at the most. I intend to make San Francisco my home." He glanced at her face. "I would prefer taking a wife with me."

"Can you support me, Paul, in the style I love?"

"No," Mason said. "Not yet. You know that. But I will, give me the time and help."

She smiled. "The prospect intrigues me, Paul. I'll give you a final answer when we leave this town."

Mason said, "Fair enough. . . . Shall we walk?"

"Not this morning," Alice Trumbell said. "Run along, Paul. Father will be down soon. I'll keep him company at breakfast."

Mason said, "I'll be back in half an hour," and left the dining room by the side door and walked along Front to the bank. Buchanan was stepping outside at that moment, giving last orders to his cashier, then facing Mason and smiling broadly.

"Good morning," Buchanan said. "Taking your constitutional?"

"Yes," Mason said. "May I offer a suggestion?"

They stood before the bank, two well-dressed men seemingly out of place in this crude frontier town.

"A suggestion?" answered Buchanan. "By all means, but make it short."

"I will," Mason said. "Hook Trumbell soon or it may be no use. He's getting impatient. When he turns that way, he might throw up the deal and go home. Will you have lunch with me?"

"A pleasure," Buchanan said heartily. "Good morning, sir."

Buchanan moved ponderously toward the hotel and Mason continued his walk up Front, smiling faintly into the upturned lapels of his overcoat. Buchanan was a cool one, and sly, but Mason held the hole card in this deal. Buchanan would make a move of some sort within two days. He found himself speculating on the method Buchanan would use to bring Trumbell into the net. A man could learn many valuable tricks, just sitting innocently on the side and watching Buchanan work.

McMahon reached the farm an hour before sunrise, left the dun horse in the barn, and crossed quickly to the house. He knocked once on the kitchen door and waited until Fletcher called, "Who is it?" before kicking the snow from his boots and answering, "McMahon, Sam."

"Good," said Fletcher and unlocked the door. McMahon walked directly to the stove and built a fire. It caught slowly and burned with a sharp, pleasant crackle.

"What luck?" Fletcher asked.

"None," McMahon said. "Abe Bloom did his best, but I know no more than I did a day ago. Will you help me pack some food, Sam? And lend me a pair of blankets. I'm for the hills."

"I'll get the blankets and a couple more heavy wool shirts," Fletcher said. "You can start on the food. Take that ham and some sausage."

McMahon was cutting thin slices of ham and making a small, tidy pile of essentials when Mary entered the kitchen, blinking sleep from her eyes and pushing her long, blond hair into a wild knot behind her head. "How long will you be in the hills?" she asked.

"Two days," McMahon said. "Got an old flour sack?"

"Yes. What are you going to do?"

"Get the flour sack," McMahon said patiently.

Mary handed him the sack and said, "Answer my question."

"Just ride and look." McMahon said. "I need a burlap sack, too."

"Then why go if you're not going to do anything?"

"I will have to talk seriously with Will Overton," Mc-Mahon said, "concerning the habits of women before marriage. Especially those who ask foolish questions."

"Very well," she said. "But I'm worried for you, John."

McMahon packed the supplies in the flour sack and dropped it into the heavier burlap bag. He picked a small cast-iron frying pan from the cupboard hook, shoved it on top of the supplies, and tied the sack mouths with a piece of leather whang lacing. He turned then, facing her, and said, "Don't worry about me. This is part of the game."

"Why don't you quit?" Mary said. "I'd think you'd have your fill of risking your life by now."

"Quit?" McMahon asked. "And then what?"

"Have you forgotten how we talked?" she said. "Or were you talking just to pass the time?"

Fletcher came from the bedroom with two heavy brown blankets, rolled and tied with a wide leather belt, a couple of heavy wool shirts over his arm. "Now you put on an extra shirt," he said. McMahon stripped off his mackinaw and put on one shirt, tucking the other into the blanket roll. Then he took the blankets under one arm, the sack of supplies under the other and moved to the door. Fletcher said, "It's thirty-odd miles north to the big river bend, John. That's reservation country. You can ride north through the Gap and then swing west. It's a long pull, but safe."

"I'll take the long pull," McMahon said. "Thanks, Sam."

Fletcher glanced outside at the deep gray of early morning and opened the door. "I'll get your horse," he said gruffly.

McMahon drank his coffee in quick, deep gulps. When Fletcher whistled softly from the barn he handed Mary the cup and said, "I never talk to pass the time. I don't forget the good talks. But a man can't quit when he has nothing much he understands in a new way of life."

She began words but McMahon was already off the

porch, running swiftly to the barn. He mounted the dun
while Fletcher tied the blanket roll and supply sack to the
saddle. Fletcher said, "Better ride hard for a few miles.
It's getting light."

"Watch yourself," McMahon said. "And her."

He waved, realizing she could not see his arm, but feeling better for the gesture. Then he swung the dun east and
rode fast down the lane. Half an hour's riding at this pace
carried him well into the Willow Gap trail, three miles
north of the farm. He was through the Gap and coming
down the north slope when full daylight spread across the
land, with the first sun in a week shining redly through the
thick fringe of morning clouds. He rode in a white land
that rolled and eddied to the north in limitless waves, a
broad plateau that extended thirty miles north and countless miles to the west. North along the river, where it made
the turn from west to south, the reservations touched one
on the other for two hundred miles. Between their boun-
daries and the Willow Ridge was the plateau land, sparsely
settled now, but waiting for the men who had the courage
to break the sod and plant the wheat and corn and small
grain this upland soil begged to nourish, change this rolling
emptiness of tumbleweed and sagebrush empire into a full
mosaic of fences and fields and farm homes, a granary vast
enough to feed a nation. Someday in the near future, Mc-
Mahon thought, a railroad would tap this land and then
the rush would be on; but not too soon. A man couldn't
rush in here. He had to plan carefully; this was still wild
country. But another ten years and farms would dot the
plateau and men like Timberlake would be forgotten in a
land changing too rapidly to remember.

Will Overton made coffee in the hotel kitchen at five
that morning and returned to the lobby desk, where he
straddled his high stool and sipped the coffee and felt even
a warmer glow, knowing that McMahon was not the drunk-

en drifter everyone in town had labeled him. In helping
McMahon, Will Overton discovered that his own judgment was quick and his courage adequate; it was a good
feeling for any man to discover within himself. He was
wondering about the next step in this dangerous game,
when she came from the stairs and stood in the alcove
shadows, her perfume preceding speech. Will Overton
turned and frowned, smelling the brandy.

"Well," Alice Trumbell said. "Coffee."

"Would you like a cup, Miss Trumbell?" he asked.

"No," she said. "Coffee's no good, Will. Not for me."

He saw her face, drawn and tired, and said, "You need
sleep, Miss Trumbell."

"Alice," she said. "My name is Alice. Can't you say it?"

She was on the edge of drunkenness, a sad and secret
kind of self-appeasement. Will Overton felt pity, then dis-
gust. He murmured, "Alice, you'll catch cold. Don't you
think . . . ?"

"Thank you," she said. "That's the first time anyone has
asked me if I think in many years. Do you believe I can
think, Will?"

"Of course," Will Overton said. "Everyone can think,
Alice. It is only the depth of thought that differs."

She laughed and steadied herself against the stair post.
"You're a funny duck, Will. A room clerk who thinks. No,
more than that. You're kind of a philosopher, Will. Aren't
you?"

"Perhaps," Will Overton said mildly. "I read the words
and repeat them and sound wise. The things I want to say
have no words. Most men are like that."

"Not all men," Alice Trumbell said knowingly. "I know
one. He has the words, Will. Too many words. Know
what I am, Will?"

"You're a fine person," Will Overton said, discovering
that he meant his words as he spoke. "But I don't think

you're happy out here. If you'll let me say so, you shouldn't drink at night, Alice."

"And in the day?"

"No," Will Overton said strongly. "I don't believe you like the stuff. Do you?"

"I hate it," she said bitterly. "Don't know why I do it, Will. So I'm a fine person. You don't know me."

"I know what I see," Will Overton murmured. "I don't judge people by their faces, their words."

Alice Trumbell stepped unsteadily behind the stove and sat on the alcove bench. Her hair fell thickly over her cheeks and curled about her fingers, twisted tightly into the folds of her robe. She coughed, and Will Overton hurried around the desk and placed his half-finished cup of coffee in her hands.

"Drink this," he said.

She looked at him oddly and drank the coffee in one long swallow. She said, "I've been sitting up there a long time, Will. Thinking. When a woman thinks, she wants to confide in someone. So I considered all my friends and who did I turn to? You, and that's funny because I don't know you, Will. At home I'd give you one look and forget you."

"You'd never see me," Will Overton said practically. "Out here it's different. Values level off. Friends are few and far between, the real ones. I learned that two years ago."

"Why don't you get mad?" she asked. "I've insulted you."

"Why blow up?" Will Overton said. "You feel badly tonight. Tomorrow you'll forget all this."

"And you?"

"I'll forget it, too," Will Overton smiled. "That's the way you'd like it, isn't it?"

"I had a question," Alice Trumbell said. "Wanted to

ask you, Will. Now it isn't necessary. You answered it for me."

"How?"

"You did," she said. "And now I can sleep. I was about to ask your opinion of a man. You told me exactly what I wanted to know. Thank you, Will, for your good advice and your coffee."

She went to the stairs and then turned. "We'll talk again, Will. That girl won't care, will she?"

"No," Will Overton said. "She wouldn't care."

"If I were she," Alice Trumbell said, suddenly clear voiced, "I would care a great deal. Good night, Will."

Eight

McMAHON RODE west and north all morning, seeing no one; at noon in a cutbank's shelter, fringed by willows, he stopped for a quick meal and smoke while the dun nosed beneath the willows, pawing for buried grass. Then McMahon angled southwest toward the now-distant ridge line. Mid-afternoon brought him to the first slope and early dusk found him deep in the ridge's convolutions, the surrounding hills dulled to vague silhouettes by approaching night. He was west and slightly north of Timberlake's place, he judged, at a distance between three and five miles. He worked east cautiously, slipping from the saddle a half hour later and leading the dun through miniature canyons that dropped into a gradual and general deeping the farther east and south he moved. He had looked closely for tracks through the day and found none; entering a steep-sided ravine that debouched into a larger, deeper canyon some distance ahead, McMahon located a pocket in the north wall and called it quits for the day. He tied the dun on a short rope, filled the nose bag with Fletcher's good oats, and made camp.

Water had gouged out the pocket wall to form a three-foot overhang; he scooped the snow from this half-roofed hole and went down the canyon, collecting pine cones and dead branches, making half a dozen trips before he had a sizable stack beneath the overhang. He used his knife to dig a small hole, a foot square and six inches deep. In this he built his fire, tiny and hot, and shaded it from the canyon by hanging a blanket on two sticks thrust in the snow. He burned down a good bed of coals on which he fried ham and boiled a pot of coffee. He sat cross-legged on the other blanket, and ate hungrily and drank all the coffee straight from the pot. Smoking three cigarettes one upon the other, McMahon then cleaned his gun and stretched himself before the fire and dozed for three hours. He woke at ten o'clock and smelled the air. It was a clear, cold night with many stars and the first thin rind of the new moon. Timberlake's place was no more than two miles to the east and slightly south. McMahon covered the remaining coals, tied the blanket roll and sack to the saddle, mounted and pointed the dun down the canyon. After an hour's riding at a slow walk he was as close as he dared come on the horse; he tied the dun and proceeded along the narrowing channel of a canyon on foot.

He smelled the faint odor of smoke carried on the wind that blew now from the southeast, a gentle and subtly melting wind, presaging the breaking of winter and the coming of spring. He was near the cup now, on strange ground, and he turned from the canyon bottom and climbed slowly to the top of the east wall. He put himself in Timberlake's place and thought as that man would. It was difficult to judge the man's scope and imagination, knowing nothing about him, only having heard his voice twice. But men like Timberlake were cut from the same cloth, and thought in much the same way. Timberlake would have his men scattered strategically around the cup on the hills tonight, and quite probably for a week to come. He took a chance, coming this near, but the night was dark despite the stars, and the south wind was lifting clouds above the horizon. He moved slowly along the edge of the canyon and came to a higher hill with a flattened top; the wood-smoke smell was stronger. McMahon drew his gun and held it against his mackinaw; they would not hesitate to kill him up here where no one lived or traveled. He walked to the crest of the high hill which, exposed to view, became a long and narrow ridge that ended abruptly some five hundred feet to the south and seemingly began farther on in the distance.

From below came the dull thud of wood hitting a sled box and then a string of curses that put many a muledriver to shame. Someone had the fire-feeding job and hated it. McMahon began crawling through the snow toward the edge of the cliff, unable to see his exact location, but guessing he was directly above the cabin and out-buildings. The wood-smoke smell was stronger, blotting out the fresh piny sweetness of the wind. He came to a slight depression that curved across his path from the right and threaded straight before him toward the cliff edge. Lying in its center, he was a foot beneath ground level. Here was something to remember. A few men could approach the cup through this natural ditch formed by wind and water, lower a rope, and be inside the cabin before Timberlake could raise one hand. If, McMahon thought, the guard at this point was taken out of the play. He heard nothing, smelled only the wind, but sensed a man's presence ahead. He crawled another hundred feet and lifted himself slightly to stare right and left and ahead where the cliff edge was no more than fifty paces distant. McMahon saw the guard to his right, sitting on a rock in the shadow of a jack pine, the faint pencil-thin line of a rifle across his knees. While McMahon looked, the man shifted the rifle and stretched both legs and grunted softly into a thick muffler. In that moment, McMahon was satisfied.

Timberlake had his guards out. That meant Mathews
and Casey were still in the area. He could pull back and
ride to town, drop the case in Trumbell's lap, and call on
the local authorities to assist in making the arrest. He
turned slowly in the narrow ditch and, completing this
swing, struck a stick beneath the snow with one boot. It
snapped loudly in the silence. Instantly steps sounded
from the side. McMahon thrust his gun inside the mackinaw and gathered himself for the first leap. He heard the
guard, then saw him stride rapidly toward McMahon, rifle
at the ready. He reached a point marked in McMahon's
mind, two steps away, and saw McMahon at the moment
he leaped from the ditch.

The rifle shot echoed and re-echoed across the hills and
through the canyons, a savage and wild sound in the night.
McMahon felt the tug of the bullet across his right shoulder and then he was into the guard, under the rifle barrel,
twisting and throwing it from the guard's hands and landing his first blow to the man's stomach. The guard was a
big man with a round stomach and a thick aroma of cigar
smoke and stale onions on his breath. He grunted once
and then clubbed McMahon on the head and shoulders,
gathering his strength to shout across the hills. McMahon
threw him by the belt and followed against his chest, fighting now with the skill and experience of years. The guard's
greater bulk was useless; he was slow and chilled, and his
opponent fought like no man the guard had ever known.
He thought vaguely as he tried to shout and felt the fingers close around his throat, shutting off the sound, that
here was a man he could never face in a stand-up fight. He
was against a man who had lived by the strength and speed
of attack the whole of his life, a man continually keyed up
and ready for perpetual danger.

McMahon felt the body stiffen and then go limp. While
he held the throat in one hand he drew his gun and laid
it solidly against the man's head, feeling him go complete-

ly limp beneath the blow. He heard the shouts all across and around the cup, and one far to the northwest, directly in his path of retreat. He changed all plans in that moment. If he turned back and successfully dodged them, closing in as they were now, they would find his tracks in the snow and follow him all night and the next day if necessary. Crouching low, he ran to the edge of the cliff and looked down on the roof of Timberlake's cabin directly below. The cliff was actually a wall here, nearly perpendicular but rough and uneven, with shrubs and stunted pines growing from the shale rock.

McMahon made his decision in this last moment of safety, hearing a man call from nearby and another answer from the opposite side of the flanking ravines. He lowered himself over the edge, found a handhold beneath the snow, and started his descent. He could not waste time; nor could he kick rock and earth loose to fall below. He heard three rifle shots from the south, evidently a rally signal, and below him, less than a hundred feet, a man ran from the cabin to the open-sided barn and began leading horses into the yard. McMahon used the moments of sound during the shots, and the ensuing noise of the horses moving from the barn, to lower himself a good twenty feet, dropping from a stunted pine to a shrub, from handhold to crevice, until, moments later, as the same man galloped up the incline toward the trail, leading a string of horses on a long rope, he was a short ten feet above the level ground, directly behind the cabin. He heard someone above him call, "Ed's bringing the horses. Fan out and find that track."

McMahon dropped five feet and stared directly into the cabin's back wall. He placed both hands gently on a log and let himself down from the rock to the snow-covered space behind the cabin, a narrow passage two feet wide, half-choked with snow and dirt. He moved to the left corner of the cabin and around the corner to the same window he had stood beside short nights past. The yard was quiet; above and fading to the north, Timberlake and his men were calling signals and spreading across the hills. Leaning against the logs, bruised and sore-muscled, he heard the voices within the cabin.

"Reckon they'll get him, George?"

"Go out and see!"

"You know what Roy told us, George. Stay here, sit tight."

"Well, you heard them flush him. He won't break away from that bunch. And maybe he'll try to circle around. I hope he does. He'll get a hot reception on the south side, too. Maybe that fat Chambers is sneaking down from the south, figuring everybody is chasing McMahon to the north. I hope Russ and Kenny shoot straight. Damn it, Casey. Don't stand there. Go out and get that wood. I'm freezing!"

McMahon drew his gun and moved to the front corner of the cabin. Casey, grumbling loudly, opened the door and stamped heavily within five feet of McMahon, moving along the path to the woodshed. McMahon slipped out and walked directly to the door, pushed it back and stepped into the cabin.

Mathews sat at a long table before the fireplace, playing solitaire, his face intent on the cards. He turned to shout at Casey, saw McMahon, and froze in place, hands twisting the cards unknowingly. McMahon closed the door, felt for the bar, and dropped it in place. The cabin was one deep, wide room with hinge bunks on three walls at one end, and the table, a dozen chairs, the cookstove, and rough cupboards at the other. There were two small windows with inside shutters. McMahon noted these factors and smiled sourly.

"Hello, fisherman," he said. "How are they biting to-night?"

Buchanan finished his noon meal and paused in the dining-room archway to exchange greetings with other merchants and to take the pulse of Warbonnet as reflected in its only hotel. Fashionably dressed drummers in bowler hats and pegged trousers up from the main line with their cowhide sample cases and catalogs, overalled farmers in for supplies after the storm, looking bulky and faintly soiled beneath home-knit gray sweaters and knee-length sheepskins, townspeople talking in small groups, somehow alien to the farmers already with their difference in clothing and knowledge that they lived in a growing community; all of them in their respective ways made the town and would, in time, strengthen it with their own growth. Buchanan had chosen to ignore Mason's warning; there was no hurry about needling Trumbell. Shortly, possibly while Buchanan enjoyed a hot lunch, McMahon would breathe his last and Timberlake would take excellent care of Casey and Mathews. Buchanan coughed gently and lit a cigar, and saw Roy Timberlake enter through the lobby door, move one hand in a secret gesture, and continue through the lobby to the washroom behind the stairs.

Buchanan took his time moving across the lobby to the washroom. Timberlake was standing at the window, drying huge fingers on the soiled roller towel. He turned when Buchanan closed the door and said, "We're alone, Ferris. All hell broke loose last night. I had to come in and tell you."

"What happened?" Buchanan said softly. "Be careful of the door, Roy. If anyone comes in, see me in the woodshed behind the bank in fifteen minutes. Now hurry it up!"

"McMahon," Timberlake said bitterly. "Damn his soul! He made a circle to the north and come down on the place from the west and north. I expected something like that after the Fletcher girl lied to me about her sore throat. I knew he was riding out from Fletcher's. I had men posted all around the cup, Ferris. I took the north wall myself.

Before midnight I heard a stick snap and went over to look. He came out of a little ditch and knocked me flat . . ." Timberlake's face mirrored his grudging admiration for a superior fighting man. "I was plumb out for a little while, but I shot when he jumped. That brought the boys, but he went up in smoke. We found no backtrack, just his trail coming in. Then I looked along the edge of the wall and saw it. Damn him! He went straight down the wall. When we hit the bottom he was in the cabin with Casey and Mathews, both of them tied and yelling at us to lay off or he'd cut their throats. You know that cabin, Ferris. I built it to my own order. It'll take blasting powder to break inside. I don't give a damn about Mathews and Casey. He can shoot 'em for all I care. But we've got to finish him. He can't get away. But we can't get him. I talked with him just before I pulled out and he said the only way he was coming out was for me to send the others ten miles north, then walk to the cabin unarmed and give myself up. He said he didn't want me for anything, but he was taking Mathews in, and Casey as a witness, come hell or high water, and I'd have to ride along as far as the wagon road to make sure the boys didn't jump him. I told him to go to hell and then he laughed. He said he could last two weeks and if he wasn't back at a certain place inside of two days, he'd have twenty men riding out."

Buchanan had listened quietly, face unmoving, as Timberlake talked. He showed the mettle of a shrewd, unbending man in this moment, refusing to castigate Timberlake for botching the job. Instead he patted Timberlake's shoulder gently.

"One of those things, Roy," Buchanan said. "Don't blame yourself. You can't be everywhere at once."

"I . . ." Timberlake said, with great relief. "Thanks, Ferris. I was scared you might shoot first and ask questions later."

"Nothing is hurt," Buchanan said swiftly. "He's been there one day, hasn't he?"

"One day tonight."

"I don't think he lied about that two-day time limit," Buchanan said. "However, Chambers and whoever else has instructions from him can't get out that way for another half day. Go straight back, Roy, and keep him busy. Don't bargain with him. Tomorrow night give him a call and agree to his deal."

"But . . ."

"Wait," Buchanan smiled. "I know this country, too, Roy. Disarm yourself, and I mean really disarm. Walk across the yard and let him tie you or whatever he wishes. Bring all the men down so he can see them plainly, and send them north. Ride with him to the wagon road as hostage. Start whenever he wishes, but no later than the following morning. Sid and Harry can circle back toward town. Have them cross the river a few miles above town and come down on the east bank to the big bluff just south and across from Olson's farm. They can take up an excellent position by crossing the river on foot and waiting in the willows. When he passes with Mathews and Casey, tell them to get Casey and McMahon, and if they miss they'll answer to me. They're to lead a third horse for Mathews. Tell them to pull the bodies off the road into the willows, hide them, then ride north to the reservation and stay at the shack until you send word. And most important, Roy, Mathews will know this without orders, but tell Sid and Harry to search McMahon to the bare skin and bring everything they find on his body. Got it?"

Timberlake said, "It's the best we can do, Ferris. A good play. When do you want me in again?"

"The night after the job is finished," Buchanan said. "Come to the house at midnight. Don't fail me, Roy. One time can be chance, two the unforeseen, and no fault of anyone's, but the third is the charm. You understand?"

Someone turned the doorknob. Buchanan immediately raised his voice and began washing his hands at the bowl, saying loudly, "If you want to talk business, Timberlake, see me at the bank. A man's privacy is something he values."

"Sorry," Timberlake said, watching a drummer enter the washroom. "I'll stop by next week, Buchanan."

"Always glad to talk business during business hours," Buchanan said. "Ah, how are you, Mr. Atherton?"

Buchanan walked from the washroom to the lobby and into the street where he paused at sight of Paul Mason coming from his noon stroll about the business district. Mason smiled and said, "A nice day, Mr. Buchanan," and moved toward the lobby door.

"Would you ask Mr. Trumbell to call at the bank?" Buchanan asked. "I have something of value for his ears alone."

"Gladly," Mason said. "Business picking up?"

"Quite rapidly," Buchanan said. "Just as you anticipated."

"Shall I come with Mr. Trumbell?" Mason asked.

"By all means. I feel you should be present to advise Mr. Trumbell against leaping into dubious investments."

Buchanan went directly to the bank and settled himself in the private office. He sent the cashier to bring the new county plat book from the vault, and then smoked in the room's stillness, planning his speech and attempting to anticipate Trumbell's reaction. In a while the cashier opened his door and said, "Mr. Trumbell and Mr. Mason to see you," and stepped aside as Trumbell entered the office, puffing volcanically on a cigar, glaring at nothing in particular, but overripe for an argument.

"Good day, sir," Buchanan said. "How are you, Mr. Mason?"

"What's all this?" Trumbell asked. "Something about that farm land I mentioned?"

"In a sense," Buchanan said. "Mr. Trumbell, ever since you were kind enough to confide in me, I've been considering all angles of your proposition with a few of my own. We seem to coincide. Have you the time to hear a story?"

"Too much time," Trumbell grumbled. "Go ahead."

"Well, sir," Buchanan said heartily. "You are interested in farm land. Oddly enough, so am I. I know the valley north of here. I know my values in this country. I'm going to show you something, Mr. Trumbell, that may strike a responsive chord in your heart."

Buchanan placed the plat map of Warbonnet County before them and tapped various sections with his pencil point. "Here," he said, "is the best way to determine the location and shape of every farm in the valley. I'm going against my better judgment now. I'm going to give you an excellent tip for the future. I have already purchased farm land in the valley north of town. I own a rather odd-shaped block extending from this western rim of hills straight across the valley to the river . . ."

"You what?" Trumbell asked sharply.

"Now, now," Buchanan chuckled. "Don't call me a fool until I explain. I had a reason for buying in this way. You see, I have felt, ever since I came here, that in years to come the valley and the plateau land north of the Willow Gap will become increasingly productive. Consider the history of this land to date, mid-February, 1887, as we stand together on it. Warbonnet was a trader's store ten years ago; the only people north of here were the Indians and a few early homesteaders. Today the valley is completely proved up and owned by farmers. The railroad sent a branch line. We are growing wheat and corn and small grain. We are feeding cattle for market and raising hogs and chickens and poultry. We have an increasing business in both directions—the raw material going out, the finished product returning. A healthy and vigorous condition. The river itself is deep enough for commerce with a bit of

channeling by the army engineers. This is a matter of poli-
tics, as you know yourself. Some day not only the river
will be open, but the railroad should extend north from
here. Therefore, I took stock in myself, faced the challenge
and the gamble, and bought this solid stretch of land across
the valley from hills to river. That gives me loading facil-
ities on the river and my own yards for my crops and cattle
if the railroad ever comes through. I own grazing land far
back in the hills northwest of here and intend to run cattle
in quantity some day, feed them fat on my farms, and ship
them direct to market. It is a dream, true, but entirely possible. I am telling you this, Mr. Trumbell, because I would
like to see you follow my plan and purchase a similar block
of farm land. Naturally, you would be wise to buy through
me and I would make the middleman's profit, as is right
and honest in good business. I am hoping, too, that by
telling you this—and no one else knows of my dream—
that you will exert your considerable pressure on your
friends in the railroad business and persuade them to extend the branch line to the Gap and on through to the
plateau. It's a gamble, but then, so is life. You could do
very well, Mr. Trumbell, with a modest investment. Have
I said too much in too little time, or are you sympathetic
with my daydream?"

For the first time in many years Trumbell was speech-
less and confused. He covered his fear by lighting a fresh
cigar and studying the map with serious deliberation,
thinking of every word Buchanan had spoken, trying to see
the catch, feeling sure that Buchanan must be the person
who had stolen his papers; and in the same thought calling himself seven kinds of fool. Here was a small-town
banker with guts and vision. But here was the block to all
his plans and, at the same moment, the chance to circum-
vent the loss of those papers and go on with the deal. He
thought of McMahon, missing for days, and no sign of
those papers. And here was Buchanan, owning one of the

sections he had purchased right of way on over a year ago. But the deeds and bills of sale were gone, and he could not prove ownership to that strip of land. He shivered inwardly, visualizing what Buchanan would do if he knew about the construction already planned and awaiting his one word to move. Then he remembered that single place at the foot of the Gap, Fletcher's, and wondered if Buchanan could purchase right of way or, if need be, the entire farm. He needed time to think, but he had to give Buchanan an immediate answer.

"It's not a daydream," Trumbell said evenly. "You have the sort of vision this country needs. Let me consider this proposition."

"Gladly," Buchanan said. "If you like, I'll have all details written out for study at your leisure."

"Do that," Trumbell said. "I'll be at the hotel."

"One thing," Buchanan said. "I want to be fair, Mr. Trumbell, but I must explain that a gentleman is due here on the evening train to discuss this self-same proposition with me. I am not at liberty to disclose his name, or the interests he represents, but I can say they are large and, to put it bluntly, eager for investments. I can have all details on your desk in thirty minutes, sooner if Mr. Mason here will remain and bring them to you. I am offering you no gold bricks, Mr. Trumbell. Frankly, I would enjoy doing business with you before all others. Your reputation has preceded you, to put it modestly. But time is of the essence. Surely you can give me an answer by six tonight."

"Fair enough," Trumbell said. "At six. Have dinner with me."

"A pleasure, sir. Dinner at six."

"Bring the papers, Paul," Trumbell said.

He nodded curtly and left the office. Mason said, "I take off my hat to you. I never heard a slicker deal in my life. I believed it, even knowing better."

"I own that land," Buchanan said. "That was my ace in

the hole, my friend, in case you crossed me after giving me
such a good thing. The deal is legitimate, Mason. If he ad-
mits his scheme to me, and asks for my assistance, such aid
and all contractual additions will be written, signed, and
witnessed. He can build his railroad. I'll help him. I wonder if you realize that in spite of your off-center shots, and
my dubious interest, if it goes through we will be engaged
in a thoroughly reputable and above-board proposition."

"Money makes money," Mason said softly. "Very true
in this case, Ferris. Trumbell has the money. We'll make
it. Finished? Good. I'll see you at dinner."

Buchanan handed him the sheets filled with the detailed
facts, showed him out, and turned to face his desk and
wipe his face with a trembling hand. He knew how a
watchmaker felt now, he thought, reviewing the delicate
pieces of this plan that were balanced on a hair-trigger and
ready to blow sky-high at a moment's notice from a single
miscalculation.

Nine

McMAHON STOOD to the left of the cabin door and
drank bitter black coffee, gun held low in his free hand,
watching Mathews and Casey. Late afternoon was soften-
ing into dusk, the fireplace gave off pleasant heat, and the
thought of Timberlake and his men squatting in the snow
was comforting. He remembered the advice of an old
deputy marshal, given years ago, about taking the bold
course when the safe turn appeared the only way out of a
trap. He had taken that bold course in the night, and now
commanded Timberlake's cabin, and not only the cabin
with its food and rude comfort, but a full sweep of the cup
which kept Timberlake's crew on the walls and behind
rocks and trees up the south trail.

Mathews was tied securely in one chair, Casey in another

at the opposite end of the big table. Their faces were studies in contrast today. Mathews was defiant, but the fear beneath moved closer to the surface every hour. Casey was utterly afraid and limp in his chair, all fight gone from his fat body, which sagged over the chair arms and against his ropes like so much sacked grain. When he entered the cabin, Mathews had been shocked into a moment's apathy, long enough to be knocked unconscious with a gun barrel while McMahon turned to the door and opened it politely for Casey and the wood sled. Casey had pulled the sled through the door, head down, grunting his reluctant thanks, and had unloaded a dozen logs before looking up and collapsing with sheer animal terror. McMahon had boosted Casey to a chair, tied him, and then taken his time lifting Mathews into another chair and tying him with the lassos hung on pegs beside the door. After that McMahon had barred the window shutters, pushed the wood sled against the door, and seated himself in a chair facing both of them. Casey was bubbling with explanations and questions, until he said, "Shut up!" and waited for Timberlake to find him.

That happened shortly, and McMahon selected two rifles from the wall rack, loaded them, and moved a small table to the right of the fireplace facing the door. Here he placed the rifles and all the ammunition in the cabin. Mathews regained consciousness while he finished his defensive arrangements and cursed him bitterly for a full five minutes. He let the man go on until someone called outside and the first shot hit the door. Then he walked quickly to the table and slapped Mathews across the face with his mittens and said, "Keep your mouth shut. I'll tell you when to talk."

McMahon fed the fire, cooked and ate a breakfast on the move, and walked around the cabin, gun ready, waiting for a sneak attack but expecting none. Timberlake's voice was not heard during the day after the parley; and now, at dusk,

McMahon wondered if the big man would try a force play. McMahon decided he had ridden into town for orders.

"John?" Casey said timidly. "You know I never wanted to come out here. They made me close up and come."

"Who made you?" McMahon asked.

"Roy," Casey said, and glanced fearfully at Mathews. "He woulda killed me if I didn't come, John."

McMahon said, "Why?" and spun the cylinder of his gun.

"I guess on account of Red," Casey said. "Listen, John. I'll do anything you say if you'll give me a chance to clear out of the country. I never killed anybody, you know that."

"I don't know it," McMahon said, "but I can believe you. It takes a certain amount of guts to kill a man."

"How true," Mathews said thinly. "When I get loose from this rope, Casey, I'm cutting your heart out."

"When you get loose?" McMahon murmured. "And how, pimp?"

"I can wait," Mathews said. "You're not riding anywhere for your health. Not for a long time."

"Maybe you've got the wrong slant on this deal," McMahon said. "If they force the cabin, my first slug goes into your guts, Mathews. You'll cut no more hearts. You'll hang or go out of here on a board."

"Tall talk," Mathews said. "You're a dead man yourself."

"I'm a dead man anyway," McMahon said cheerfully. "We're all dead, Mathews. It just takes time to reach us all."

He turned to the door and heard the rifle shots and the thump of bullets against the outer wall. From the darkness Timberlake shouted, "McMahon?"

"Yes?" McMahon called.

"I'll take your deal," Timberlake answered loudly. "Your terms. When do you want it?"

McMahon smiled and saw Mathews struggle futilely

against his ropes and curse Timberlake savagely under his breath. Casey was visibly relieved. McMahon called, "Tomorrow morning in full daylight. Bring your crew down, let me count them, then send them north. You come unarmed to the barn, bring the horses in front of the cabin door, saddled, three tied together with a long end on the rope. We'll go on from there in the morning."

"I got your promise to let me go at the wagon road?"

"You go free," McMahon said.

"Fair and square," Timberlake shouted. "And don't eat all that ham. Give Casey the bologna."

They laughed raucously in the outer perimeter of darkness and Casey's face turned red. McMahon came to the table, facing them, suddenly hard and angry.

"You hear that?" he said. "Rats leaving the sinking ship, Mathews. Can you feel the rope?"

"Never felt better," Mathews said. "I'm not done, McMahon."

"Who is he, Mathews?" McMahon asked abruptly.

"Who's who?"

"You know who I mean," McMahon said. "The big boy, the man who gives the orders. His name and I'll recommend clemency for you. That means twenty years in prison, eventual pardon."

"You," Mathews said distinctly, "can go to hell!"

"Well, Casey," McMahon said. "Your turn."

"I don't know, John," Casey said. "Honest to God, I don't know."

"Then Mathews has a boss?" McMahon said.

"I never said that . . ."

"Cut it," McMahon said harshly. 'Don't feed me that plumduff. Who is it?"

"I don't know," Casey said weakly. "Timberlake gives the orders. We just follow them, John. That's all Red knew, and he was my best friend."

"He was," McMahon said. "You know who killed Red, don't you?"

"I . . ." Casey said.

"You can spit on him," McMahon said. "Why don't you? If I cut you loose and give you a knife, what will you do?"

"Nothing," Mathews said scornfully. "Saying I killed Red, which I didn't, he still wouldn't do nothing."

"You killed him," McMahon said quietly. "Let's not talk foolish, Mathews. I know it. You know it. Nobody heard us that night but you. Casey, I'm taking a killer to town tomorrow. He'll hang as sure as I stand here. You're going along to testify at his trial . . ."

"No," Casey said. "No, John. They'll . . ."

"Oh," McMahon murmured. "Now the wind blows hard. They'll get you when you walk outside, is that it? Know who I am, Casey?"

"I . . ."

"A fly cop," Mathews said. "A damned Pink."

"Was," McMahon said. "One of the damned Pinks who ran the rats off the railroads a few years ago, Mathews. I'm not a Pink now, Casey. I work for another boss. He backs me to the limit, just like the Pinks, and the limit is the noose for Mathews and ten years for you as accessory—unless you testify."

"Don't let him scare you," Mathews said. "You've got friends, Casey. Just remember that."

McMahon was silent for a minute, allowing the fire sound and the wind to fill the room like mice scampering across dry leaves. "Casey, would you like to get out of the country?"

"You mean that?" Casey said eagerly.

"Yes. Now listen to me. I'll untie your right hand. I want you to write out a full statement concerning events leading to the murder of Red Egan, the manner in which it occurred. Sign your full name. I'll take care of it. When we reach the wagon road tomorrow about noon, I'll turn you loose. You'll have a horse and your health. Ride over the Gap, out of the country. Your statement is good in court with me witnessing it."

Mathews raged against his ropes and shouted, "You sign anything, Casey, you're a dead man!"

Casey looked at McMahon and said, "You mean that?"

"I keep my word, Casey. What do you say?"

"Give me that paper," Casey said. "I'll write it all."

McMahon concealed his elation and searched the cabin for paper and pen, or pencil, finding a cheap ruled tablet and a tooth-marked pencil above the fireplace. He loosened Casey's right arm and pushed tablet and pencil under the stiff fingers. Casey flexed his hand and said, "What'll I write?"

"I'll talk it out for you," McMahon said. "You write."

He stood behind Casey and spoke slowly, following the erratic pencil as it spelled laboriously through the words and sentences. McMahon dictated a full statement and Casey finished the last phrase, wrote the date and place, and signed his name. Mathews watched him covertly and McMahon hid a smile as he walked to the fireplace and tossed two logs atop the blazing pile. He checked their ropes after he had retied Casey's arm and then took the chair behind the small table, facing the door, and dozed comfortably, chair tipped against the wall. He had filled both lamps and they burned low and steady. Once during the early-morning hours a chair scraped and McMahon opened one eye and said, "Don't try it, Mathews," and immediately dozed off again.

He woke in the pre-dawn grayness and built up the fire, cooked and ate breakfast, cooked another breakfast and spoon fed it to both men. He was drinking his third cup of coffee when Timberlake called, "Getting daylight, McMahon! You want us to set things up?"

"Go on," McMahon answered. 'Get your boys down and start the ball."

He moved to the east wall and unbarred the heavy plank shutter and opened it half an inch; then moved to the door and opened the peephole that gave a full view of the yard. Men were riding down the trail into the cup and grouping before the cabin. Timberlake dismounted and placed his rifle, revolver, and a skinning knife on the ground, then strode deliberately across the yard to the barn. McMahon heard him talking to the horses, slapping blankets and saddles over cold backs, fumbling with something that had to be the tie rope, and finally leading three horses directly in front of the cabin. Two were tied, the other stood alone. Timberlake called, "I'll get my own," walked to his horse, led it back and tied it into the string. He turned then and counted his men, six in all, and called, "Ready and waiting, McMahon!"

McMahon said, "Stand clear of the horses, ahead of them on the right. Tell those bucko boys that in case they figure on potshooting me, you'll get every shot I can pump before I drop. And that'll be more than enough."

"They know that," Timberlake called hoarsely. "There'll be no potshooting. You made your promise. I keep mine."

"All right," McMahon said. "Send them off."

Timberlake waved one arm and the riders wheeled up the trail, disappeared over the ridge and around the bend, then appeared minutes later on the west ridge, riding six in line. All waved and went on to the north and west. McMahon murmured, "Very nice," and then retied Mathews and Casey with new knots, releasing their legs and pushing them erect.

"We'll go outside," he said, "to the lead horses. Timberlake will boost you up. Casey, your hands are tied over your belly so you can handle the reins. Mathews will follow."

He walked to the door and called, "Face the horses and raise your arms, Timberlake."

"Ready."

McMahon swung the door back and said, "All right, let's go!"

They walked stiffly into the yard, McMahon holding his gun directly on Timberlake's wide back. He said, "Boost them up, Timberlake," and watched the big man lift Casey to the lead horse, push the reins between his clenched fingers, and toss Mathews like a paper bag onto the second horse.

"Get up." McMahon said.

They faced each other for the first time. McMahon saw the brutal face, the thick mouth and cruel eyes and tremendous body that had once been hard and thick, and now was swollen with fat.

McMahon mounted quickly, gathered in the rope that ran to Timberlake's horse and on through to the others. He cocked his gun, the sound loud in the morning silence, and said, "We'll go out of here at a walk. When we clear the Gap trail, turn east for the wagon road. Then we'll start moving. All right, let's go."

Buchanan enjoyed dinner immensely that evening. Alice Trumbell wore a striking maroon gown that set the other women in the hotel dining room grinding their teeth in envy. Paul Mason was the suave middleman, offering his own polite opinions whenever speech tapered off around the table. When coffee was served and Mason sent the waitress for brandy, Alice Trumbell excused herself and retired to the lobby. The dining room was empty now; other guests had swallowed their final view of her white shoulders and gone away muttering about the injustice of life. Trumbell sipped his brandy, coughed thickly, and spoke.

"I've studied your proposition," he said. "It makes sense."

'I agree," Buchanan smiled. "But have you reached a common viewpoint?"

"Yours, you mean?"

"Naturally, Mr. Trumbell. Profit for me, profit for you."

"My capital," Trumbell said.

"And my assistance," Buchanan said, smiling once more. "Come, Mr. Trumbell. A gentleman is waiting for me at the bank. What shall I tell him?"

Trumbell had spent a restless afternoon, considering the deal. McMahon was gone somewhere, the papers were seemingly lost forever, and time was running short. He had estimated that particular factor to the last day during his mental argument. Everyone said it would be an early spring; that meant construction could push off March first, the tenth at very latest. This was mid-February and outside, following the storm that had begun with anger and petered out unexpectedly, a southeast wind blew across the land. Buchanan had placed the alternative solution squarely in his lap. If he could purchase right of way through Buchanan and buy the Fletcher farm without giving the banker too large a cut of the eventual profits, the deal would still go through to his ultimate satisfaction.

"A deal," Trumbell said. "I authorize you to arrange purchase of farms adjoining your own in a similar block."

"From hills to river," Buchanan said. "I commend your foresight, Mr. Trumbell. When shall I start negotiations?"

"Immediately," Trumbell said. "I'll transfer funds to your bank tomorrow. Now, about your commission?"

"By all means," Buchanan said, "shall we get to the root of all evil? Ordinarily, Mr. Trumbell, the farmer would pay me the commission for selling his land. However, several of the farms in question are owned by satisfied men. That is to say, they are satisfied with their present lot, but no man will refuse a high price for his land. At present land is selling from fifteen to twenty-fiive dollars an acre in the valley, depending on the improvements. A bonus of ten dollars above their asking price will fetch most of them. We may run afoul of the individualist who demands more. I feel sure that you won't quibble over a few hundred dollars?"

"Certainly not," Trumbell said testily. "Make the deals."

"I'll start tomorrow," Buchanan said. "Mr. Mason will undoubtedly assist me, will he not?"

"Yes. He handles everything of this nature."

"Then we are agreed," Buchanin said.

"Do you want a contract, an agreement?" Trumbell asked.

"From you, sir?" Buchanan said. "Your word is good anywhere."

Trumbell paused and looked around the empty dining room. "Buchanan," he asked, "what would you say if I told you all this farm land business was so much child's play?"

"For you, sir," Buchanan said, "it must be. When a man has your wealth and connections, this sort of business amounts to a mere bagatelle, a hobby."

Trumbell smiled wryly. "Do you remember the railroad you spoke of this noon?"

"Remember!" Buchanan said. "I can't forget it."

"How soon would you say it is plausible to build such a road?"

"Now," Buchanan said. "Right now. Get me the money, Mr. Trumbell. I'll build you a railroad that will pay out within ten years after the first tie is laid."

"How do you credit this assumption?" Trumbell asked.

"Will you allow me the floor for considerable time?" Buchanan said. "You've touched one of my pet dreams, one I have studied for years. Let us assume you wish to build a road from here, north through the valley to the Willow Gap, through the Gap, into the plateau country, and end it on the boundary of the reservation land. Sixty miles of road, the chance to start two new towns, one, certainly. People are coming out here steadily. Farm land is rising in price. Produce will be swelling the bins, waiting for a convenient means of transportation. Take the farmer fifteen miles north of here. He has a thousand bushels of corn in surplus. He wants to sell. Very well, here in town we have agents for various large milling concerns. They offer a price, the farmer accepts, and then he is forced to take two, possibly three days, and haul that corn here by wagon over a rough, bumpy road, closed part of the year by snow and mud. The further north that farmer lives, the greater the saving a railroad would mean to him. Consider the man who built that railroad. He could set reasonable, yet highly profitable rates, for a short haul. With connections, he could effect the proper relationship between his road and the main line's branch. The farmer might cuss a little over paying a freight rate for the short haul, and another for the long haul to market, but think of the time he would save for a reasonable expenditure! And eventually, if the builder of such a road showed good profit and the region began to fill with more people, he could strike a deal with the big railroad and come out with a tremendous profit. All he need do is safeguard the building of a competition line by purchasing a block of land across the valley. Do you follow me, Mr. Trumbell?"

Trumbell was no longer the slightly interested customer; now he leaned heavily on the table. "And what would such a railroad cost, per mile, in this region?"

"Well, now," Buchanan murmured, "from here to the Gap, considering everything, around sixteen thousand dollars per mile. To cross the Gap—a 3.2 per cent grade—that is, three-tenths per cent below the maximum, your cost should not exceed twenty thousand per mile. Sidings are not included in this original estimate, but will run about the same. Excessive curvature might be reduced, if necessary, for thirty thousand dollars additional."

Trumbell concealed deep surprise at this fat, slow-appearing man who had named the cost of the road within a few thousand dollars. He said, finally, "You're not far off."

"Thank you," Buchanan said. "You flatter me, Mr. Trumbell. I'm a mere amateur playing with big figures. You know them."

Trumbell came to a final decision. The fat was in the fire and he had to move one way or another. Get in or get out, he thought grimly, and pay the price.

"What would you answer," Trumbell said, "if I authorized you to purchase a right of way from Warbonnet north across the Gap to the reservation boundary?"

Buchanan placed a look of complete amazement on his fat, round face. He said, "You're joking with me."

"Damn it!" Trumbell said. "I never joke. Can you do it?"

Buchanan whispered, "You want to build this railroad?"

"If you can keep it to yourself and co-operate with me."

"I'm your man," Buchanan said. "Give me the green light and I'll go through mountains." Speaking, Buchanan wondered if McMahon was digging through a mountain to escape; the thought cleared his head and made him doubly alert.

"About the right of way," Trumbell said. "I assume you will sell me rights across your land and purchase the bulk from the owners. Also, this Fletcher?"

Buchanan smiled. "Now, sir, we come to the crux of this deal. Put yourself in my position. What would you say to that?"

"Name your price," Trumbell said. "Anything within reason."

"I'll be reasonable," Buchanan said. "My commission for buying all farm land and right of way is ten per cent of the total . . ."

"Fair enough."

"And fifty per cent of the stock in your railroad."

"You're mad!" Trumbell shouted. "Crazy!"

"I think you have been trying to pull the wool over my eyes," Buchanan said amiably. "I think you have planned to build this railroad for a considerable time. Remember that block of land I own, Mr. Trumbell. From hills to river. You cannot lay a single rail unless you pay to cross my land. Fletcher is another fly in your ointment. You can't handle him. I can. Come, come. Let's deal. There's profit for all, and more."

"I can force you to sell," Trumbell said harshly.

"After extended litigation," Buchanan said imperturbably. "During which time I shall be spreading the news and land values will be rising astronomically. No, Mr. Trumbell. That would be the fool's way. Admit I have you. Admit I'm not too greedy. Let's close this deal and get to work."

"Ten per cent," Trumbell said, "plus your commissions. That's a fair price only because I have no choice."

"Fifty," Buchanan said evenly.

"Fifteen then, but that's my top offer."

"It has been pleasant," Buchanan said, pushing his chair back. "My gentleman is waiting. I'll not mention anything you have told me. I respect your trust in me. However . . ."

"Sit down!" Trumbell said savagely. "Let's see it through. But not fifty per cent. This is my railroad and I keep control. Name me a reasonable figure and we'll do business."

"A man cannot lose by reaching for the moon," Buchanan laughed. "Very well, forty per cent."

"God damn it! I said reasonable. I'll give twenty."

"Thirty then, Mr. Trumbell. I'll make the concession."

"No."

Buchanan lost his smile and frowned. "Meet me on the bridge. Twenty-five and, I warn you, I go no lower."

Trumbell cursed fluently for half a minute. "Twenty-five."

"You have a deal, sir," Buchanan said. "And a man who'll back you to the limit. When shall we draw up the papers?"

Trumbell had the grace to chuckle. "My word isn't good?"

Buchanan smiled. "In cabbages, sir, but not in kings. Shall we sign the agreements in the morning at the bank?"

"I doubt if we can draw them up by then," Trumbell said.

"Mr. Mason is a lawyer," Buchanan said. "I suggest he meet me at the bank early, at eight, and we will draw up the papers jointly. If you can join us at eight-thirty or nine, everything will be ready."

"Very well," Trumbell said wearily.

"Then good night, gentlemen," Buchanan said. "You'll never know what this short evening has meant to me."

Trumbell shook the offered hand, nodded to Mason, and left the dining room. Mason waited until Trumbell's steps died away and then shook his head with admiration.

"My hat's off to you," Mason murmured. "I'd hate to be on the other side."

"You are straddling," Buchanan said, "and I suggest you maintain your balance. I'll have the agreements ready when you come tomorrow morning."

"We have something to discuss," Mason said. "My share."

Buchanan said, "Yes?"

"Half, Buchanan."

"Half of what?" Buchanan asked. "Everything?"

"No, not your land commissions. Half your profit from that stock. Twelve and a half per cent. You're in no position to argue. We'll sign a paper before Trumbell arrives in the morning, or I queer the deal."

"Five per cent," Buchanan said. "Don't be a fool."

Mason was calculating rapidly, He had been willing to settle for five, but now he laughed softly and said, "Make it seven, Ferris, and ten thousand in cash for my good will, payable tomorrow morning."

"A deal," Buchanan said. "Good night."

He turned the thick velvet collar of his coat against his ears and walked slowly from the hotel into the night, and directly through town to his house on the river bank. He was filled with the heady exhilaration of triumph that could only be heightened by proof of McMahon's death. Even if McMahon got away, somehow or other, it would not matter. He had completed the deal without revealing his possession of Trumbell's papers; now they could lie untouched in the warehouse while he proceeded with the business at hand. McMahon had to go, and Casey, and Mathews, if the need arose. Fletcher was someone to consider thoroughly and then act upon without hesitation or scruples. As for Mason—Buchanan smiled at his hands—Mason would receive his ten thousand in the morning, but very soon he would suffer a fatal accident. After that it would be legitimate business. Chambers was no longer important. The man knew nothing definite and could be ignored. Buchanan poured a glass of brandy, lit a last cigar, and rose to scrutinize his library and select a book for an hour's reading before bed.

Ten

THEY HAD RIDDEN fast through the morning, strung closely together in a strangely intimate line of four horses and men. No one spoke but McMahon, who twice called a sharp warning to keep strung out and moving. Casey needed no spur on his seat; he kept the pace, but Mathews deliberately retarded his horse, attempting a pile-up, but doing it in such an open fashion that McMahon wondered about the man's thoughts. Timberlake had agreed too eagerly the night before, and reaching the wagon road as they would at noon hour, there remained twenty miles of riding beside the river to Warbonnet. McMahon followed them over the last rise and saw Fletcher's farm half a mile to the east and north, with the wagon road's beaten path extending south from the Gap. He moved both arms, sloughing off stiffness, and called, "Hold up!"

"Good time," Timberlake said. "You keeping promises?"

"Pull off to the side, Timberlake," McMahon said curtly. "Head backtrail. You want some good advice?"

"Always open for that," Timberlake said. "You got some?"

"Pack up," McMahon said. "Shake the dust and leave the country."

"If I like it here?" Timberlake asked.

"It won't be healthy," McMahon said evenly. "Better clear out."

"I'll think about it," Timberlake said. "So long."

Timberlake reined around McMahon, and rode west on the backtrail. McMahon murmured, "But you won't," and then said, "All right, let's ride."

"A man get any rest from you?" Mathews said peevishly. "Ride!"

Timberlake had disappeared into the west hills when they reached the wagon road. Casey stopped and looked at McMahon hopefully. "You ain't forgettin' what you said last night?"

"No," McMahon said, "but I've been thinking, Casey. I might as well turn Mathews loose, too."

Mathews said, "What . . . ?" then closed his mouth tightly and stared at Casey, the murder badly hidden behind half-closed eyes.

"Turn him loose!" Casey said. "You can't do that, John. He'd kill me the minute you left. You're joking. I know you are. Cut me loose, John, and let me clear out of here."

"I've been thinking," McMahon said easily. "It's a twenty-mile ride to town from here. Let's just do a little supposing. I turn you loose, Casey, and ride for town with Mathews. Suppose a couple of Timberlake's boys circled around and took the shortcut across the valley to the river a few miles above town. Mathews and I come riding down the road, cold but happy, and somebody potshoots me from the willows. Understand, I'm just supposing. Now then, you'd like to make certain I got Mathews to town and safe in jail, wouldn't you, Casey?"

Casey said, "I got to have time to get out, John."

"That's why I'm thinking," McMahon said. "Why don't I turn Mathews over to you, Casey? You cross the river here, circle wide to the east, come into town after dark from the south. I'll be waiting at Mathews' shack, and take him off your hands. You get the chance to collect anything you want from the saloon, cross the river south of town, and hook the night train for Weeping Water. You'll be clear and Mathews'll be in jail."

Casey was weighing both sides of the argument now and finally he nodded reluctantly. "You're right, John. But I'm not taking him without a gun."

"You'll have a gun," McMahon said. "If you agree to this. I warn you, Casey. Mathews will try to change your mind. He'll offer you money, a lot of money, to let him go. You can do that. But remember, Casey, life is worth more than money if you don't have life to spend the money. If you don't bring him in, I'll be on your trail in ten minutes. And then you'll never come in. What do you say?"

"It's a deal," Casey said thickly. "Give me the gun."

McMahon moved the gun carefully around Mathews and cut Casey's ropes. He handed the lead rope to Casey and drew the saloonkeeper's own gun from his mackinaw pocket. Casey accepted it gingerly, unbelievingly, and checked the cylinders. "Loaded," he said dully. "I thought you were fooling."

"Get behind Mathews," McMahon said. "Keep your eyes open and your gun out. You understand?"

"I got you," Casey said. "Make a big circle, meet you at his place after dark. I'll do it, John. I'll do it!"

McMahon saw the rider come from Fletcher's barn and gallop down the lane toward them. He said, "Come on, show some life!" and slashed Mathew's horse across the rump. Mathews bounced in the saddle and cursed McMahon in a flat, vicious voice, the words floating back as Casey chased him down the path to the river, through the willows, across the snow-covered ice. They were mounting the other bank when Fletcher pulled up beside McMahon, holding a rifle ready for any and all action.

"John," Fletcher said. "I recognized you half a mile up the trail. I had to come down. I didn't know . . ."

"What's the time, Sam?" McMahon asked calmly.

"Few minutes past twelve."

"Fine," McMahon smiled. "Let's go up and have some coffee, and I'll tell you the funniest story you've ever heard."

Mary met them on the porch and took McMahon's hand as he mounted the steps. "We were getting worried," she said.

"I'm hungry," McMahon said. "And thirsty. Will you feed a starving man while he brings you up to date?"

"You need sleep," Fletcher said shrewdly.

"No time," McMahon said. "No rest for the wicked." He stretched his legs fully and relaxed in the barrel chair, eating and drinking, telling them everything from the moment he rode away to the present.

Fletcher asked, "You reckon Casey will bring him in, John?"

"He's got to," McMahon said. "He can't let Mathews go, not for any money. Mathews will kill him the first chance he has. Casey will bring him in. I was thinking fast all morning, trying to work this deal as Timberlake would be thinking, or maybe I ought to say Timberlake's boss. I've got Mathews. I don't need Casey. His signed statement is good in court. Timberlake is a different proposition. I don't want him right now. Sam, get your best team and that wagon box sled. You'll have to take me into town. I can lie down and you can sit on the seat, just going in for supplies. I'll bet my life a couple of them are waiting along the river."

"I'll come too," Mary said.

McMahon wanted to say no, but changed his mind. Timberlake was moving fast while they sat here, doing something that could start at this farm or end too close for comfort. Mary would be safer with them.

"We've got to make town before dark," he said. "Will Overton will be starting this way if I don't show up."

Fletcher hurried to the barn while McMahon finished a fourth cup of coffee. Mary changed clothes and came from her bedroom dressed in the boy's bibbed overalls, blue shirt, and heavy boots she had worn the day he saw her in the hotel. The rough clothing changed her, McMahon decided, but all to the good. He had never known a woman who wore overalls and made them look like a gown.

Fletcher had his big team of Morgans hitched to the wagon sled, the bottom of the box filled with fresh hay and half a dozen blankets. McMahon squirmed comfortably into the hay and pulled two blankets over his body while they climbed to the seat above his head. He could see to right and left through the bangboard cracks, and the tailgate covered observation from the rear. He held his gun across his chest, said, "Go to it, Sam," and closed his eyes.

McMahon dozed and planned alternately. The night ahead meant a great deal. He wanted to get rid of Casey and then put Mathews in a safe place and work on him until he cracked and talked. Trumbell could be told tonight; in fact, he had to be told. For Trumbell wanted those papers and had to give them permission to keep Mathews under cover until they could find the big fish, the boss, the man they wanted most of all. McMahon had no definite plan, but it would shape up as the hours passed.

Buchanan had his noon meal in the privacy of the big office. On his desk, propped against the cigar humidor, were the signed papers that gave him twenty-five per cent of the shares in Trumbell's valley, Gap, and plateau railroad, plus an agreement which gave him ten per cent commission for all purchases of land, right of way and farm for Trumbell. Mason had arrived early and checked the agreements; Buchanan had given him ten thousand dollars in cash, and signed a personal agreement between the two, stating that Mason, for services rendered, would receive a seven per cent share of all profits derived from Buchanan's profit in the road. Trumbell, after signing, had wired a message to his office in code, starting the initial steps of the new construction. Buchanan had promised to purchase all right of way within three weeks.

Buchanan worked all afternoon. He called in his cashier and tellers, swore them to secrecy, and then allotted certain farms to each man. He promised bonuses for every man and arranged with his cashier to have two extra clerks assist at the bank for the next three weeks while the tellers and his cashier were making the right of way purchases; only Fletcher remained unlisted. That would take a different method. Buchanan would drive north and personally swing that deal or, failing, would call on Timberlake. Without McMahon to give them his newfound friendship and assistance, Fletcher might not be such a tough nut to crack.

Buchanan left the bank at five-thirty, making a wide circle that carried him along the river and gave him a clear view of the bridge and fish huts and the town. He had changed clothes after a hot bath and shave when the bell tinkled and Timberlake came through the hall into the library, half running in his haste.

"Well . . . ?" Buchanan said.

"Something's gone wrong," Timberlake said. "I did just like you told me, Ferris. He bit on the scheme. We followed it to the letter. The boys headed north, Sid and Harry doubled back, and I rode east with the three of them. When we got near the wagon road, McMahon turned me loose. I headed back to the first draw and then circled around down valley, and joined Sid and Harry. We tied the horses on the east bank and got set in the willows just like you said. We waited all afternoon, Ferris, and he never showed up. Only people we saw were farmers coming and going, just a few, and Fletcher came by with his girl, driving in for supplies. I told Sid and Harry to sit tight until full dark and then come to town. I figured it was best to get in fast and let you know. How do you see this, Ferris? What did he do?"

"Sit down, Roy," Buchanan said mildly. "You expect me to give you hell. Oddly enough, I won't. Roy, you did the best job any man could do. Don't feel that you made mistakes. Since nine this morning we no longer need worry about McMahon."

Timberlake sighed with deeply apparent relief. "Then you made some kind of a deal with Trumbell, Ferris."

"The best deal we've ever made," Buchanan said happily. "Once we finish it, you're on easy street the rest of your life, Roy. It makes no difference about McMahon. Trumbell's committed himself to me, and the papers are worthless."

"But McMahon?" Timberlake said. "I want him, Ferris."

"And you'll have him," Buchanan said. "When Sid and Harry ride in, tell Sid to register at the hotel. McMahon doesn't know him. Send Harry north to the reservation. Tell him to bring all the boys down, have them ride into town one or two at a time, register at the hotel, and have some fun. In the meantime, you watch the jail. When Mc-

Mahon brings Casey and Mathews in, let me know immediately. It will take McMahon and Chambers a day or two to clean up the case. That will give us sufficient time to take care of everybody concerned. But move carefully, Roy, and with a minimum of noise."

"We'll do that little trick," Timberlake said. "I'll handle McMahon myself."

"You check into the hotel, too," Buchanan said. "McMahon has nothing against you. He can't prove you were hunting him down, and I don't believe he cares to pursue that side of the case. Roy, Trumbell is building his railroad."

"But ..."

"And I am purchasing right of way for him, Roy. For a certain percentage of the profits, which you will share with me. You understand what this means. I can buy right of way straight through to the reservation boundary with one exception. Fletcher. I'll visit him myself. If he won't sell, you take over."

"That will be a pleasure," Timberlake said harshly. "Damn them, taking that McMahon in and helping him. I'll handle Sam Fletcher for you, Ferris. Don't worry about that land."

"Then we have everything arranged," Buchanan said. "Except for one thing. Our friend, Mr. Mason, who has sold his soul to me. I've paid him fifteen thousand cash so far, Roy, and signed an agreement with him, giving him seven per cent of my profits from the road for his assistance. Next week I'll see that Mr. Mason takes the train to St. Louis on important legal business. It will be your job to see that he has an accident en route."

"Fatal?"

"Decidedly, Roy," Buchanan said. "He'll have my money and that agreement. You'll have to do a good job, you or Mathews or Sid, whichever one takes it. Get my money, that agreement, and make Mr. Mason disappear completely. The money is yours to split with the boys any way you see fit. Is everything clear?"

"All clear," Timberlake said. "I'll stop Sid and Harry before they get here. Then I'll be hanging around town tonight. I'll report back soon as McMahon comes to the jail."

Fletcher crossed the tracks and said, "John, wake up. We're in town."

McMahon turned over quickly and murmured, "Stop before the hotel. Mary, go in and get rooms for you and your father. Will Overton should be in the lobby. Tell him I'm here. Sam, drive around to the livery barn on the north side. I'll get out while you take the team in."

Fletcher said, "All right, John," and clucked at the Morgans. McMahon lay tensely in the hay while Mary got down before the hotel, and did not relax until the wagon sled stopped beside the livery barn and Fletcher called for Tom. It was dusk now and McMahon slipped over the tailgate and followed the horses into the barn's dark alleyway. Tom was ahead, holding his lantern, pointing out an empty stall to Fletcher. McMahon slipped into the end stall and waited until Fletcher and Tom rubbed the Morgans down, fed them, and went to the office. Fletcher knew exactly what to do; McMahon had given him instructions during the last hour on the road. Fletcher would find Chambers and both men were to go directly to Abe Bloom's and prepare the kitchen cellar for a visitor.

McMahon waited ten minutes in the barn and then left by the side door and began his circle of the town, following around to the river bank, down the river and waited in the trees north of Mathews' shack. Half an hour later he heard the horses and then Casey's voice, tired and worried, saying, "Shut up! You been saying that all day. McMahon treated me square, I'm doing the same."

"Ten thousand," Mathews said. "Cash, tomorrow morning."

"No."

Casey jerked viciously on the lead rope and Mathews reeled backward in his saddle and then cursed Casey with all the remaining strength and fury he possessed. McMahon came from the trees at this moment and stood beside Casey.

"All right," McMahon said. "You kept your word, Casey. That's worth something to a man."

Casey jumped involuntarily and said, "I never saw you come up. Here he is, John. I guess you're right about that word."

"You'd better cut the dust," McMahon said. "The train leaves in about half an hour. I'll take him now. Here . . ."

Casey dismounted and groaned with pain, and McMahon shoved a wad of bills in his coat pocket. Casey said, "Thanks, John. I figured you'd do the right thing."

"One word," McMahon said. "It won't do much good, I suppose, but keep out of trouble, Casey."

"By God!" Casey said sincerely, "I sure will, John."

McMahon watched him lumber stiffly toward the river and out of sight down the bank. He pulled Mathews roughly from the saddle and gagged him tightly. Mathews mumbled through the handkerchief and McMahon said, "Keep that up and you'll choke."

He lifted Mathews into the saddle, mounted Casey's tired horse, and began the last mile of his long ride, around the town to the west and behind Abe Bloom's house. The window rose silently and Chambers murmured, "Welcome home," and helped hoist Mathews through the window.

"Fletcher?" McMahon asked.

"Inside."

"Send him out."

Fletcher dropped through the window and stood beside McMahon, sighing with suppressed excitement. Mc-

Mahon said, "Take both horses to the livery barn, side door, just turn them in and don't let Tom see you. Go to the hotel and sit tight."

"On my way," Fletcher said, and moved to the horses.

McMahon murmured, "Help Abe put Mathews in the cellar. Then join me at the hotel, upstairs. We've got to talk with Trumbell."

"Ten minutes," Chambers said, and closed the window.

McMahon trotted from Abe Bloom's house, found the alley mouth, and ran the full distance, entering the hotel by the back stairs and standing at his room door in the hall's familiar shadows and smells, anxious to see Trumbell and bring this case to a climax. He knew the next step; it was the worst side of this business, but had to be done. He was turning the key in his lock when she came from the front stairs and called her greeting with a warmth that surprised him.

"Mr. McMahon," Alice Trumbell said. "Where have you been hiding?"

"Miss Trumbell," McMahon said. "Will you tell your father I want to see him within fifteen minutes?"

"Yes. Where?"

"His room," McMahon said.

Her eyes were bright. "Did you . . . ?"

"I'll talk then," McMahon said. "It's better that way."

"Of course," she murmured.

"Please," McMahon said, "don't mention my name. Just ask him to come upstairs."

"I see," she said. "Very well, in fifteen minutes."

McMahon entered his cold and stale-smelling room, opened the window, poured water into the bowl, and washed his face and hands. He smoked two cigarettes, heard Trumbell's steps and deep voice mingled with those of Alice and Mason, then Chambers coming softly from the back stairs; he snubbed the cigarette against his boot heel and opened the door. Chambers murmured, "Ready?" and they crossed the hall.

Eleven

THE ROOM was unchanged but the faces had undergone subtle change since he last saw them; a change that permeated the room and put him instantly on guard. Chambers assumed his inconspicuous seat against the wall and nodded to Trumbell and Mason. He smiled at Alice, who sat on the bed, eyes bright with expectation. Trumbell had a self-satisfied look that thinly underlaid apparent anger.

"It is nice to see you," Trumbell said sarcastically. "For a man in my employ you take your sweet time about reporting."

"Not in your employ," McMahon said. "Get that straight before we talk."

"All right," Trumbell said. "What have you got to say?"

McMahon said, "I've got your killer."

"You . . . !" Trumbell stared with complete surprise. Mason remained on the other chair, face expressionless, only his eyes shifting quickly from McMahon to Chambers, and back again. Trumbell said, "You've got him?"

"Yes."

"And the papers?"

"No," McMahon said. "I wanted to explain everything to you before I take steps to recover the papers."

Trumbell was strangely unexcited. "This is a fine time to tell me, McMahon," he said. "So you can recover the papers?"

"Give me one week," McMahon said evenly. "Do you want to know who the man is, who he works for, the rest of the truth?"

"If you wish," Trumbell said.

"Very well," McMahon said. "Now we'll talk business, Trumbell. You sent me after a killer and some papers. You wouldn't tell me what they represented. I went after a two-bit killer and landed in a pack of wolves. I'm here by the grace of God and good luck. Chambers wired the Colonel concerning the circumstances of this case. The Colonel wired him. The gist of this is simply that you paid the Colonel for finding peanuts and expected us to turn up elephant tusks. Chambers, what did the Colonel wire you? Tell him."

"Strictly business, Mr. Trumbell," Chambers said mildly. "The Colonel wishes me to inform you that your fee is inadequate. There will be an additional charge of five thousand dollars for carrying through the investigation."

Trumbell laughed sourly. "There will be?"

"Yes, sir," Chambers said, "and quite fair. To put it bluntly, there's more to this case than meets the eye. If you expect dangerous work done, you'll have to pay the price."

"I'm to understand," Trumbell said, "you have this killer, the man who stole my papers. You can prove he did the job?"

McMahon said, "I have proof. All that remains to be done to hang him for his part of the deal is to fill out the warrant and take him to St. Louis. But that's the beginning, not the end."

"I see," Trumbell said. "You'll take this man, see him hung for the fee paid thus far. But you won't continue the case and find my papers unless I pay five thousand more. Correct?"

"Yes," McMahon said. "Those are the Colonel's orders."

"Fine," Trumbell said sharply. "In that case, take him back and hang him. I have no further use for your agency."

McMahon had felt the words coming and even before Trumbell spoke was thinking back and placing the scat-

tered pieces of this case together in a twisted, incomplete
puzzle that to him, for the first time, encompassed many
people in its devious folds. Now, stronger then ever, was
the conviction that Trumbell's papers were connected with
something important about to happen in this valley. Even
stronger than this conviction was the feeling that Mathews'
boss, Timberlake's boss, had got to Trumbell and forced
a secret deal that voided the original papers. He had no
proof but it could be no other way. McMahon was filled
with bitter anger that refused to be allayed by any word
or command; the injustice of his position, the risks he had
taken, could not be shunted aside and forgotten at this late
date. He had to see this through to the finish, not for
Trumbell, not for the money, but for his own pride. He
remembered talking with the Fletchers and telling them
he had never failed to get his man. Well, he had one man
but two others had sprung up, hydralike, even now laughing in the dark.

"We have a contract . . ." Chambers began.

"No," McMahon said. "Let me say this, Chambers.
Let's tell Mr. Trumbell a little more. I think he should
know us better than he does. He doesn't understand the
Colonel's rule. It's simple, Trumbell, and it has been
drummed into us, and we agree, that once we start a case
we finish it, even if the employer shows the white feather.
Very well, Trumbell, our business associations are closed,
as of tonight, but I intend to stay here and follow this
thing to the finish. Three men in this town will try to kill
me within the next three days if I stay. I'm staying. I know
two of them. The other one, the big one, I want to know.
If you're connected in any way with this man, and I find
that connection, no matter what the deal is, I'll fight you
to the end. You have no sense of honor, Trumbell, no feeling of consideration for any man. You've forgotten a poor
damned bookkeeper, you don't care about a man named

Red Egan, dead and gone. But you won't forget me. I promise you that."

McMahon turned to the door and jerked it open savagely. Chambers rose and rubbed his hands together gently and said, even more gently, "All this goes double for me," and walked with surprising dignity into the hall. Behind McMahon, Trumbell said, "Get out and stay out!"

The door slammed and McMahon crossed to his own room, with Chambers.

"Damn him!" McMahon said. "Damn them all like him! How many times have we run into the same ending? Not many, but enough to remember and keep count. It's beginning to pile up, Chambers. What good's the pride, the honor, the satisfaction, in your work? All we get is a living and no thanks. I've felt it coming a long time. Maybe I've been overdue and didn't know it. I'm finishing this job and then I'm through."

"You're red-hot," Chambers said. "So am I. We'll see things in a better way tomorrow."

"No," McMahon said. "Now forget it. We've got work to do, the dirty, stinking, miserable work we've dodged long enough. We're going to Abe's and make that rat tell the truth if I have to roast him over a slow fire. Come on!"

"Don't go off half-cocked," Chambers said. "Remember, Will Overton and Abe and the Fletchers are in this. We've got to consider them. I'm confused about this business. Trumbell doesn't make sense. But I'm sticking with you until everything makes sense. So let's do it right. I'll go downstairs and tell Will Overton to keep his eyes open. The Fletchers have got to take it easy. You go out to Abe's and do what you have to do. And here's something else to consider. Trumbell is ripe to tell this town marshall and county sheriff about our killer. That means trouble. Start thinking, John. Time is running out."

McMahon smiled then. "Sorry, Chambers. It takes the old head to cool the young. I'm all right now. You take care of this end. I'll head for Abe's. And just for fun, check the register and see who signs in tonight."

"A suggestion," Chambers said pleasantly. "Abe and I placed Mathews in a tight-fitting little cellar beneath Abe's kitchen floor. He is flat on his back, tied and gagged, but his eyes are open. Toasting his feet might cause undue alarm if his gag slips. Why not use the water cure?"

McMahon said, "That's the best advice I've had tonight," and slipped away into the hall.

Front was loud with the mid-evening sounds of a big night. Timberlake's men in heavy boots and chaps, mackinaws or sheepskin coats topped by fur caps or hard-worn Stetsons, were much in evidence. They swaggered, cursed and drank freely. No matter how heavy their clothing, every man was armed, some with two six-shooters. The farmers, more quietly dressed, kept out of their way.

McMahon moved north through the alley and abruptly changed direction behind the town jail, which occupied a corner lot one block beyond the bank and directly across from Jensen's livery barn. McMahon paused beside the north window, saw Hickerson, the marshal, playing solitaire at the desk, and came around to the door and walked inside. Hickerson looked up and frowned.

"What you want, McMahon?"

"Are we alone?" McMahon asked.

The marshal dropped his cards and said, "You're not drunk?" and in the same breath gave McMahon a closer look.

McMahon said, "You've had one opinion of me for two months, Hickerson. Let's set the record straight." Talking rapidly, McMahon pulled all the shades and opened his money belt and spread his credentials on the desk. "You know who I am now," he said quickly. "I could not explain before tonight. Now I want your help. I want to help you."

Hickerson examined the papers and nodded. "Seen these before, McMahon. Sloane's ranks beside Pinkerton in my book. What can I do? Who are you after?"

Hickerson's expression was painfully clear; the man smelled reward money and knew, from long experience, that Sloane's men did not accept such money. McMahon's first gamble had paid off. He had to play on the man's cupidity with reward money so large that no political string would hold the marshal.

"It's a big case," McMahon said softly. "A pack of killers with a big man behind them. We've trailed them for two years. They've killed a dozen people to cover their tracks. We followed two of them here. I've been watching for nearly two months. We're getting close, but you know how we work. There's reward money totaling fifteen thousand to break this case. Give us your help and it's yours. You know my word is good. Sloane's has always made certain reward money goes to local officers."

"Fifteen thousand," Hickerson murmured. "McMahon, I'm your man. I'll see that Sheriff Bishop helps all the way."

"I handle it?" McMahon asked.

"You bet. You tell us how to play this. We'll follow orders, don't worry. Now, who are they?"

"You know George Mathews?" McMahon asked.

"By God! I always figured him."

"And Red Egan," McMahon said. "And Timberlake. They're the boys who take the orders, Hickerson. I'm going to tell you a lot now, in a few minutes. We think the big boy lives in or near this town. We've got to make the others talk. Timberlake has a dozen men working for him up their in the hills. I don't want him yet. Now, I've got Mathews . . ."

"You got him? There's a cell back here he'll never break."

"Thanks," McMahon said. "But listen. This Mathews

is a rat. I've got him in a safe place. I'm going to work on
him until he talks. In the meantime, warn the sheriff, tell
him to keep this between the two of you, and stand ready.
Watch for Timberlake. I think he'll come to town. Let
him alone, but try to mark every place he visits, every man
he sees. If I can't force Mathews into talking, we'll have
to go after Timberlake. Are you with me? It may get
dirty."

"Son, I'm with you," Hickerson said. "And I can get
all the help you need. Let me tell you something. I'm
kind of an old goat. I got this job through pull. But that
don't mean I'm against making this a good town."

McMahon grinned, unable to conceal his feeling. "Then
you don't care about the reward money?"

"Man's got to be sensible," Hickerson said. "Maybe you
did figure me wrong when you come in. Sure, I want that
money. For my wife and daughter. Is that wrong?"

"It never was," McMahon said. "It never will be. Got
a back door?"

"Sure. Come on."

Shaking hands and slipping into the darkness, McMahon
thought of Trumbell and murmured, "Try to stop that
end of it, fat man," and moved cautiously up the alley
toward Abe Bloom's. He had told a monumental lie about
reward money, but he would take care of that himself if
the Colonel refused to help.

Abe Bloom led him into the kitchen and pointed to the
floor beneath the round oak table. "A bad one, that man."

McMahon said, "Bad clean through, Abe, but not the
worst. I've got a lot to tell you, so listen carefully."

McMahon told him everything, speaking without pause
for ten minutes. Abe listened and nodded and finally, when
McMahon finished, shook his head and said, "This Trumbell—to treat you and Chambers so shamefully! You say it
would be of great help if you knew who Trumbell has seen

the past days? I have friends. One is coming here within the hour. He may have information. Until then, shall we amuse ourselves with Mathews?"

"Get a big can," McMahon said. "Make a very small hole in the bottom so that water will drip from it, steadily but slowly."

Abe said, "Ah," and went across the kitchen to his cupboard. McMahon moved the table aside, lifted the trapdoor, and looked squarely into the red, murderous eyes of Mathews, who lay on his back in the small rectangular hole. McMahon said, "Casey has left, Mathews. That leaves you. I'm only telling you once. I want the man's name and you'll get off with a sentence. Keep your mouth shut and you hang."

Abe touched his shoulder and handed him the large can. McMahon placed one finger on the hole Abe had pierced in the bottom and held the can above Mathews' face. He said, "If you want to tell me now, shake your head."

Mathews cursed him wordlessly and remained rigid and tight-fisted. "Very well," McMahon said. "Do you see this can? It's filled with water. There's a little hole in the bottom. Here's how it works." He released his finger and a drop of water fell soundlessly and splashed on Mathews' forehead. McMahon held the can steady and five seconds later another drop collected and fell. Mathews flinched and glared at him. McMahon said, "We'll close the trap, make a small hole in it over your face, set the can in place, and let time do our work. You're thinking water never hurt anybody. Mathews, you'll be stark, raving mad in twelve hours. I see you don't believe me. All right, we'll give you a treatment. When you begin to understand, roll around and let us know."

Abe and McMahon closed the trapdoor, bored a hole in the floor, and placed the can of water on it.

"Now for some coffee, McMahon said. "Strong and hot, Abe."

"Do you mean to . . . ?" Abe asked.

"Drive him crazy?" McMahon said. "I've no mercy for a killer, Abe. He's the worst kind of killer. He gets his man in the back. I'll do anything, Abe, to get that name."

"He may not crack," Abe said thoughtfully. "If he becomes violent, John, may he speak then without curbing his tongue?"

"Only one way to determine that," McMahon said coldly. "Either he talks sanely, or he'll babble later on."

Timberlake moved about the upper end of the business district in the shadows that cloaked Casey's saloon, watching the marshal's office across the street and stepping into the alley regularly as Sid passed and spoke in whispers and moved away on a round of the saloons and other buildings. Timberlake had watched McMahon enter the marshal's office, realized soon after that McMahon had gone away by the back door, and wondered if Mathews and Casey were now in the jail. Timberlake stood bulkily in the darkness beside Casey's. He was turning toward the alley, eager to tell Buchanan and receive orders, when Sid ran from the south calling softly.

"Roy, there's something damned funny going on tonight. Chambers is sitting behind the stove in the lobby with that night clerk. He just looked at the register a while back. He knows you came in, and me too. I don't know where McMahon is. If he's out, I missed him. But Fletcher and his girl are in the hotel for the night, and McMahon must be figuring something."

"We'll know about that pretty soon," Timberlake said. "Can't rush this, Sid. You go back and stay in the alley behind the hotel. Come back here in an hour. I'll be waiting."

Sid murmured, "An hour, Roy," and disappeared down the alley.

McMahon heard the soft tap on the bedroom window an hour after he had started the water treatment for their invisible guest. Abe murmured, "Sit still," and returned a minute later with a slender, gray-haired little man who blinked apologetically in the lamplight as Abe said, "John, this is Henry Slater. Henry's a good friend, and a good man. He's been wanting to meet you for some time."

"You work in the bank," McMahon said.

"Yes," Henry Slater said. His voice was soft and curiously mild. "I am cashier, Mr. McMahon."

McMahon said, "Can Mathews hear us, Abe?"

Abe murmured, "Not if we move beside the stove."

Henry Slater glanced curiously at Abe and walked to the stove and began filling a large-bowled briar pipe. McMahon asked, "How much does Henry understand?"

"Enough to help," Abe said. "Henry has been watching the people concerned as much as possible. I think he's near to bursting with news."

Henry Slater smiled and his thin, serious face became alive and younger. He got the pipe burning strongly and said, "Perhaps my information is of little value, but I want you to hear it. This Mr. Trumbell and his lawyer, Mason, have called on Mr. Buchanan several times. All in the way of business, probably, and quite natural for Mr. Trumbell. However, this morning Mason came to the bank again and assisted Mr. Buchanan in preparing several papers. Mr. Trumbell arrived at nine o'clock and they were closeted in the private office for some time. Then Mr. Buchanan called me—I am also a notary public—to witness and affix my seal to an agreement between them. Usually Mr. Buchanan does not care if I read the papers, but this morning he had them arranged in such a way that I could read very little while affixing the seal. But I read all I could.

The papers were an agreement between the two men, giving shares in something to Mr. Buchanan and also a commission for services to be rendered. I nudged one paper while affixing the seal—which required me to stand and exercise some weight—and caught the words 'Valley, Gap, and Plateau Railroad.' Then Mr. Trumbell left. Mason remained a few minutes and went out. Mr. Buchanan then called me and the two tellers, Jones and Witherspoon, to the private office and swore us to secrecy on bank business. Mr. Buchanan is evidently assisting Mr. Trumbell in preparing the way for a new railroad. We have been promised excellent bonuses for prompt work. This is perfectly legal business and I do not wish it spread about, but somehow I felt I should tell you. That is all I have at present."

McMahon almost whispered, "You say that's all Henry?"

"I'm sorry," Henry Slater said mildly. "That's all.

McMahon said, "Who knows you came here?"

"No one but my wife and daughter."

"Can you depend on them?"

Slater seemed to grow taller. "Mr. McMahon, my wife and daughter are—well, sir. Yes, I can."

"Excuse me," McMahon said humbly. "Don't misunderstand. I am standing here trying to find a way to thank you, Henry. And I can't. Man, I want to jump through the roof and hit the sky. My God! I've been running in circles and you had it for me, Henry. Look, you don't understand, and I haven't time to explain now. Abe will tell you. But I want you to know that anything I have is yours, and I mean that. Now listen, if anyone knows you came here, your life isn't worth a plugged cent. Abe, do you see it?"

"I see it," Abe Bloom said sadly. "I have been fooled too long."

"We can move now," McMahon said, almost happily. "Henry, when Abe tells you, you'll understand these orders. First, is Buchanan's bank solvent?"

"I don't know," Henry said. "Our cash reserve is small. Quite naturally we do not have sufficient cash to pay out all depositors. But Mr. Buchanan is a wonderful business-man."

"I want a run started on the bank not later than tomorrow afternoon," McMahon said. "Do it any way you can, both of you here, so that no one knows where the rumor starts. Then watch Buchanan, Henry. Arrange to get word to Abe of anything out of the way in his actions. You understand?"

"Yes," Slater said.

"Tell him the whole story, Abe," McMahon said.

He smiled and went to the trapdoor and removed the can, and went through the house to the bedroom window. They heard the window rise, clothing scrape softly, and then the window was down and they stood in silence.

McMahon went to the upper end of Front and walked boldly along the sidewalk to the hotel, into the lobby and across to the stairs, and directly to Chambers' room. He knocked and was talking before the door closed. Chambers said, "Slow down, slow down. You've got something, haven't you?"

"Have you seen the cashier at the bank?" McMahon said. "You have. A mousy little man. Listen, he just came to Abe's and told me everything and didn't realize what he was saying. Do you know what those papers were, Chambers? Now I can tell you. This morning Trumbell and Buchanan signed an agreement. Trumbell has given Buchanan shares in his new railroad to be built north through the valley and Gap to the reservations. Buchanan's tellers and Slater, the cashier, are going out to buy right of way starting tomorrow. Now tell me God doesn't smile on the good and the meek and the lucky. Mostly lucky, Chambers. That's us, shot in the pants. Do you see it?"

Chambers spoke the name. "Buchanan."

"He's our man," McMahon said. "He's got to be. Trumbell's stolen papers are bills of sale and deeds, postdated, for right of way land he bought over a period of time, undoubtedly through agents. I remember Fletcher telling about a man offering him a high price for his farm, finally a strip along the river. Fletcher refused and heard no more about it. Buchanan saw the possibility of a railroad, discovered Trumbell's plan. Matthews did the job in St. Louis. We know that. Buchanan knew about me from the beginning. He was confident I'd never run him down, so he sat back and waited for Trumbell to come his way. Trumbell had no choice. He wants to begin work this spring, but the papers were gone and with them his legal title to right of way. I couldn't find them soon enough, so he came up here and forced me. We moved but not the way he expected. I think he realized that fact before he arrived and planned on something else. We don't know which one opened up first but I'd say Buchanan tricked him and carried the deal through, making Trumbell think it was his own idea. I wonder what he'll say when we tell him that Buchanan has played him for a fourteen-karat fool?"

"We know all this," Chambers said quietly, "but what do we do?

"Move," McMahon said simply. "Starting tomorrow."

"Timberlake and a man named Sid checked into the hotel tonight," Chambers said.

"Good. That makes everything ring true. I want them all here. I saw the marshal. A good man. He's with us. I spun him a tall tale about a big gang and plenty of reward money. He'll back us when I give the word. It may cost the Colonel, or me, a lot of money. I had to play it that way."

"The Colonel will back us," Chambers said. "You know that."

"Maybe," McMahon said. "But he may balk at losing fifteen thousand."

"Fifteen . . . !"

"Reward money," McMahon smiled. "It would be nice if there was a price on the three of them. Wire the Colonel in the morning. Ask him to investigate all men answering to Buchanan's and Timberlake's descriptions. Tomorrow morning the ball begins. Now go to bed. We'll need this night's sleep."

McMahon stepped quietly into the hall, moved to the main stairs and paused on the top step, hearing muted voices in the alcove below, indistinct above the fire sound from the big stove. It was an ordinary scene in the hotel after midnight; the shadows thick in all corners, chairs empty and cold to the eye, and Will behind the stove, his legs stretched comfortably on a box, talking with an unseen person. McMahon stepped around the stairpost and saw Alice Trumbell, swallowed surprise, and murmured, "Will?"

Will blushed faintly. "What is it, John?"

McMahon nodded at Alice Trumbell. "Like to see you alone."

"She's all right," Will Overton said.

"I'm all right," Alice Trumbell repeated. "Didn't you know that, Mr. McMahon? I'm all right. Will has been telling me about things I've forgotten."

McMahon wondered if she had been seeing Will Overton often, and in the same thought remembered Mary. He asked, "Timberlake in his room?"

"Across the street," Will Overton said. "With that man named Sid. In the Antlers."

"Where's Sam?"

"104," Will Overton said. "Mary's in 106. Down the back hall, John. I figured they'd be safer on the main floor."

"Possibly," McMahon said. "I'll be talking with Sam."

"When you need me," Will Overton said, "just say the word."

McMahon said, "Thanks," and backed away from the lobby into the darkness of the back hall that ran to the rear of the building and served eight rooms on the main floor. Will Overton's room was 108, placing Mary between her father and Will in a protected spot, while across the hall were rooms held permanently by clerks who had yet to find a house or build. McMahon tapped on 104's door and Fletcher murmured, "Who is it?"

"John," McMahon said. "Open up."

Fletcher had jammed a chair under the knob, and now pulled it away and opened the door. McMahon entered the room and closed the door and said, "Get back in bed, Sam. No cause for alarm."

"Timberlake and Sid checked in," Fletchers said.

"Will told me," McMahon said. "You see them?"

"In the lobby," Fletcher said. "Timberlake wanted to say something, but didn't."

"He won't," McMahon said. "Tomorrow I want you to sit around the lobby and see who checks in before noon. More of Timberlake's crew will be drifting in from the north. Visit Abe's before noontime. He's got a lot to tell you. I need sleep or I'd tell you tonight," McMahon smiled. "If I told you tonight, you wouldn't sleep. How's Mary?"

"Worried," Fletcher said. "About you."

"A fine girl," McMahon said. "But you know that, Sam. She'll make a wonderful mother, a fine wife, for some man."

"My opinion," Fletcher said. "Of course, I'm prejudiced. How old are you, John?"

"Thirty-three," McMahon said. "If you're thinking what I have a hunch is in the back of that mind, don't think it."

"And why not?"

"She'll want a man her own age," McMahon said. "A steady man who stays in one place."

"Not the way she explains what she wants," Fletcher said, dryly. "But like you say, we need sleep."

McMahon went up the stairs. Will Overton's feet were once more resting on the box and Alice Trumbell's soft voice murmured in the alcove.

Alice Trumbell heard the steps fade along the upper hall and turned to Will Overton. "He's a strong man, Will."

"The best," Will Overton said simply. "He knows what he wants."

"Something is going to happen here," she said. "I feel it. I hope it doesn't hurt my father too much."

"Do me a favor," Will Overton said. "Don't go out tomorrow, Alice."

"Very well," she said. "I'll stay in my room and get drunk. Does that suit you?"

"I didn't mean that." Will Overton said. "I mean—please believe me—tomorrow may be the worst in this town's history."

"I like Mary Fletcher," she said unexpectedly. "She's a lovely girl, Will."

"I guess so," Will Overton said awkwardly.

"Do you love her?"

Will Overton said, "I guess it isn't that kind of love. We grew up together back home. We've always been close friends. Out here things are different. We talked this afternoon."

"About what, Will?"

"Me," Will Overton said. "Her. And McMahon. She's in love with him."

Alice Trumbell laughed gently. "The lion and the lamb. And how does McMahon feel?"

"She doesn't know. But she wanted to tell me. Six months ago I thought if Mary ever picked somebody else, I'd feel like hell. Now I know different. I just feel good, for her."

"So you're a free man?" Alice Trumbell asked.

"I guess so."

Alice Trumbell said, "I'm going upstairs and rest a while. If I can't sleep, I'll come down again. If you want me to."

"If it helps pass the time," Will Overton said, "come back down, Alice."

Twelve

McMAHON WOKE in late morning sunlight that warmed his room and placed a long oblong of gold across the floor. He dressed quickly in the dirty, still damp clothing he had worn constantly for too many days, and stood in the window, staring across Front at Abe Bloom's store. He saw two men step from Abe's door, stand a moment on the sidewalk in serious conversation, and move across the street toward the bank. One was the harness-shop owner, the other a contractor recently arrived in town to build and open Warbonnet's first lumberyard and brick works. McMahon saw two men come from Jensen's stable and move toward the hotel, heavy holsters and shell belts worn openly over their sheepskin coats. McMahon left his room and walked swiftly to the stairs. The lobby clock above the desk, always ten minutes slow, read eleven-thirty. He rounded the stove, intent on breakfast, and brushed against Timberlake, who stood square and unmoving beside a chair.

"Didn't take my advice," McMahon said.

"Advice?" Timberlake said. "I don't recollect you giving me any, friend."

"I'm not passing it out," McMahon said curtly. "Just once, Timberlake, just once. No return trips on this line."

"No return trips," Timberlake murmured. "Where are you keeping them, friend. In the jail?"

"I wouldn't know," McMahon said. "Do you?"

Timberlake smiled without humor. "I'm sure relieved

to see you, McMahon. I figured I might have to chase you a thousand miles."

"A short distance," McMahon said evenly. "Ask the big boy what comes next?"

Timberlake moved his shoulders and said, "You . . ." and McMahon shook his head and said, "Don't forget to ask the boss first, Timberlake. Wouldn't want to make a mistake, would you?" Smiling, he entered the dining room and took a corner table facing the lobby door and the windows. It was too quiet, he thought. He ate hurriedly and left the dining room by the street door and crossed directly to Abe Bloom's.

"How is he?" McMahon asked.

"Resting comfortably," Abe said. "When you left, John, I took a look. It was fortunate you removed the water. He was beginning to crack. I spoon fed him this morning, banked the fire, and wished him well. My friends are withdrawing cash from the bank as you directed. When shall we start the run?"

"One o'clock," McMahon said. "I'll see Trumbell in twenty minutes. When I finish our conversation, things will start to happen."

"What?"

"Nothing today," McMahon said. "Tonight will be the beginning of the payoff. I want that valise you stored for me and the use of your back room to change clothes."

Abe Bloom smiled happily. "You are shedding your skin?"

"It's time," McMahon said. "I want to dress like a man, and see this out like a man."

Abe Bloom murmured, "I understand your feeling, John," led the way to a small back room adjoining his office and placed McMahon's valise on the work table. From the bag McMahon removed polished black boots and fine gray trousers and good shirts. He stripped to the skin, wadded his torn, dirty clothing into a sodden ball, and threw it into

the darkest corner beneath a rack of mackinaws. He put on
clean underwear and socks, and slipped into a dark green
shirt, trousers of the latest cut and his tailored shortcoat
with the gun pockets sewn inside and under the arms; then
the boots of finest leather. He lifted the black hat from
the bottom of the valise. Changing into these clean, expensive clothes, moving money and gun and ammunition into
the various pockets, he seemed to become a different man.
Abe Bloom opened the door and said, "When they see
you on Front, I would like to see their faces"—Abe grinned
—"from loafer to gentleman."

McMahon walked through the store and stepped onto
Front and pulled the hat brim lower over his face, shading
his eyes. The night man from Jensen's passed with a brief
look, then stopped and turned and said, "Jesus! Is that
you, Johnny?"

"Time you were sleeping, Tom," McMahon said. "A
nice day."

He crossed Front and entered the bank. Henry Slater
rose from his small desk behind the railing and spoke without visible recognition. "Good morning, sir. What can we
do for you?"

"Buchanan," McMahon said.

"I'll see," Henry Slater said. He walked to the door at
the far end of the big room and knocked.

"Mr. Buchanan will see you, sir," he said.

McMahon opened the door, closed it softly, and faced
Buchanan, who sat behind the desk against the far wall,
smoking a fat cigar and smiling benignly. Buchanan said,
"Mr. McMahon?"

"Yes," McMahon said. "I have a message for you, Buchanan."

"For me, sir?" Buchanan said. "I'm very much afraid
I've not had the pleasure of meeting you before. State your
business and I'll give you my time if it's worth while."

"Drop the pretty words and the cigar." McMahon said,

"Mathews talked, Buchanan. Casey did a little talking, too."

Buchanan rose slowly. His face maintained the smile but now the great bulk was alert. Buchanan said, "I don't know the gentlemen you mention, sir. Perhaps you'd better explain further."

"You're good," McMahon said honestly. "I can see why you've lasted this long in Warbonnet. Let me tell you about Mathews. He's the best man for the work he does. He's fast with a knife and a gun"—McMahon grinned—"and a fish spear, but he's got the instincts of a packrat. When he took the papers he couldn't bear the thought of leaving the antique trunk behind. You know, the trunk they were in—in Trumbell's office safe. Trumbell prizes that trunk. When I give it to him today, tell him where I found it, what Mathews told me, I wouldn't be surprised if he has fifty men up here within two days' time."

"You speak in riddles, sir," Buchanan said.

"Keep your hands above the desk," McMahon said. "Go for that gun and I'll finish this business now."

"Saying I understand what you're talking about," Buchanan said, "what chance would the word of a man like Mathews have against mine?"

"Now," McMahon said harshly. "Now we're getting to it, Buchanan. His word against yours? No chance, without proof. But I'll have that. I'll have it so fast you won't have time to think up arguments. Timberlake won't stop me. I'm going to blow you wide open in this town, Buchanan. I'm going back to the hotel and see Trumbell. That'll give you time to think fast and pull another cat out of the bag. If you'd care to see Trumbell's trunk, drop by the hotel later today. I'll show it to you."

McMahon backed to the door, stepped onto Front and went to the hotel. When he entered the lobby, Paul Mason came from a wall chair and said curtly, "Mr. Trumbell wants to see you, McMahon."

"I want to see him," McMahon said. "In his room?"
"Yes. Come on."

Trumbell turned from the window and said, "Where the hell have you been?"

McMahon stepped to the right and stood against the wall, facing Trumbell and Mason. He said, "Busy, Trumbell. No need to send your errand boy for me. I was on my way up. Do you remember what I told you, Trumbell? That I'd finish this case, pay or no pay? Let me tell you something I forgot last night. I've had your trunk in safe-keeping several days . . ."

"My trunk?" Trumbell said.

"The little one with the beautiful designs," McMahon said quietly. "The one in your safe in St. Louis, with those papers under the top drawer. I found it in Mathews' shack the other night. Mathews was the one who killed your bookkeeper and took those papers. Mathews works with a man named Timberlake. Timberlake takes his orders from a man named Buchanan. The local banker, in case you don't know him . . ."

"Damn him!" Trumbell roared. "Damn me for a fool! I couldn't see it! I . . ." Trumbell could not speak, but stood in trembling rage, his face choleric with rising blood, hands raising and falling against his stomach.

"You couldn't wait," McMahon said. "You had to build your railroad. You didn't care about your bookkeeper or your promise to give me the time I needed. You bought right of way and Buchanan let you go. How much percentage are you paying, Trumbell? And what makes you think you can get right of way from Warbonnet to the reservation? Did Buchanan mention Sam Fletcher? I'll tell you how much of his land you can buy for the right of way with Buchanan doing the purchasing. Not one square inch. Buchanan said he'd force Sam to sell, didn't he? Let him try, Trumbell. Let him come down the hill to scare

Fletcher. I'll be there, and so will fifty more like me. I don't care about your railroad, Trumbell. We're not working for you any more. I don't even know why I bother to tell you the truth. Maybe because I'm going to get Buchanan, and you deserve warning. Stay away from him. You can't fool with the devil and come off without a touch of the brush. That's about all. I'll bring your trunk here later in the day. It's yours and I'll return it. No need to get those papers now, is there?"

McMahon turned to the door and Trumbell stood in shocked silence. McMahon wondered at Mason's closed mouth and narrowed eyes; the man had not reacted according to his character. He opened the door and stared once more at both men, and then went away quickly, down the hall to the stairs and below into the lobby. He felt better and cleaner, for getting that much of the dirtiness off his fingers; and in the same thought, moving behind the stove in the alcove's shadow, came another. Trumbell would come downstairs in a few minutes, raging mad, and head for the bank; once there, facing Buchanan, he would realize the truth. Buchanan was a tough and thoroughly ruthless man, fully aware that no direct proof was held against him, and as such, would not budge an inch from their agreement. Then Trumbell would have to move; and that move could be made in just one direction. McMahon wondered how much he could charge Trumbell to bring the man's fingers out of the fire. He was considering this possible turn of affairs when Trumbell and Mason charged past him, through the lobby and into the street. Chambers was entering the lobby and stepped aside quickly, then crossed to the alcove and smiled at McMahon and rubbed his fingers together over the stove.

"Timberlake's crew are all here," Chambers said softly. "Seven men. I just came from Abe's. His friends are spreading the word, starting their run on the bank. Abe is going over in five minutes to withdraw his entire account. What comes next?"

"I don't know," McMahon said, "but it will happen by dark. Will you give Abe one more message? Have his friends scatter along Front in the stores. Upstairs whenever possible, with rifles. Half on tonight, half tomorrow morning, all tomorrow afternoon. Buchanan will finish with Trumbell and then he'll call on Timberlake. And then we'll finish that part of it. Let them worry this afternoon. After dark tonight we'll have a talk with Mathews. I've got an idea there. It depends on things this afternoon. I'll be here in the hotel, either upstairs or down. You see Abe and then come back and stick close until dark. How are your nerves?"

"Excellent," Chambers said. "And my eye is clear, if you are questioning my trigger finger."

Buchanan's immediate reaction upon McMahon's departure was a vicious, nearly uncontrollable urge to find and kill Mathews with his bare hands. For how else had McMahon learned the truth? He had believed McMahon was lying, shooting in the dark, when they began talking; when McMahon mentioned the trunk, Buchanan knew it was out in the open. Even so, he would not stand in this office and admit defeat, the ruin of years, in the words of one man. McMahon needed proof, and had none. The Trumbell papers were safely hidden in the warehouse; Mathews could be taken out of the way in a short time. Buchanan smiled grimly, entered the banking room, and received the worst shock of all. Henry Slater came from the back room and stood beside him, gnawing nervously on his lower lip.

"Mr. Buchanan," Henry Slater said. "Something funny is going on, sir."

"What?" Buchanan asked harshly.

"Sorry, sir," Slater said meekly. "People are withdrawing

their accounts. It started just a short time ago. I thought nothing of it until more began coming in. Look, here are two more, Mr. Buchanan. You've got to do something."

Buchanan turned and saw the men approach the second teller's window and demand their accounts in full, in cash. Buchanan walked ponderously to the teller's cage and forced a smile. "Withdrawing your accounts, gentlemen?" he said. "Is there another bank opening for business?"

"No," one said. "We just want our money."

"Gladly," Buchanan said. "Hoyt, close out the accounts for these gentlemen"—Buchanan raised his voice and his words cracked in the sudden stillness—"and when they wonder at the foolishness of rumors in a few days, tell them we do not care for their business when they wish to open their accounts again. Perhaps they wish to do banking sixty miles away at Weeping Water. Well, don't stand there. Get their money."

Neither man moved from the window. Buchanan watched both men accept and count their money and leave the bank; and before he could hurry to the back room, three more entered the bank and approached both windows with a grim determination. Buchanan glanced at the wall clock; just two. Bowing to the men, he walked slowly into the bank room and closed the door. Henry Slater had opened the big safe and Buchanan mentally totaled the inadequate supply of cash on hand. About sixty thousand remaining, he knew minutes later after a quick check. It would do little good to explain that their money was safely invested in other places and drawing interest for the bank; and more important, known only to him, was the fact that much of that money was not invested but used up, spent in various ways. Buchanan faced the windowless walls and pictured McMahon laughing half a block south in the hotel lobby. McMahon had started this in some fashion; the man was totally dangerous and incapable of pulling back.

Buchanan walked to the big room and touched Henry

Slater's arm. "If this becomes general, instruct the tellers to double-check accounts, count all cash twice, do everything as slowly as possible. I'll wire Weeping Water immediately for more cash. We close at three sharp today for auditing. How much will we need, Henry? Quickly, now?"

"A hundred thousand should turn the tide."

"Delay everyone," Buchanan murmured. "I'll send that wire."

He walked to the private office for his overcoat and hat, paused briefly in the big room to exchange greetings with a steady trickle of incoming customers, and turned north from the bank toward the depot. He had to send this wire himself, and not to the bank in Weeping Water. He could not get a hundred thousand from that bank; not more than twenty. He had one chance and, failing that, had no choice. If Trumbell could be persuaded to advance the money, he could keep the bank open and weather this storm; if not, there was but one alternative. Buchanan walked to the depot and sent an innocent wire to an address in Kansas City, inquiring the price of hogs from a commission office. He turned then and moved south, walking slowly on the snowy walk. Timberlake appeared in the livery barn door and jerked one hand to the rear. Buchanan nodded slightly and crossed the street, moving behind the livery barn in the general direction of his house. Timberlake said, "Hell's popping, Ferris."

"I know," Buchanan said steadily. "Ready for action?"

"Whatever you say, Ferris."

"Spread your men around the hotel," Buchanan said. "Follow McMahon and Chambers wherever they go. A thousand dollars to the man who finds Mathews and brings him to the house tonight."

"He talked, didn't he?" Timberlake said.

"Yes. McMahon came in and laid his cards on the table, Roy. Mathews must have talked. I want Mathews tonight.

I want McMahon. If you have to go into his room, I want him finished. You understand?"

"It'll break things wide open," Timberlake said. "You got to have it that way, Ferris?"

"Yes," Buchanan said shortly.

"If things break bad," Timberlake asked, "do we pull out?"

"Come to the house at midnight," Buchanan murmured. "If you fail, we'll have to leave."

Buchanan turned and went back to Front and south to the bank. He forced a path through the roomful of people, nodded cheerfully to everyone, and stepped into the private office. He was lighting a cigar and trying to compose his nerves when his door opened with a smash and Trumbell entered the office with Mason following him.

Buchanan said, "Kindly close the door, Mason. Well, sir? Why the forced entry?"

Trumbell advanced to the desk and placed both hands flatly on the ebony cigar box. He said, "Buchanan, our deal is off."

"Off?" Buchanan said mildly. "The agreements are signed. I'll fight you through every court in the land and win hands down."

"The deal is off," Trumbell repeated hoarsely. "You damned killer! I'll see you hang, Buchanan, before I'm done with you. Don't sit there sanctimoniously and try to lie out of this. I know all about Mathews and my trunk and the papers. You're clever, Buchanan, damn your soul, you're clever. But not quite enough. McMahon got to the truth."

"Just a moment," Buchanan said coldly. "I understand you want this railroad. I did not realize you were squeamish about business. I'll get your right of way. I'll help build your railroad. Cross me now and you'll never lay a rail. I haven't a lot of time to discuss wild stories and harum-scarum killings and what-not ·I seem to have committed. Hear that crowd outside? They're pulling a run on my bank. You know damned well I don't carry sufficient cash to meet all accounts. No banker does. If I'm forced to close and lose everything I've worked to make for many years, I'll do one last thing: I'll spike that railroad for good. Trumbell, I need a hundred thousand cash by morning. Your signature is good in Weeping Water. Will you credit me with that amount to stop this run?"

Trumbell stepped away from the desk and folded his arms and regarded Buchanan with some calmness. He said, finally, "McMahon was right. He said you'd try everything. No, I'll loan you nothing, Buchanan, not even to save the railroad. Do your damnedest, Buchanan, because I intend to do the same within twenty-four hours. Come on, Mason."

Buchanan said, "Mr. Mason, I'd like a word with you."

"Give me a minute," Mason said, touching Trumbell's arm. "Perhaps I can . . ."

"You can do nothing," Trumbell said coldly. "But stay if you wish. I'm leaving."

The door closed and Buchanan glanced at his wall clock; two minutes of three. He smiled sourly at Mason and seated himself behind the desk.

"Mason," said Buchanan.

"Will you take the night train to Weeping Water for me?" Buchanan said. "The bank there has received my wire and is collecting a hundred thousand in cash. They'll start it north on a special train. Meet that train, and bring me that money by eight in the morning."

Mason shook his head. "No thanks, Buchanan. It won't work."

"Then loan me the fifteen thousand I gave you," Buchanan said gently.

Mason's right hand moved slightly, touching his side. "Sorry," Mason said. "I sent that to my own bank two days ago."

"Like a rat," Buchanan said softly, "you are leaving the ship. Am I correct?"

"Not like a rat," Mason smiled. "Just a sensible man."

"I will take great pleasure in telling Trumbell of you," Buchanan said. "How will that fit in with your plans?"

"Do so," Mason said. "And I will counter with my own plan. I am going directly to the hotel and explain how I attempted to trick you, and nearly succeeded. After that, do your best."

Outside the heavy door the shouting increased and became a steady roar that drowned all ordinary speech. Buchanan glanced at the wall clock. Henry Slater had just closed the bank for the day.

"How do we stand?" Buchanan asked.

"We did it, sir," Slater said proudly. "Twenty thousand cash is still in the safe."

"Good," Buchanan said warmly. "Send everybody home. Sweep out the customers and go home yourself. I'll close up."

The door closed and sound grew louder outside, then died away slowly and became a whisper that vanished in the enveloping silence of the emptied bank. Mason regarded Buchanan curiously and said, "Sorry, Buchanan. It might have been a great scheme."

Buchanan's right arm hung loosely over the arm of the big chair. "I'll take that fifteen thousand, Mason. I need it."

"You talk like a fool," Mason said sharply.

Buchanan raised his arm, hand holding the small pistol steadily, and shot twice, the sound deadened and absorbed in the room's draperies and thick walls. Buchanan rose quickly, watched Mason take a short step, clutch his side, and collapse on the thick rug. Buchanan dropped the pistol in his coat pocket and walked around the desk and knelt beside the body. "A shame," he murmured to him-

self. "Fifteen thousand is such a little sum for a life—but
I need it badly."

Thirteen

McMAHON SPENT the early part of a long, tension-
packed afternoon in the narrow confines of his room facing Front. He was lighting a cigarette and feeling the chill
of nearing dusk when the knock came, soft but firm. He
dropped the match and said, "Come in."

Mary Fletcher opened the door, slipped quietly into the
room, and wrinkled her nose against the heavy layers of
smoke. "You've been here all afternoon, John."

"Waiting," McMahon said. "You shouldn't be up,
Mary."

"Why not? I'm a part of all this, John. I want to know
what will happen tonight. Father told me part, Will told
me a little more, Mr. Chambers told me nothing. John,
isn't there something I can do to help?"

"Yes," McMahon said gently. "Sit on the bed—there—
and talk with me."

She nodded and sat on the wrinkled mass of heavy
blankets and regarded him with solemn gravity.

"Tell me more about the farm, Mary," McMahon said,
"I was just getting to know it, and you."

An hour passed, and another in which Mary talked of
the joys of creating a living farm from the wasteland. It
had never entered his conscious mind that any woman
could enter his mind, let alone his heart. Now he became
frightened, not for himself, but for her.

"It's time to go," McMahon said, abruptly, suddenly
afraid to hear her talk longer.

"I thought . . ." she said.

"You thought I wanted to hear you talk?" McMahon

said. "I did, Mary, but not too much. We'd better go downstairs and see how things are shaping up."

She stood quickly beside him and said. "Don't lie about tonight, John. There'll be shooting, won't there?"

"Who knows?" McMahon said. "It depends on them, Mary."

"What will you do with Mathews?" she asked.

"It depends on them," McMahon murmured again. "I want you to stay in your room, Mary. Now listen to me, will you?"

"I'll be careful," she said. "But don't expect me to sit twiddling my thumbs if you need help."

McMahon smiled. "Would you come breathing fire and brimstone?"

"For you?" she said. "I would, John."

For a moment he did not speak, standing so close her hair touched his mouth, her eyes wide and unblinking. He touched her arm and she turned, facing him, and said, "Please be careful." He kissed her, holding her gently, her mouth soft and warm, trembling with some emotion he wanted to understand and was completely afraid to go on and discover fully. He stepped back and walked quickly to the door.

"That was foolish," McMahon said. "It will get us nowhere."

"Why do you think I came up here?" she asked simply, and walked to the door and opened it before he could answer. "I'll go now," she said, "but I'd better tell you that I won't stay in that room if you need help."

She turned and walked swiftly to the stairs. McMahon waited until her steps died then followed her out, sober now and worried about his own thoughts. He stepped to lobby level and saw the groups of men talking seriously, their cigar smoke hanging in a thin blue veil above the closely gathered heads. Only Will Overton, just come on duty and busy with the books, showed a familiar face. The others were townspeople and a scattering of those dark-faced men who possessed the wild-rider look and cowboy clothes to match. He counted seven strange faces and as he stood beside the stove and rolled a cigarette, one by one those men drifted from the lobby into the street and disappeared. Timberlake entered from the street almost immediately saw McMahon, and grinned mirthlessly. McMahon saw Chambers then, sitting obscurely in a corner chair, reading a Chicago newspaper; that paper covered Chambers' lap and the unseen gun, ready for use. McMahon felt the warmth of comradeship, knowing he was backed by this small, harmless-looking man and the others who even now waited throughout the town. While he watched Timberlake, the man at the desk was speaking with Will Overton and his words reached McMahon, meaning nothing, but clear.

"Special comin' up from the main line," that man was saying. "She'll pull off at Seven Mile Siding for the south-bound, and she better. Know what's on her list?"

"No," Will Overton said disinterestedly. "What?"

"For the quarry company," the man said. "One car with ten tons of giant powder. Next car two thousand gallons of naphtha, next car ten tons of hardware and steel rods, next car full of tiling. Regular rocket in the making."

"Good pay load," Will Overton said. "Let's hope the brakes hold."

McMahon heard this conversation absently, watching Timberlake all the while. The big man finally crossed the lobby and stopped on the far side of the stove and smiled; his smile had that forced quality of the man who had waited patiently to shoot a wolf and now saw fulfilment in the near future.

"Nice night," Timberlake said softly.

"You want to start it here," McMahon said, "hop to it, Timberlake."

"That wouldn't be polite," Timberlake said. "We'd

bust up the lobby and scare the ladies. Any time you want me, I'll be at the north end of Front. Any time, all night long."

"You can expect me," McMahon said. "Get out of here, Timberlake, or I'll throw you out. You think not? Remember that night on the bluff? You had a rifle, one shot, and all your boys. I took you in one minute in the dark. In here, seeing you so plain, I'll take more time, do a thorough job. Get out!"

Timberlake said, "Only because I'm polite, McMahon. I'll be looking for you—and your fat pal, Chambers."

"Tell Buchanan I'll be seeing him soon," McMahon said. "What's the matter? Didn't you know the game was finished? You're a dead man now. No matter if you get away, Timberlake. I know you like you know yourself. Where can you go, what can you do, how can you change the finish? This year, next year, ten years—it'll be the same for you, for me. The gun, Timberlake, at the end, the gun."

Timberlake showed anger and first uncertainty in his eyes, and then turned away. He walked heavily from the lobby, his great bulk reflected against the window for a moment, then gone into darkness as he passed along Front and swung into the first saloon and signaled for his drink. He was worried now, thinking of his men, wondering if he had brought them to a peak of anger necessary for this night of inevitable violence; with this doubt came a flood of pent-up anger and rage, pushing at his arms and chest, crying for outlet in the only manner he understood, savagery and action.

Timberlake studied the room calmly and seemed to dismiss every man as he turned the glass slowly between his hands. Whisky had slopped along the bar from another man's careless drinking and Timberlake nudged one blunt finger into the wet streak.

"You ever wash this dump out?" he asked the room at large.

"Quit smelling your own hide," someone called. "We never smelled nothin' until you came in."

Deep in the brain centers of Timberlake's mind outrage grew and exploded and burst into the violent action he needed; he turned with one easy motion and threw the glass across the room toward the unknown voice. He followed the glass, broken into shards and lost among the sawdust piles, and picked his man from the group around the stove, a big one with burly shoulders and a red face disfigured by a bold, fleshy nose. He pushed that man against the wall and smashed one clubbed fist squarely on the nose that seemed, to him, utterly repellent and vaguely accountable for all his unhappiness on this miserable night. The man bounced dully against the wall and a dozen of them, up and roaring anger, charged him from three sides. Timberlake threw a chair at them, caught the nearest man with a full arm swing that sent him reeling against the stove with a womanish scream; and then half a dozen of them were on him and over him, kicking, hitting, biting, yelling with the animal outlet of their rage. He hit the floor with both shoulders and came into sitting position, fists before his body, face already bloody and twisted, eyes clear and watching them all. He saw two of his men burst through the front door, understood this scene immediately, and react with quickness. One wheeled back into the street, calling as he ran, and the other dove into the crowd, clubbing his revolver and striking out viciously. Timberlake rolled his body under a table, came upward with brutal power, and upset the table over two men. He caught a chair, knocked out the nearest light, and began bellowing with enjoyment, standing now with his back to the wall, clothing ripped and dirty and wet, knees flexing automatically as he waited for them to come to him.

Sid was the man who came into the saloon, clubbing with his revolver, estimating this fight with the experience of a hundred past battles in similar rooms. Sid watched

Timberlake throw men away and hit others, and stagger when another came from the side and broke a chair over his head. Someone caught Sid on the face with a ringed hand, cutting a deep gash and throwing Sid from his course, which lay undeviatingly across the room to Timberlake's side. Sid struck this man and came on, shot out two more lights, leaving only the wall bracket lamps, six in number, to illuminate the long, smoky room; and ramming between two men, reached Timberlake and pushed closely beside him and called then, for the first time:

"Lazy T!—Lazy T!"

Timberlake grinned savagely beside him and shouted between split lips: "Ho, Lazy T!"

The front door came open and this time broke off the hinges and flew toward the bar's end, striking one man and throwing him to the floor as five of Timberlake's riders came into the fight, swinging before they could see clearly in the semi-darkness. Timberlake saw them come and thought, "They've got some guts after all," and shouted a full-throated defiance at the entire room. Outside, along Front's cold, windy length, doors opened and men poured into the street and swung toward the saloon. Timberlake's men came on into the center of the room, swinging blindly, then methodically as their vision cleared and they saw him against the wall. "Lazy T!" they called then. "Ho, Roy!"

The fight spread across the room as Timberlake and Sid were separated by sheer force of numbers and weight, and the other Lazy T riders were bounced apart and set upon individually and in close-backed pairs. Another bracket lamp went out and then another, and the bartender dived beneath his overhang, grasped his weighted club, and crouched in the temporary safety of the heavy wood wall, waiting for the inevitable to occur when they fought around the bar ends and converged on his sanctuary. This was the worst he had ever witnessed, this fight brought on for no good reason, and he wished for just one thing—a clean shot at Timberlake with his weighted club. Above him, the mirror broke in a thousand glittering bits and showered his quickly bent head with glass and whisky from the broken, falling bottles.

Sid was bulled across the room against the bar, struck from behind, and snapped down forehead first on the rounded rail. He clawed at the bar and slipped downward to the floor, fought back on his feet, and clung helplessly, unable to move his arms. Timberlake roared from a long distance away and Sid felt, but could not see plainly, his advance through the welter of bodies and flying bottles and chair legs and rungs swung carelessly now against any and all heads. Timberlake came up behind a big man, turned him, measured him, and struck the jaw with one straight full-shouldered blow. Even in the half-frantic sound of this complete furor the bone made a distinct and clean sound as it snapped. From somewhere nearby a woman screamed, and the bartender made his first entry into the fight, slugging a man who came charging up the alley behind the bar. Above the bartender, Timberlake lifted Sid under one arm, walked unfeeling over the inert body of the man he had just hit, and fought toward the rear door. Behind him, the man with the broken jaw began to cry in an agonized, horrible voice. Someone shouted, "Hickerson's coming!" and around Timberlake men turned and instinctively ran for all exits.

"Lazy T!" Timberlake shouted hoarsely. "Lazy T here!"

The other joined him at the rear door, battered half a dozen or more men away from that narrow opening, and followed Timberlake into the alley, across the alley through a vacant lot, and away from the sound into the darkness behind a shed. Timberlake said, "Wake up, Sid," and felt the man's body move beneath his hands. "All right," Timberlake said. "All right, Sid."

They stood around Timberlake and Sid, breathing gustily, rubbing bruised faces and spitting blood on the snow, their boots moving as if they could not stand motionless until the fighting fever dissolved and softened in their minds. Timberlake watched them, collectively, then singly, and was satisfied and finally cleared of all anger. His face, battered and swollen, stained with his own and the blood of a dozen other men, moved into a satisfied smile.

"All right," he said. "We've had our fun. We feel better for it. Now get back to your places and we'll start the big show."

McMahon stepped to the desk as Timberlake disappeared and said, "Where's Fletcher, Will?"

"Dining room, with Mary. Trumbell and his daughter are eating, too."

"And Mason?"

"Hasn't shown, John. I've got something for you. Abe and Chambers brought that trunk over."

McMahon said, "I'll take it, Will," and then turned as the fury of the fight came clearly from the saloon. Moments later a man burst through the front door and shouted, "Timberlake and his crew are fightin' the whole town!"

"He's started it," Will said.

"No," McMahon murmered. "Just their fun, Will. Timberlake had to blow off steam. Ask Trumbell to come out here."

Will Overton lifted the small trunk across the desk, nodded reluctantly, and went to the dining room. McMahon moved into the alcove behind the stove and sat with the trunk balanced on his knees, listening to the fight through thin board walls, smoking a cigarette and dozing comfortably in the stove warmth. He remained in this relaxed position until the distant battle had run its course and died away, and Trumbell's voice sounded in the lobby, "Where is he?"

"Back here," Will Overton said.

When Trumbell rounded the corner, McMahon lifted the trunk and pushed it unceremoniously into the man's slack fingers. Trumbell stared, unbelieving, and pulled the trunk against his chest as if testing its reality.

"I thought . . ." Trumbell said.

"We were lying?" McMahon said. "There it is, Trumbell. No papers, but you don't want them, you told us earlier. Let me offer a suggestion. Stay inside tonight and tomorrow. Keep your daughter and that lawyer under cover."

"Trouble?"

"You should know, man," McMahon said roughly. "It's your doing."

"I've been thinking," Trumbell said reluctantly. "I'm a damned fool. No, a stubborn fool. That's worse, McMahon, I'm not backing water, but I'll take care of all expense for this. Wire Colonel Sloane and explain for me. I've been eating, sleeping, and dreaming this railroad. I let it get the better of common decency. You understand what I'm trying to say?"

"Save it," McMahon said. "It's no longer in your hands. We bury our own dead. Watch yourself."

McMahon crossed to the dark corner and took the chair beside Chambers and said, "I'm going to Abe's. Are his friends placed?"

Chambers spoke behind the newspaper. "All along Front. Down by the depot. Around his house."

"Timberlake is waiting for me at the north end of Front," McMahon said. "All night. We'll take him in turn. I'm going to break Mathews, make him talk, then turn him loose. I want to see what happens. Maybe he'll save us some trouble. Timberlake and Buchanan want him bad. He'll fight back. See Marshal Hickerson now, Chambers. Tell him to stand ready all night with his deputies. This can break wide open at any minute."

McMahon crossed to the street door and turned south on Front, walking openly in the yellow light from the Antlers. He passed from the business district into the first block of houses and trees, stopped dead in the middle of the block where the flickering gas lights did not reach, and plunged quickly between two houses, running west across the alley, between other houses, and into the cleared ground that lay about the town. Sid would be the man waiting in the alley behind the hotel; and it could take no less than five minutes for the lookout on Front to spot him, estimate his course, and hurry around to give the warning. McMahon drew his gun and angled northwest, quartering around the town in a wide curve. He stopped at a point exactly on line and west of the hotel, in the shadow of a cottonwood growing amid low brush, and waited for the expected sound.

It came two minutes later, the flat thudding of boots on the crusty snow, growing louder, then slowing as one man took the lead and the other fell behind to cover the rear. McMahon dropped on his knees, placed his left arm against the thick bole of the cottonwood, and leveled his gun across that steady forearm. He saw the two figures, twenty feet apart, walking now. The first man turned and called, "Stake out here. You take the tree. I'll go on to that little hump." McMahon recognized Sid's voice and sighted on his legs.

"Far enough, Sid," McMahon called. "Throw that gun down and get your arms up. You too, you behind!"

His voice stopped them, stiff and dark statues against the faint glow rising above Front. Sid said, "Damn you!" and dove suddenly to the ground, shouting, "Circle him, Bill," and firing toward the cottonwood.

McMahon placed one shot on Sid and moved away from the tree and to the right, watching the other man, Bill, running out and around in the darkness. Sid shouted unintelligibly and answered McMahon's shots with two of his own, both striking the tree. McMahon was ten paces back now, on hands and knees, crawling rapidly toward Bill, who had come behind him and was out of sight, on the snow, and moving forward. McMahon dropped on his stomach between two snow-crusted bushes and waited. Sid was holding his fire.

Bill called from a short distance away, "Ho, Sid!"

McMahon saw him, a black and oblong shape on the snow. He said softly, "Drop it, Bill! Don't play it foolish."

Bill twisted convulsively and fired, the bullet cutting dead twigs from the bush above McMahon's head. He felt an inner satisfaction, akin to joy, having the right to return that fire and even the odds. He shot twice, hitting Bill squarely. Bill managed one last call, "Sid!" and then lay still, a sprawled mass of arms and legs, a body that would not move again. McMahon was moving away from the bush as Sid shouted, "Bill, Bill!" and made a rush for the cottonwood, realizing his mistake. McMahon rolled behind another ridge of brush and dead, scattered branches, lay on one side and reloaded, watching the cottonwood and wondering how Sid liked the odds now. Far away, on Front, someone was calling and other voices answered. Sid's friends would not come out here; this was not their duty.

"Bill!" Sid called from behind the cottonwood.

"He's done," McMahon said, holding one hand before his mouth. "You're no good at this game, Sid. One more chance. Come out with your arms up."

"Go to hell!" Sid answered, and immediately shot three times in the direction of McMahon's voice.

"Last chance," McMahon called. "I'll count five, Sid. Then I'm coming for you."

Sid's answer was another shot. McMahon fired once, rolling to the left as the echo died, coming on his knees and moving away westward along a small ditch that offered partial protection. Sid shot twice at McMahon's gun flash;

that was six. Sid had to reload. McMahon left the ditch and, crouching low, ran straight north until the cotton-wood was directly on line with his right shoulder. He had angled inward and was some thirty paces away, and could see Sid crouched low behind the trunk. McMahon shot twice, jumped three long paces to his left, shot twice more, and dove full length on the snow. He heard the startled shout and then a cough. Sid changed position and shot blindly over McMahon's head, said something in a thick-ened voice, and suddenly stood erect beside the tree, grop-ing with one hand for the trunk, gun arm leveled and sag-ging as Sid coughed once more, cried out with anguish and crumpled into the snow. McMahon said, "You had your chance," and closed in without worry. Sid was a dead man, gun muzzle down in the snow near his right hand. Mc-Mahon pocketed that gun, turned Sid over and searched him quickly, rolled him against the tree, and started north. Two down, he thought, and the night's young. The weeks of waiting were forgotten now. He was like the snake shed-ding a worn, tattered skin, the bear smelling fresh grass after a long winter; this was the time when he could throw off all restraint and fight with no holding back.

He came to Abe Bloom's house openly, holding one arm over his head, calling out softly, "Hold it, men. I'm com-ing in." From the outer darkness a strange voice called, "It's McMahon—go ahead, McMahon. Abe's inside."

"How many of you?" McMahon asked.

"Five here. Fifty downtown. We're all with you. What happened over south?"

"You'll find two near that big cottonwood," McMahon said tonelessly. "No hurry, they won't go away."

When he stepped onto Abe's porch, openly for the first time, he heard one man saying softly, "God! He shoots two men and doesn't raise his voice." Then Abe had the door open and he was inside the warm, familiar kitchen, shaking Abe's hand and moving immediately to the chair where Mathews sat, bound tightly and gagged with a clean handkerchief.

"We took him from the hole," Abe said. "No need to give him pneumonia, John."

McMahon ripped the gag from Mathews' mouth, slapped the white face twice, and spoke without preamble, "Buchanan's done, Mathews. Timberlake will clear out or I'll have him by morning. You hear the shots south of here? I got Sid and Bill. You've got one minute to decide. Write out a full statement, everything I order, everything you know. Sign it and I'll give you more chance than you deserve. The train leaves in half an hour. You can be aboard. Don't think Timberlake and Buchanan will pull you out, Mathews. I told them you confessed everything. They'll shoot first when they see you, ask the questions in hell. This is the showdown, Mathews. If I didn't want Buchanan legally, I'd push you through a fish hole and forget you. The minute's up. Make your choice."

Mathews was in terrible shape, thin and frightened by body weakness that refused to combat dripping water and lying gagged and bound for what had seemed all eternity. Until this moment he had kept hope alive. When McMahon spoke Buchanan's name, Mathews felt all hope die. He wondered weakly if McMahon was devil or just a man. His decision was made by his flesh, not his mind, but even his mind savored the future taste of freedom and overrode all ties of allegiance to Buchanan.

"I'll write," Mathews said hoarsely. "Get the paper."

Abe Bloom murmured softly, "Checkmate," and hurried to the corner desk.

Fourteen

TIMBERLAKE WAS STANDING just inside the side porch door of Buchanan's house, talking with Buchanan, when the shots came from the west side of town. Buchanan was dressed in rough clothing and thick boots, with a muffler wrapped twice about his thick neck. He said, "It's started, Roy. If we only knew where they had Mathews."

"Ferris, you got to listen," Timberlake said. "We're busted higher'n a bobtail flush on the call. Get all the cash you've got and we'll be clear by morning. The others don't count. Hell with 'em. I've got a light sled and a fast team tied under the bridge. You get what you need and wait for me there. We can be on the reservation by morning. By night the whole damned army won't find us."

Buchanan murmured, "Still a chance, Roy. I hate to give up all this. So much work. So much to win. If Mathews doesn't talk, and Trumbell changes his mind, there's an outside chance."

"Have I ever backed down for you?" Timberlake asked softly.

"No, Roy. We've been through thick and thin for a long time."

"You know I don't take water for any man," Timberlake said desperately. "And not from this McMahon. I'll get him tonight, Ferris. I promise you. Then we got to clear out, Ferris. I can fight one man, two men, but not a town."

Buchanan sighed and rubbed one gloved hand against the wall, feeling the solid and lasting structure of his house, the first home he had ever built and lived in; and his bank, and the warehouse, and the farms, bought and erected with money that, true enough, was the bank's, but could have been replaced within a year and no one the wiser. Buchanan considered these tangible results of a good life and shook his head.

"You're right, Roy," Buchanan murmured. "I'll get all the cash and meet you under the bridge. How long will you be?"

"He'll come no later than midnight," Timberlake said, thinking aloud. "I'll be at the bridge by one, Ferris. If I'm not, head north for the shack, leave the sled and team, take two horses and ride west. Get into the river hills, cross at the big bar and keep riding until you can cover your trail. Heslet's place is on the north bank, thirty miles west of the bar. You wait for me there."

"And if something happens to me?" Buchanan said.

"Shouldn't," Timberlake said. "Just be careful, Ferris. Don't show yourself."

"Very well," Buchanan whispered. "One thing, Roy. If you have the chance, take care of Mathews too."

"With my bare hands, Ferris," Timberlake said viciously.

Timberlake shook hands and slipped into the darkness. Buchanan watched him for a moment and smiled, admiring the big man's devotion and twisted sense of honor. Even now, with everything gone, Timberlake had arranged the getaway and thought of Buchanan's safety. Buchanan murmured, "Sorry, Roy," and moved soundlessly through the house to his library, locked the door and turned the lamps up bright and yellow.

On the big desk in neat stacks lay the end of a dream. Fifty thousand he had kept in the library safe; fifteen thousand he had taken from Mason's money belt which, in all honesty, was his own; then thirty thousand, all remaining cash in the bank. There was one more thing to do: he must get those papers from the warehouse. Buchanan moved swiftly about the room, packing the money in a small valise, filling and thrusting a long flask of brandy into his hip pocket, dropping a tiny sack containing three diamonds and his pearl shirt studs into an inner coat pocket; and finally, after placing the valise on the desk, loading and checking two short-barreled .32's which rode near his hands in a model vest similar to the Wesley Hardin quick-draw vest just beneath his heavy mackinaw. These few possessions, he thought bitterly, and no more. In this moment he hated McMahon with an intensity that flushed his thick face and made his fingers tremble when he stopped to lift the valise under his left arm. He moved to the east window, pulled the drapes a trifle so that anyone outside could see the bright lamp and assume, he hoped, that the banker worked late to save his bank; and then, glancing once more around the room, he hurried into the bedroom, closed the door and left the house on the river side by a window. He wondered if Timberlake would head north when he reached the bridge later that night and found no one waiting in the sled; that was the most difficult part—leaving Timberlake. But ninety thousand was a respectable stake, and Timberlake was in actuality a dead man for all purposes. Buchanan intended to remain hidden in the warehouse that night, the next day, and then follow his own long-arranged plan of escape. Across the river, half a mile south of town, he had hidden a section crew handcar in a ravine over a year ago; the ravine came down from the bluffs on the west side of the tracks, a narrow, rain-washed gully good for nothing and never explored. He had spent ten nights digging the small cave, then greasing the handcar, shoving it into the hole, and sliding rocks and shale over the entrance. Tomorrow night, with McMahon and the others following a cold trail north, he could slip from the warehouse, cross the river, and pump south toward the main line. It would take two nights, with a day spent in hiding along the track, to reach Weeping Water; but once there, arriving at night, he could go directly to a certain house and, for a price, get safely out of the country. Perhaps he should leave tonight, but he wanted Trumbell's papers. He wanted to send those deeds and bills of sale to Trumbell two or three years from now, after the railroad had cost Trumbell much more than he estimated. Nothing could change him from that belated revenge.

Timberlake circled north along the river to the tracks,

and crossed them into the complete darkness that enveloped that part of the railroad yards. The night train was loading farther west, engine puffing and snorting, moving cars onto the main line and shoving them into the forming train. Timberlake had thought out his plan during the day while sitting in Jensen's barn, studying the depot and tracks and short sections of cars. Front ran straight north, crossed the tracks just east of the depot, and became the wagon road that followed the river up the valley. He could take up a position behind one of those cars and cover the entire length of Front, the depot, and the yard. McMahon would come for him, there was no doubt of that in his mind, and all he asked was the first shot.

Timberlake angled north from the siding and crossed the wagon road well beyond the light cone of the last street lamp shining over the grassy plot beside the depot. He returned to the first siding and took up his position between two sheep cars, with a clear view of the depot and the full length of Front. Timberlake settled himself against the coupling, rolled and placed an unlighted cigarette in his mouth, and waited patiently, tasting the sharp tobacco and rubbing the hand-warmed butts of his guns in both mackinaw pockets. Before him on the main track, the night train took final shape. Timberlake wondered if the shots heard on the west side of town had meant the finish for one or more of his own crew, or someone with McMahon. He argued with himself, hoping McMahon had been shot, and yet hoping strongly that McMahon still lived to come up Front and finish their personal fight.

The night train was ready now; the engineer pulled his cord and the whistle sounded shrilly as the brakeman moved toward the caboose far back in the west end shadows of the yard. In this moment, watching with the still fresh curiosity of the small boy, Timberlake saw a man run quickly across his front and swing onto the slowly moving train, three cars behind the engine. Timberlake came erect, recognizing Mathews without question, knowing his run and slight, wiry body. Timberlake saw him swing behind the third car, a freight car, and drop into the open-topped blackness of the fourth, an empty coal car. It meant only one thing to Timberlake, his senses acutely sharpened to all possible developments of this business: Mathews had sold out, written and signed a statement, and had been given a chance to get clear by McMahon. Timberlake acted immediately upon the surge of rage that filled his body. He ducked between the sheep cars and ran across two siding tracks, turned in parallel to the train, and swung himself up between two cars. Most of the train had passed by that time and he was one car from the caboose and at least eighteen from Mathews.

Timberlake clung to the ladder that banged and creaked against the car's flat end, balancing himself with one foot on the lowest rung and one foot atop the coupling. They rumbled over the bridge and Timberlake thought of Buchanan, then McMahon, and changed his plan. He would get Mathews, but it might take some time; in that time Buchanan would be waiting under the bridge with every right to head north at one o'clock. Timberlake smiled in the darkness; Ferris would get away. He would take care of Mathews and, if necessary, spend another day or two finishing with McMahon. Making his decision, Timberlake climbed carefully to the top of the swaying, snow-slickened car and began his advance toward the engine.

McMahon stood in the total darkness of the upper yard and watched Mathews board the night train; and moments later saw the big man run, like an angry bear, from the line of cars and haul himself up and out of sight between two cars. Abe Bloom shivered involuntarily and murmured, "You were right, John."

"Had to try it," McMahon said. "Timberlake was sure

to wait for me here. He'll go after Mathews and then come back." McMahon smiled. "He owns a twisted sense of pride and honor, Abe. He'll walk sixty miles up track if necessary to have his shootout with me. This takes care of Mathews."

Abe Bloom shivered again, not with cold. McMahon was utterly remorseless in a way, Abe thought, a man who went straight to the heart of a problem and broke it into the most simple pieces. Mathews had written and signed a statement, telling all they knew, had guessed, and much more about Buchanan. Mathews was turned loose, undeserving that freedom, and Timberlake would soon finish the man in his own way. Harsh justice, Abe thought, but the only kind for men like Mathews.

"And now?" Abe asked.

"There will be five or six of Timberlake's crew in and around town," McMahon said. "Root them out, Abe. Turn your friends loose on them. Notify Hickerson. Tell him it's time to close the gate. I want you to take every unknown man to jail and keep him there. Chambers will be at the hotel. Have him wire Weeping Water, using Hickerson's name and official approval, alert their marshal for a pickup of Timberlake or Mathews, or both, if they decide to pull freight."

"And you?"

"I'm going after our fat friend," McMahon said evenly. "There's the man who has the mind of his own. I can't outguess him. I'll have to bull right in and start looking."

"I think," Abe said, "that Buchanan will attempt his getaway within a day. I have more than enough men, John. Wouldn't it be wise to block all roads and search thoroughly for horses and teams?"

"Do that," McMahon said. "I'll be near or inside Buchanan's house or somewhere along the river."

He squeezed Abe Bloom's shoulder and moved down track at a lope, passing through shadow, then appearing in silhouette against the depot lights, running along the cindered platform and crossing the road into the darkness. Abe Bloom shook his head in silent wonder and hurried away to do his share of this business. Within twenty minutes Hickerson, with five deputies and fifty volunteers, was scouting the town, shining lanterns in alleys and vacant lots and darkened buildings. Chambers sat in the depot office, dictating a wire to Weeping Water's marshal, then moving down Front with Will Overton and Fletcher, watching the formation of a new order as demonstrated by the solid people of the town. Abe Bloom and fifteen men were searching all barns, dropping off men in pairs to cover the three roads and two trails leading out from the town like irregular spokes from a greasy wheel hub. Coming to the river bridge, they found the sled and big team, and posted four men at this spot. At the moment Abe Bloom hurried downtown to ask advice of Chambers McMahon stood a short distance from Buchanan's house, studying the thin line of yellow lamplight pouring through a crack in the drapes. He could not see inside the room, but he had the impulse, coming suddenly, to smash the glass and go through the empty frame into the house. McMahon ran quickly to the trees, selected a heavy limb some three feet in length, and returned to the window. He swung the limb in a full-armed smash, striking the window squarely in the center. The wooden sash gave inward, dropped away, and glass showered and fell on McMahon's hat. One circular motion of the limb, crashing around the inside window frame, dislodged all jagged particles of glass from the hardened putty and glazier points. He dove over the sill, was enmeshed momentarily in the drapes as one tore loose and fell baggily about his body; and then came erect, facing an empty room, a library walled with books and lighted with two large lamps, both burning brightly.

He saw two doors and discounted one immediately, that

plainly leading to a hallway; the other had to be the bed-room. McMahon crossed the library, pushed that door open quickly, and stood aside to face total darkness and stillness. When he struck a match and tossed it into the dark bedroom, the red glow illuminated, for one moment, the large bed, chest of drawers, and no more. Buchanan had pulled out, leaving his house, his possessions, every-thing behind. McMahon returned to the big desk and went rapidly through all drawers, then made a thorough search of the room, finding the safe, now open and seem-ingly laughing at him, and nothing else of pertinent value. McMahon cursed then, softly and without anger, unable to decide on a plan. Buchanan had a dozen alternatives, all capable of taking him out of town in safety. McMahon ground the cigarette viciously in Buchanan's ash tray and left the house by the broken window, drawing the drapes to the same position, leaving the sliver of light showing. He had turned north and moved nearly to the depot when Abe Bloom came up Front, calling his name, and joined him on the platform.

"We found a team and sled under the bridge," Abe said breathlessly. "I put four men on guard, did not touch horses or sled, and went for Chambers. He ordered it left as is, under guard. He is of the opinion Buchanan and Timberlake will use it to head north."

A little more of this blackness was clearing for Mc-Mahon. Buchanan was in town, somewhere within five minutes' walk, waiting for Timberlake to do one more job. But Timberlake had taken another tangent, going after Mathews, feeling that enough time remained to finish him, return and face McMahon, and then meet Buchanan under the bridge for the getaway. McMahon spoke quietly.

"Your name is Buchanan, Abe. You're waiting for Tim-berlake. You hide somewhere in town. Just where would that be?"

"Many places," Abe murmured sadly, "but only two are

likely. Mathews' shack. Myself, knowing Buchanan slightly, I would say the warehouse. But that warehouse is a rabbit warren with a hundred places to hide. It would be best, I say, to surround it and wait."

"I'll take a look," McMahon said. "How is the wolf hunt coming?"

"Five of them," Abe Bloom said. "Locked in jail. Hickerson is still combing the town."

"Post ten men in the yards and along the wagon road north of the bridge," McMahon said. "Timberlake will be coming back within two hours or not at all, if I know the man. I'll take a look at the warehouse."

He turned despite Abe's protest, and trotted down that same alley toward the warehouse and the back step where Red Egan had died and started everything.

Timberlake had crawled forward over ten cars when the whistle blast came back to his ears and the train began a jerky slowing motion preliminary to stopping. Holding firmly to the brake wheel five cars behind the engine, Timberlake saw the lanterns flashing half a mile down track and remembered the Seven Mile Siding. A special, he thought, waiting for a clear track into Warbonnet; and with this realization came the hope that the night train would stop and allow him a few minutes to crawl forward on the slippery boards until he was poised above that open coal car. The night train ground to a slow halt abreast the dark oblong of the special, halted on the siding. Brakemen were exchanging loud greetings and moving to the special's caboose for coffee and a cigarette.

Timberlake rose carefully to his feet and moved forward, stepping with double caution over the space between cars; halfway along the top of the last car behind the open coal car, he went again to his knees and began the painful crawling that bruised his knees and made his thigh muscles ache. He reached the end and looked down

upon the black interior of the coal car, trying to pick
Mathews from the shadows; and failing this, knowing
Mathews would be unarmed, made his decision and moved
into action. He swung down until his feet touched and
found balance on the top rim of the coal car, then turned
and jumped, landing heavily in the bottom of the car,
coming up and rushing toward the front end where
Mathews must have been crouched out of the wind. The
shadows fell away at this range and Timberlake stared in
complete surprise at a vacant end; and as suddenly, body
reacting with anger and haste, wheeled in time to see
Mathews swing over the side and drop lightly to the
ground. Timberlake bellowed his rage, a deep and rising
anger at his own stupidity. Mathews had crouched in the
rear end and he, like a fool, had jumped over his head
and given him another chance. Timberlake leaped, caught
the car's side edge and vaulted over and down to the snowy
right of way. Mathews was a catlike streak in the darkness, racing madly toward the engine of the special on
the siding, then ducking between two cars and disappearing from view.

"All right," Timberlake said. "All right."

He drew one gun and ducked behind the special's caboose to the far side of the tracks. In this moment, standing just beyond the upper grade, the night train's two
brakemen came from the special's caboose, laughing and
calling good-byes, swinging their lanterns and moving toward their own caboose. The engineer whistled twice and
the night train tightened all couplings, groaned and moved
forward, then began its trip to the south, grinding away
from the siding. Timberlake moved around and watched
closely between trains. Mathews did not appear. Only then
did Timberlake smile. Mathews was somewhere near or on
this short special. Timberlake counted the cars; six, with
the engine and caboose. He saw the brakeman's lantern
on the other side, flashing to the engine as the brakeman

began his cold walk forward to throw the switch on the main line. Timberlake had no choice now; that switch would go over in five minutes and the special would be off the siding and heading for Warbonnet before he had a chance to find his man.

He ran past the cars and swung himself onto the engine's lower step, holding the rail with one hand and standing firm, facing the engineer and fireman who turned and stared blankly at his gun. Timberlake said, "Come on down," and when they did not move, leaped into the cab and smashed the engineer to the floor with one vicious sweep of the gun. The engineer struck the padded seat, bounced away and down, falling without outcry. The fireman said, "What the . . . ?" and lifted his shovel, then dropped it with a sharp clatter as Timberlake crossed the cab and slapped it from his hands and whirled him around like a child, with one big arm.

"I don't mean no harm," Timberlake said thickly. "I just don't want to hurt you bad, friend. Stand where you are."

Timberlake searched him quickly and pocketed the short-barreled revolver he found in the fireman's overalls. He stepped backward to the engineer's window and saw the brakeman's lantern giving the come-ahead signal from the switch. Timberlake searched the engineer, found another revolver, and then took the fireman's mackinaw collar and forced him to his knees. "Stay here," Timberlake said. "Remember, I don't want to hurt anybody, but try something foxy and you get hurt plenty bad."

"It's your funeral," the fireman said huskily. "There's nothing of value on this train."

"I know," Timberlake said. "I don't want your cargo."

The brakeman came from the switch, lantern bobbing crazily as he took the ties four at a time. He swung into the engine and called, "What's the matter, Jake?" and stiffened into frightened silence as Timberlake waved his gun and said, "Stand right here, friend. All right, the two of you pick up this one. We'll take a walk to the caboose."

The brakeman was an older man, experienced and wary. He stepped back and stood beside the engine, watching Timberlake cautiously, holding the lantern before his stomach. He said, "I don't know your game, brother, but it don't make sense."

Timberlake nudged the fireman, who lifted the engineer and eased him down the steps to the brakeman. They walked toward the caboose with Timberlake following three paces behind; walking now, he studied the cars and noted their type and number. They passed the fourth car and Timberlake said, "Hold up," and rubbed along the door edge with his free hand. This car held freight and the door latch, under his fingers, hung open.

Timberlake murmured, "Go on," and hurried them past the two remaining cars to the caboose. They carried the engineer inside and placed him on the padded bench and turned, white-faced, watching Timberlake.

"Your cars sealed?" Timberlake asked.

"At the start of the run," the brakeman said. "Checked 'em myself."

"Come out here," Timberlake said. "Uncouple this caboose."

"Brother," the brakeman said softly. "You're going to terrible pains for a load fifty men couldn't cart away."

"Uncouple," Timberlake said harshly.

He watched them uncouple the caboose, checked the connections himself, and pushed them back into the caboose. He said, "I don't want to hurt you, but I'm taking this train up track about a mile. I'll bring it back in an hour, maybe less. I don't suppose you'd sit here and wait, would you?"

The brakeman smiled coldly. "You know better, brother, Switch open on the main line, stealing railroad property, half-killing Fogarty. Step in our shoes, how would you answer?"

Timberlake sighed heavily, time resting on his shoulders and passing too swiftly for argument. He said, "Then it'll be this way," and stepped three paces and hit the brakeman flush on the jaw with his free fist. The brakeman staggered the length of the car, struck the back door, and collapsed. Timberlake had the fireman down and out as the brakeman fell. He moved swiftly then, throwing both men against the wall and tying them with a blanket; ripped into strips and wrapped roughly around arms and legs. Then he left the caboose open a bare two inches, and cupped one hand over his mouth.

"George," Timberlake called softly. "Come out and face it like a man. I know you're inside."

Mathew's voice came faintly from the front part of the car, muffled by distance and the car's contents, "I like it in here, Roy. Come in and get me."

Timberlake could not bargain with this man. He said, "You don't have a gun, George. You don't have that knife. McMahon sent you out stripped to your hands. You made a statement, didn't you, George? I told Ferris you were a yellow rat. Come out and take it the quick way, or I'll come in and make it slow, with my hands."

Mathews laughed softly. "Come ahead, Roy. Reach inside and feel the shipment of goods. Hardware, Roy, and I'm standing in the middle of it with my hands full. I'll give you a tip, Roy. I've got a new Winchester in one hand and shells in the other. It's warm in here and I like it fine. I can wait as long as you can, Roy. Here's my calling card."

The shot was muffled but the slug tore splinters from the door and pushed Timberlake back with a leap and curse. He pushed the door shut and crouched low; and then anger took complete possession. He latched the door and ran for the engine. Steam was up when Timberlake checked the gauges; five minutes later he nursed the train

slowly into the switch and north on the main line toward
Warbonnet. He went up track a good mile before stopping; and then, coldly furious, moved along the cars,
wrestling with this unexpected turn of events. Passing the
first car, a tanker filled with naphtha, the idea became
desire; and when he reached the second car and found the
big red cards tacked in five pieces, he smiled broadly. The
cards read "Explosives." Timberlake broke the seal and
pushed the door back and felt inside. This car was loaded
with a good ten tons of giant powder and the special, with
naphtha, giant powder, and a car of hardware, was a per-
fect projectile lying quietly on tracks, harmless but deadly
to the touch of a match. Timberlake had his mad thoughts
in this moment, hatred and impatience overriding the
last vestige of decency. Back in the Warbonnet yards, the
switch engine was shunting empties and loaded cars along
the main track, preparing them for the next train south.
Buchanan waited for him, trusted him, and Mathews was
locked in the fourth car back, grinning like the rat he was,
knowing that Timberlake had just so much time. Timberlake made his decision and ran for the engine.

He brought the darkened special north at a crawl until
Warbonnet's lights rose clear across the river. A mile from
the long curve that approached the river bridge, Timberlake stopped and climbed atop the engine, then dropped
inside and moved the special to the start of the curve, half
a mile from the depot. He could hear, and faintly make
out, the switch engine chuffing and moving in the yards,
and finally saw a string of freight cars moving on the main
track beside the depot, blocking the wagon road and extending almost to the west end of the bridge. He opened
the firebox and shoveled coal furiously, watching the steam
gauge as he worked; when it began to rise slowly as the fire
caught and burned high, he dropped from the engine and
ran to the fourth car and raised his voice.

"Mathews, can you hear me?"

"Sure," Mathews called. "Taking us back to Warbonnet, Roy? Good idea. McMahon'll be glad to see you."

"Listen," Timberlake shouted wildly. "I'll give you one last chance. Are you coming out?"

Mathews answer was another shot that scraped full length along the inside of the door. Timberlake said, "All right, George," and returned to the engine.

The gauge was rising rapidly when Timberlake backed the train a quarter mile, stopped, stood trembling until the boiler shook and began leaking steam, and then opened the throttle. The driver wheels spun and whined, caught and moved, and the special's light load gathered speed into the curve. Timberlake pulled the throttle on the gate and leaped for the steps; and crouching to make his dive into the deep snow along the grade, took one last glance at the gauge. The special would not be moving too fast for the curve, but fast enough to smash into the freight cars and blow the naphtha sky high. Timberlake laughed and dived outward into the darkness, ducking and rolling onto one shoulder to absorb the shock of landing; as he left the steps in a long clearing arc, the special passed behind him, wheels singing now as the speed increased with every revolution. He thought, "It'll blow the town flat," and then struck soft, yielding snow and rolled over and over, coming to a halt against the thick brush-choked snow that lined the right of way.

He lay for a moment, moving his body cautiously before scrambling to his feet and shading his eyes with both hands to watch the special. The engine reached the bridge, then engine and cars careened across with a thunderous roar, seemed to leap forward toward the depot and smash into the string of empties on the main track. Timberlake saw the engine lift upward and fall on one side; he saw the naphtha tank burst and almost immediately, it seemed, flying coals from the broken firebox had ignited the oil. Flames shot upward with a sound he could hear across the river, then raced along the special's cars. Timberlake said savagely, "How do you like that, George?" and ran for the river.

Fifteen

McMAHON CIRCLED the warehouse twice, looking closely for doors and windows recently opened; the rear door facing the river, through which Mathews had escaped after spearing Red Egan, was locked tightly, the snow undisturbed on the step and the path to the river untouched that night. McMahon estimated the time Timberlake would need to catch Mathews and return, and allowed himself no less than an hour to search Mathews' shack and the bank itself for Buchanan. He moved swiftly on a thorough round and check of the shack and then up Front to the bank. Abe Bloom and Hickerson came from the livery barn.

"Everybody's rounded up," Hickerson said, with pride. "What comes next, McMahon?"

"In here," McMahon said. "I want a look around."

Hickerson smiled. "Bank's locked."

"Can't seem to find the banker," McMahon said dryly. "Would you object if I just walked on in?"

"Not tonight," Hickerson said. "I'll bust that lock for you."

McMahon nodded and stood aside until Hickerson smashed the door glass, reached through gingerly and turned the inner lock and pushed the heavy door open. McMahon entered the main room, lit a bracket lamp, and walked to the private office. Ten minutes' quick search convinced him that Buchanan had stripped all cash from the safe and left this place for good; and turning, staring angrily across the office, he saw the dark spot on the rug before the desk. Abe Bloom, waiting in the open doorway, watched him drop on one knee and rub the spot hard with a forefinger.

"Blood?" Abe asked.

McMahon nodded curtly and began a circle of the room. One door led to the main room, he knew that, and the other, smaller door opened into the heavily timbered back room where filing cases and the safe lined the inner wall. Another door opened from this room into the main room, and yet another seemed to give access to what was undoubtedly a broom closet. McMahon twisted the safe handle, found it locked and off combination, and walked absently to the small door and jerked it open. He saw the body of Paul Mason doubled into the far end beneath a dirty smock and a pair of overshoes hung on a hook by their buckles. He was staring at Mason's body, understanding yet another tangent of this case, when Hickerson called "Great God!" from the front door, and the shattering crash and ripping crescendo of the special's ramming into the empties filled the town and his ears.

McMahon followed Abe Bloom into the street and saw the flames rising, then licking along the smashed cars of the special. Running toward the depot with Abe Bloom, pushing through the suddenly crowded street, McMahon saw the red explosive cards on the second freight car at the moment the depot agent and the switch engine crew came running toward them, waving arms and shouting a warning.

"It's the special," the depot agent called. "She came in without a crew and blew the naphtha tank. There's ten tons of giant powder and a car of hardware and steel rods right behind. She'll blow us to hell in ten minutes."

McMahon murmured, "So he had to do it that way."

"Do what?" Abe Bloom asked.

"Timberlake," McMahon said. "You'll find Mathews in one of those cars."

"My God," Abe Bloom said. "The man is crazy."

McMahon hit the agent's arm sharply and called, "We can't stop that fire. The powder'll go in a few minutes. Clear your yard." McMahon turned, grasped Hickerson's arm and said, "Everybody out of town, down along the river south of here. And fast! You've got ten minutes, maybe fifteen. Move out!"

Hickerson said, "Right," and ran down Front, shouting orders, firing his gun at the sky. Other men fanned out across town, shooting and yelling. Abe Bloom ran beside McMahon toward the hotel and said calmly, "I'll get everyone away from the bridge."

"Save that team and sled," McMahon said. "Don't waste time."

He passed Tom, standing before the livery barn, and called roughly, "Get help, Tom. Get those horses south of town."

Tom nodded fearfully and began turning his livestock into the street. McMahon whirled a man and said, "Help with those horses," and moved into the lobby of the hotel, meeting Fletcher and Mary. Trumbell came from the dining room, and Alice Trumbell stood quietly in the alcove, watching Will Overton close the hotel safe and scoop up the cash. McMahon said, "Come on, all of you."

"I'll be there," Will Overton said. "I've got to check all rooms, John."

"Make it fast," McMahon said. "Come on, Mary."

"She blew!" Fletcher gasped, running heavily beside McMahon. "What train is it?"

"Special," McMahon said. "Came in and rammed some empties. Car of powder going to blow in no time. Don't ask questions. Run!"

McMahon led them toward the river and came to the bank just beyond Mathews' deserted shack, a good half mile south of the depot. The bank at this point was thirty feet above the ice, offering protection against the flying hardware and timber that would follow the blast. Mc-

Mahon half-slid, half-ran down this steep incline, holding
Mary Fletcher steady with one arm and balancing himself
with the other. On the narrow footpath that followed the
river's edge, McMahon stopped them and called to
Fletcher and other people now pouring over the bank and
forming along the river. Flames from the burning cars
were visible in the sky, even at this distance, and against
the backdrop of their red brilliance McMahon watched
the people of Warbonnet come streaming over the bank
in a steadily increasing rush that soon became a solid,
bobbing mass of shoulders and heads silhouetted fleetingly
against red light, then jumping, rolling, tumbling down
the snowy bank to the river's edge. Chambers came sliding down on his buttocks, dusted himself calmly, and
came along the path calling, "McMahon—McMahon?"

"Here," McMahon said.

Chambers stood beside him and murmured, "Timberlake."

"Had to be him," McMahon said. "Look for the agent,
will you? Ask him if the special waited for the night train
at Seven Mile Siding. If it did, we have the story."

"I'll join you again if possible," Chambers said, and vanished into the crowd along the river.

Trumbell's voice came to him from the darkness along
the bank, "McMahon, if anything happens to Alice, I'll
hold you responsible."

"Where is she?" McMahon said. "She has ears."

"Stayed to help that fool night clerk," Trumbell said.
"Of all the damned fool tricks."

McMahon smiled in the darkness and said, "She shows
more compassion than her father, Trumbell. She'll be
here in a minute. Lie down!"

He turned to Fletcher and said, "Get down, Sam.
Mary . . ."

"Yes?" she said quickly. "What is it, John?"

"Get down," McMahon said. "Both of you. On your

stomachs. Cradle your faces in your arms. Stay there."

Two people slid down the bank and fell in a confused mass near them. Will Overton's calm voice came from this jumble, "You all right?"

"Perfectly," Alice Trumbell said. "Except for bruises I can easily afford."

"Will," McMahon called. "Get her over here and down on the ground, Trumbell, get down here with your daughter. Will, pass the word along the bank. Everybody down, head in their arms. Maybe they think this will be a firecracker. It'll bounce them like chips. It'll be worse than anything they can imagine."

"Right," Will Overton said.

Another man came sliding down the bank and struck Will Overton a glancing blow, regained his feet and chuckled softly. He said, "Sorry, Overton. Your hotel is all clear. I checked that back room."

"Thank you," Will Overton said. "Help me get these people down, will you?"

Passing McMahon, saying to Will Overton, "I'll go north," the man smiled at McMahon in the flaring red light. "Fine way to greet a stranger in town. They do this every Saturday night?"

"Just every other Saturday," McMahon said. "Thanks for the help, friend. You'll do."

McMahon started up the bank and Mary Fletcher said, "Don't go up there, John."

"Get down," McMahon said sharply. "You think I want you hurt?"

"Or you, John?" she asked quietly.

"I'll be all right," McMahon said.

He touched her face with one hand and then climbed the snowy bank and ran into the trees north of Mathews' shack. The special was burning full length and the yard had caught fire, buildings and wrecked cars and naphtha gas burst into towering, dancing flames that cast a reddish glow over the town, showing last stragglers running for the river. Urging the last two from behind, two fools laden with equally foolish possessions, Hickerson and Abe Bloom came into the trees, running with stiff-legged, exhausted strides. McMahon called, "Over here," and waved them into the trees.

"Town's clear," Abe Bloom gasped. "How long did it take?"

"Not long," McMahon said. "Good work, Hickerson. My hat is off to you."

"Thanks to you," Hickerson said. "My God! How did this happen, McMahon?"

"Got a dry match, Abe?" McMahon asked.

He rolled a cigarette and leaned against the nearest tree, lit the cigarette and drew smoke deeply into his lungs. He stared at the flames soaring above the town and said, "What happened? Chambers should join us in a few minutes. I'll tell you then. In the meantime, sit down and smoke a cigarette and take a good look at Warbonnet."

"Will it . . . ?" Abe Bloom asked thinly.

"Sorry," McMahon said. "The north part of town will blow flat. Your house is gone. Your store might stand. Jail empty, Hickerson?"

"Everybody's out," Hickerson said. "Got 'em under a twenty-man guard."

Steps sounded behind them and Chambers came puffing from the bank and dropped on his knees beside them. He said, "The special was to take the siding until the night train passed. Agent says both crews would stop to say hello and have coffee. Seven Mile Siding was the special's spot. Engineer, fireman, brakeman was the crew. All three missing when the special came in wild. Agent can't understand it. He and half a dozen men are going south to the Siding right now."

"I can guess at it," McMahon said quietly. "When

the night train stopped, Timberlake went after Mathews, found him, but Mathews ducked off and sneaked into one of those cars on the special. It has to be that way. Timberlake tried to get him, but couldn't pull him out of one of those freight cars. We can see the result. Timberlake cornered the special's crew, probably tied up in the caboose at the siding, and then something snapped in his mind. He had to get Mathews and this was the way he thought—run the special toward town, build up pressure, turn it loose and jump. Never mind innocent people, property, anything else. Chambers, you and Hickerson get down below the bank. After it blows, wait until the air is clear, then start looking. Timberlake will be somewhere in town. Buchanan has got to be there. I don't care how we get them. We get them. Hurry now!"

"Very well," Chambers said. "We'll come along the river. Meet you uptown"—he chuckled without humor—"or what may be left of town by then."

Chambers and the marshal ran stiffly toward the bank. McMahon dropped to his knees and then stretched full length on the snow beside Abe Bloom, loosening his body, knowing from past experience the shock that would touch them all when the powder blew. Beside him, Abe Bloom shivered like a wet puppy and murmured, "Perhaps this is for the best, John."

"You mean the town will rise again," McMahon said.

"Like the phoenix," Abe Bloom said. "Clean and burned free of all the old dirt."

"It's a good dream," McMahon said. "I hope you're right, Abe."

"How much longer, John?"

"Relax," McMahon said. "Think of something, anything."

"I'll think of my family," Abe said softly.

McMahon thought of the past, his own years now spent and forgotten, the hours of days that blended into months

and congealed over the endless plains of time into the
years that every man possessed and strode across with
such careless waste. If he could only be sure, he thought,
of the worth he had gained from those years, if he could
wind together once again the million gray and dusty
threads of that vanished time and appraise them with a
miser's eye for karat weight in the scale of man's true
worth! How could he know if those years of work and
fighting and traveling and loving, those years of doing all
that man can do in life, were worthy of the inner man, the
soul, the secret desires and longings cherished by every
man? Thirty-three years now gone forever, half his life
turned from the open hand of time and scattered from the
big river to the Pacific, from the sweep of Mexico to the
equally wild sweep of the Canadian plains, through a
thousand cities and towns and crossroad stores, and farms
and ranches and mountain cabins, carried on the strength
of countless meals and gulps of water and sacks of brown
tobacco, spiced with a million spoken words, too many
faces and shapes and steps on board walks and dusty streets
and leaf-covered slopes in the wet-grassed dawn, the high
noonday sun, and the slow, silent tunnels of the night.
Thirty-three years, and why? And what? What was he
reaching for, wanting with the secret part of his heart,
his mind, his body and eyes and hands? What did a man
search the streets and hills and meadows for? It had to be
his dream, and for every man there lived a different dream
of peace, of wealth, of all the material and spiritual wealth
offered by the earth and the people on the earth. And he
was wandering across the earth, pausing here and there,
leaving the ghost of his presence in the white china wash-
bowls of stale hotel rooms, in the empty glasses on the
wet-topped bars of a hundred saloons, in the clothing
bought and worn and thrown away, boots walked through
and discarded, words spoken and his guns, and the curses
of men who had pursued their own dreams and were

brought up short by him, the man who shattered their dreams and sent them where nothing existed but walls and the oval shadow of the knot and the noose and the water-tipping trap set for the weight of he who stepped once and went through to his final dream. He was wandering across the earth, and his ending would be no greater, nor worse, than anyone before or after him. He thought of Fletcher and Mary, and in this clear memory of their life found a quiet pleasure that had grown unfelt in him for days; and in this memory, and the face of the girl, came the feeling that had escaped him until the moment he sat in their kitchen and drank their coffee and saw plainly the future of their unspent years. McMahon, he said wordlessly, McMahon is a name, a body without substance, a man who has got to stop now.

"Twenty-five minutes now," Abe Bloom said. "How much longer?"

"I don't know," McMahon said wearily. "One minute, two, maybe . . ."

The earth beneath them rocked and seemed to move away; the roar of twenty thousand pounds of powder exploding in one unbelievable blast and flash of flame tossed them up, then down against the earth and the suddenly rock-hard structure of their arms. McMahon lost consciousness for a brief moment, felt blood from his nose stain his face and cover his mouth. Abe Bloom had been thrown, or bounced, up and over McMahon's shoulders, and lay inert, arms loose, legs thrust outward at a drunken angle. McMahon heard the shrill whistling sound above them, a sound that had a thousand separate reeds, each sliver of shrillness that made up the whole representing something flying through the air, arching high and returning to earth. McMahon rolled savagely, pulled Abe Bloom's limp body to the snow and threw himself over the smaller man. Something thudded dully into the snow a short six feet to his left, and below the bank along the river a woman screamed with pain, and immediately was joined by other women in a rising, falling, frantic scream of tension and fear.

"Abe," McMahon said. "Abe, wake up!"

"I'm all right," Abe Bloom whispered. "I'm all right."

"Look up," McMahon said. "Look at the town, Abe."

Abe Bloom was trembling with nervous reaction as he pulled himself around and sat like a small boy, cross-legged, in the snow. He stared north toward Warbonnet and said, with awe and fear, "My God, my God!"

Hickerson's voice floated upward from the bank edge: "She's all done, McMahon. What comes now?"

"Keep everybody in the south end of town," McMahon shouted. "Get your men together. Fire will start. You'll have to save what you can."

McMahon ran toward town, drawing both guns as he cleared the trees and entered the south end of Front. Moving between the houses, he slowed to a walk and went slowly into Warbonnet, staring at the flames now rising slowly in the north end of town which, with shocking suddenness, was no longer an orderly section of buildings but a flattened area where nothing stood and nothing lived. Everything north of the bank was crumbled like a deck of cards smashed by a man's flat hand; the brick bank building bulged and canted over the sidewalk, and when McMahon passed, moving up the exact center of Front, the wall collapsed into the street and the bank building shook and dropped into complete rubble, only the rear wall standing in jagged shards. Jensen's livery barn was a sway-backed ruin and Abe Bloom's store was a windowless building pushed southward and filled with a tangled mass of goods. Buchanan's warehouse stood across the alley, roof caved inward, north wall pushed ten feet out of line, but standing uncertainly as if afraid to fall and unable to remain in that position much longer. This uneven line of half-ruined buildings extending from east to west

marked the space between the utterly ruined northern
third of Warbonnet and the remaining buildings of the
town to the south. McMahon ran for the depot and stood
in the middle of Front, fifty feet from the main line, and
looked with unbelief at the wreckage. The powder car
had crashed to a halt directly over the wagon road; and
here was nothing but a forty-foot crater some twenty feet
deep. The special's engine was a mass of twisted iron,
tossed into that place where the depot had stood, burning brightly, still making almost human sounds in the
night. The remainder of the special train and all cars in
the switch yards had disappeared, gone into complete dis-
integration. The river bridge, clearly visible in the fires
now burning and rising along the track, was twisted and
pushed from shape, unsafe to carry even a wagon load of
freight. McMahon guessed at that moment, and learned
the next day, that every window for twenty miles around
in farm homes had gone out; Weeping Water, sixty miles
to the south, had shaken with the blast; it was the most
terrible explosion McMahon had ever witnessed; it was
frightening him more, standing in the midst of this ruin,
after the force and blast was finished.

He saw a man step into the street from the shelter of
Abe Bloom's store, look directly toward him, and duck
from sight. McMahon recognized the broad shoulders and
heavy body. Timberlake had kept his word; he had come
back for the finish. McMahon wondered how the man
could stand the sight of the destruction he had brought
about with his own wild anger, and with the thought,
forcing himself to move, McMahon ran to the west side
of Front and began a slow advance toward Abe Bloom's
store. Two things to do, he thought bitterly, two more
jobs to finish. He reached the ruin of Jensen's livery barn
and veered into the alley now littered with burning wreckage and the smashed walls of half a dozen buildings.
Casey's saloon littered the dirty snow, whisky barrels now

blown to pieces and scattered over the twisted, upthrust timbers and boards. McMahon stood motionless in the half-shadow of one hanging wall section; and from the darkness a hundred feet down the alley, Timberlake's voice, hoarse and almost inhuman, shouted at him, "I'm stepping out, McMahon. Make your play."

McMahon called, "Don't be a fool, Timberlake. Throw your gun away and give up. You can't get clear."

"No," Timberlake shouted. "Are you scared, McMahon? Face a showdown. I told you I'd be here. Come on out!"

McMahon checked his guns quickly, held them under his arms and stripped off his gloves and flexed his hands. He dropped the gloves and lifted the guns and felt their solid, balanced weight against his fingers. This was the way it had to finish with a man like Timberlake; this was the end any man could expect if he followed the long trail. McMahon thought of other times in the past, remembered other men who had turned to face him, and wondered if his luck would hold good just once more.

"Show yourself first, Timberlake," McMahon called "I'll be coming down the alley."

"I'm your man," Timberlake roared.

McMahon saw his bulky form leap from the darkness and stand wide-legged in the alley, with the warehouse and Abe Bloom's store forming a topless frame for the picture of him, cap pushed back from his battered, blackened face, guns held low and stiff-armed. McMahon admired him in this moment, the only one of his pack with the guts to face the showdown; and then lost this foolish admiration, seeing the man as he really was, a killer all the way through, stripped of any decency, any pride, any honesty, years ago. McMahon cocked his guns and stepped into the alley and began his walk.

Behind him and to the west, Abe Bloom called, "Chambers, they're in the alley!"

Timberlake grinned and the lifting flames from the burning buildings painted his face and teeth red. He walked forward and as he reached the corner of the warehouse, he called, "Get clear, Ferris. I'll be with you soon." His shout made no sense to McMahon then; the distance between them was seventy feet, sixty, then fifty. McMahon stopped and said, "Time to start the ball, Timberlake."

"Time to start!" Timberlake said. "Make it close, McMahon. If you're thinkin' of Mathews, he went up with the powder . . ."

Timberlake lifted both guns and began shooting. McMahon dropped on his knees and shot his right gun empty, went to his stomach as he shot, dropped the right gun and took the left with his long-practiced flip, and continued shooting until the hammer struck sharply on a spent shell case. Smoke covered the alley before him and far off, then very near, Abe Bloom said, "Nice shooting, John. You are a tough man to face, day or night, any time."

Rising wind blew the smoke up and away; a hundred fires illuminated the alley when McMahon rose stiffly to his feet and touched a rip in his left mackinaw sleeve. He murmured softly, "Not this time, McMahon," and looked at Timberlake's body sprawled face downward in the frozen, dirty snow. Hickerson came from behind Abe Bloom's store and stood over Timberlake, shaking his head and holstering his own gun. When McMahon reached the body and studied its suddenly shrunken bulk, Hickerson coughed gently.

Hickerson said, "Dead center. You saved eight hundred people the trouble, McMahon. This man is better off dead."

"A week ago he could have lived," McMahon said. "The break comes and they can't pull back."

"All down," Chambers said behind him. "One to go, John. Where is Buchanan?"

McMahon reloaded both guns and faced the warehouse. "This man," he said flatly, looking briefly at Timberlake, "was faithful to the finish. Buchanan didn't deserve his friendship. This man was the better of the two. Surround the warehouse. I'm going in. He's got to be in there."

He walked from the alley, along the north wall of the warehouse, and turned the northeast corner toward the river door. He lowered his right shoulder, and made his charging smash that ripped the lock from its seat and burst the door open. McMahon struck the floor in a headlong dive, rolled out of doorline, and came to his feet in total darkness. He smelled the assorted odors of long-stored articles, furs and lumber and household goods, the stale and dusty scent of possessions shaped and formed by hard work and dearly saved money, and traded to Buchanan and placed here in limbo, in exchange for a few bits of papers that had value and yet, when time had passed, ceased to mean anything to anyone. McMahon faced the deep void of this building, twisted and blown out of shape, and raised his voice to a shout.

"Come out, Buchanan!" he called. "I'll give you the chance. Come out and face the music."

Silence swallowed his words and ran soundlessly through the long room. McMahon spoke again, "Timberlake's in the alley, Buchanan. Mathews went up with the powder. Your sled and team are a mile from the river bridge. I'll give you one last chance. Come on out!"

He could not be sure, but from the depths of the warehouse came a low rustling sound, almost a ghost of a real sound, the dry murmur of something moving in fear and freezing in place, bound and held by fear in the darkness.

"Very well," McMahon said loudly. "I'm coming for you, Buchanan. We'll play the game out in the dark. I'm a better shot than you, Buchanan. Make a move and I'll give you my answer. I could go outside and set this place on fire, but that wouldn't be playing it square, would it,

Buchanan? You never played anything square in your life, did you? Fine, let's play this one to the finish. Get ready, Buchanan. I'm coming in."

Sixteen

BUCHANAN HAD SETTLED himself comfortably in the small but reasonably decent room he and Mathews had constructed months ago in the warehouse. He had entered through the alley window, drawn the ladder up and inside after him, and barred the window securely. He had planned this room so that its shape was hidden by stacks of goods arranged in orderly rows along the south side of the big room. The little room was built of planks, flush against the south wall of the warehouse. The interior was lined with tar paper, five layers, which sealed it completely; the door was only a trap large enough for his own body; inside a large blanket hung above the door and could be nailed down to shut off all light that might possibly leak through the cracks between door and casing. Ventilation was provided by a stovepipe running upward within a false section of warehouse wall to the roof. Buchanan had furnished this tiny eight-foot square cubicle with a cot, a small oil heater, and sufficient canned and dry food to last a week. He had a five-gallon can of water, cigars, matches, even an extra overcoat. His fear of the dark was allayed by a box of fifty large candles which, burned in a special candle lamp with a reflector, furnished reading light and illuminated the entire room. As a final touch, he had placed a thick rug on the floor.

Buchanan lit a small lantern and walked slowly around the large storeroom, checking the doors and windows, and then edged carefully through six layers of packing boxes, replacing each moved box as he advanced, until he reached the small door. He entered the little room on hands and knees, turned and replaced the last packing box which hid the door from the outside; he barred the door and tacked the heavy blanket in place, lit a candle and snuffed out the lantern and sat on the cot with the valise held tightly between his knees. He lit a cigar and allowed himself one short sip of brandy from the flask, and then transferred Trumbell's papers from their hiding place beneath the cot into his valise; as an afterthought he counted his money once more and then stretched full length on the cot to pass his alotted time in this cramped room. He dozed off and awoke twice, smiled at the candle burning steadily, and was thinking with unctuous sadness of Timberlake when the special smashed into the empties and sent a rumbling, twisting shock throughout the warehouse.

Buchanan sat up and straightened the flickering candle, understanding the crash though unable to see why a train should run wild into the yards; but nothing was affected by this diversion, which could be helpful. Buchanan chuckled softly, wondering where McMahon was at this particular moment, and again stretched out on the cot. The entire town would soon be milling around the depot, watching the trainmen and section gang straighten out the wreck. He heard a crackling sound and guessed correctly that a fire had started in the wrecked train; that would give them something more to think about. He was lighting a fresh cigar some twenty minutes later when the world turned upside down and blew apart before his shocked eyes. Something smashed against his head and he dropped into a whirling black pit of nausea; regaining consciousness, he found himself on the floor, in total darkness, with a section of splintered plank across his chest.

Buchanan felt a cold draft on his face as he struggled from beneath the plank. He stood abruptly and bumped his head against loose planks that once had formed a solid roof; his hands felt the warped, broken ends and moved hurriedly around the walls, now bowed inward. Buchanan was frightened; something unforeseen had blown the outer world into fragments and his warehouse, as well as he could tell, seemed to be pushed far to the south so that the main building walls creaked and groaned and hung by mere threads to shape and shelter. He groped for the spilled box of candles, and lit one with shaking fingers. The tiny flame rose and remained steady, and Timberlake's voice came suddenly from the alley, shouting at McMahon—it had to be McMahon—and finally Timberlake called, "Get clear, Ferris, I'll be with you soon."

The night was filled with gunfire. Buchanan pinched the candle with two fingers and crouched beside the cot in darkness that grew horns and faces of imagination in his mind; and as he listened to the voices in the alley, those dark faces began their relentless attack on his body and mind. He heard McMahon ordering men to surround the warehouse; at that moment he was scratching a match to relight the candle. Now he dared not show a light in this room, with the walls no longer tightly fitted. Buchanan drew his guns and sat in the middle of his thick rug, in the hiding place that was no longer secret.

He fought against the fear of darkness with the greater fear of McMahon's approach; when the river door smashed open and McMahon began shouting at him, Buchanan felt all hope shrivel and die. He remembered the valise at this time and began clawing about the floor; and then McMahon called, "Get ready, Buchanan. I'm coming in," and he dared not move his hands and make a sound.

His mind seemed to freeze and refuse him the gift of clear, lucid thought; there must be a way out, had to be —for how could he fail now with everything planned so carefully and the way to the south clear just beyond the river? He mastered his fear momentarily and thought, "I'll sit here and let him grope in the darkness. I'll plan something." And then he thought of the darkness, once more thick and living about him, and felt the vomit of fear rising in his throat.

When Buchanan refused to answer, McMahon felt the clean flush of utter success in this dirty, weary affair. That meant but one thing: Buchanan was ready to pull out and was guilty of everything that had taken place. McMahon considered the final result of this case and decided that Buchanan could not escape punishment no matter how much money he might spend in his own defense. Accessory to two murders—the bookkeeper's and Red Egan's and the Lord only knew how many others covered by time; killer of Paul Mason, that was certain, and for reasons bound to come out within hours. Enough to take care of him, McMahon decided, and then wondered if Buchanan would give up.

He moved one foot along the floor, then knelt and removed his boots. The cold seeped through his thick socks, but his feet made no sound when he rose and took an experimental step toward the front of the warehouse. In the back of his mind was a memory of Buchanan's library and bedroom, not a picture so much of furnishings and size, but the small lamp burning in the bedroom for no good reason. It might be that Buchanan, like several people McMahon had known, kept a lamp burning while he slept. He might do this for a variety of reasons, but it was possible he did not like the darkness. McMahon dropped carefully to his knees and searched about with one hand until his fingers touched and lifted a short piece of splintered wood. He threw this three foot length of timber toward the far wall; it struck a high pile of boxes, from the sound, caromed against a tin bucket, and clattered loudly along the floor. In the silence that followed, McMahon waited for any reaction; none came.

"All right," he thought, "you want to wait me out. We'll see who lasts. Buchanan."

He was trying to keep his unseen enemy on edge, toss-
ing a few boards or cans around the warehouse until Buchanan's nerves were grinding with an agony of fear. When
a man sat hidden, waiting for a break, and nothing happened but the irregular banging of boards and cans and
bottles against the inner perimeter of his self-styled citadel,
sooner or later he would crack and make a move. Mc-
Mahon moved to the left and edged cautiously around
and through tumbled masses of boxes and barrels and packing cases until he reached the south wall. Here he holstered both guns and began a systematic search for all
loose objects. Luck was with him. He pawed over and
recognized by touch a full case of empty bottles, then a
box filled with scrap iron and old harness buckles and other
assorted junk. He hefted a bottle and tossed it toward the
north wall; the crash and clatter of broken glass was a
sharp, grating sound, followed by the spreading tinkle
of smaller glass pieces falling on the floor. McMahon settled himself against the wall, rolled a cigarette and placed
it between his lips unlit, and began timing himself. At
five to ten minute intervals he tossed bottles, scrap iron,
and other articles all over the warehouse, sucking on the
cigarette and gleaning dry relief from the paper and tobacco. On impulse, half an hour later, he lifted and threw
the remainder of the case to the left; the bottles fell on
something solid, did not break, and rolled off what must
be a big packing case or stack of boxes to the floor.

McMahon began an advance along the south wall, inch-
ing forward with one gun drawn, detouring around rubble
and wreckage, until the wall turned before his face at a
ninety-degree angle, evidently forming a partition of some
kind in this end of the warehouse. He flattened against
this heavy plank wall, twisted badly out of plumb, and
listened to his own heartbeat and the faint, distant sounds
that filtered inside from the town. Below this steady cur-
rent of noise that was felt more than heard, McMahon

caught the tiny sound that seemed to come from behind
the plank partition; this sound reminded him of a small
animal or a baby whimpering in its sleep. He moved farther along the partition and touched a vertical crack where
the planks were sawed off cleanly and faced with a door
casing and then the buckled but intact rectangle of the
door itself; and behind the door the whimpering became
coherent and shaped into faint words that came to his ears
in snatches, then singly, as the speaker seemed to swallow
thickly, remain silent for a minute, then murmur once
more. McMahon listened and heard the words, "Damn
him . . . Damn him," repeated many times. When another
phrase came, "I can outlast him. . . ." McMahon smiled in
the darkness.

He stepped away from the door and placed one hand
against the planked partition and began a steady push;
the planks held, then squeaked slightly, and suddenly
groaned and shook as he placed full pressure of his body
behind and into his arm. He dropped his hand and listened; within the whimpering had stopped and silence,
almost audible, filled the warehouse. McMahon moved
backward along the partition three steps and cleared his
throat.

"Nice little rat's nest you've dug, Buchanan," he said
loudly. "Are you coming out or do I come in?"

He heard a shuffling sound, that of a man surprised and
turned by instinct, boots moving on a carpet or rug, and
then the silence again. McMahon waited five minutes by
silent count and spoke again:

"Lonesome, Buchanan? I'll give you a minute to come
out. Then I'm coming in."

He waited a minute and Buchanan, behind the partition, did not move. He examined the partition and felt a
quarter-inch crack between two planks; and placing his
gun muzzle here, pulled the trigger. The shot echoed and
reverberated through the warehouse, magnified and harsh-

ened by the walls; and inside, suddenly come to life, Buchanan fired blindly at the planks. The slugs thudded into three-inch thick wood. McMahon slipped backward another three steps and called, "Still kicking and alive, Buchanan. Just wanted to smoke you out."

Buchanan spoke for the first time, his voice trembling with some unknown fear entirely separate from any fear he might have of McMahon. "You can't get me, McMahon," he said. "I can stay here forever."

"You can?" McMahon said happily. "I doubt it."

Buchanan seemed to find vanished courage in the sound of his voice, "I suppose it would be useless to offer you a deal, McMahon?"

"Can't hear a word you're saying," McMahon said. "I'll offer you a deal. Come out and I'll see you live to stand trial."

"And after that?"

"No guarantee, Buchanan. I found Mason a while ago. I've got Casey's statement, and Mathews'. I'm just showing the tender side of my nature, talking with you now. Take your choice: come out standing up, or be carried out on a door."

"In that case," Buchanan said, "come and get me if you've got the courage you've been boasting about. Or will you call for a dozen more to help?"

"Just sit back and keep your fingers crooked," McMahon said. "I'll join you in a little while."

McMahon moved away from the area of the door and stood beside the partition that was actually one wall of a small room built cleverly within the warehouse, of that fact he was now certain. Buchanan had constructed this hideout for emergency; as such, being windowless, the room needed ventilation. McMahon reached high and curved his fingers over the top of the wall, feeling the first plank of the roof over this little room. He holstered his guns and, moving quietly, drew his body upward and wiggled onto the roof. Crawling beside the south wall of the warehouse, which formed the south wall of this room, he came to that slight bulge in which the stovepipe fitted, and ran upward to the warehouse roof. McMahon reached a quick decision; he continued along the wall to the west edge of the small room's roof, let himself down to the floor and crossed to the window that faced the alley. This window shutter was hanging at a drunken angle, latched and closed, but held in place by one twisted wood screw in the top hinge. He turned the screw with his fingers and pulled the window shutter open; outside and across the alley, from Abe Bloom's office, somone called, "Keep an eye on the window, boys," and a rifle barrel gleamed momentarily in the light from a dozen fires still raging to the north.

McMahon cupped his hands and spoke softly, "Abe?"

"Wait!" Abe Bloom said, from the alley darkness. "John?"

"Under the window," McMahon whispered. "Quick."

Abe Bloom ran from his alley door and stood beneath the window, face pale and anxious. "Did you find him, John? We heard the shots."

"Yes," McMahon said. "He built a cubbyhole along the south wall. Won't come out. There's a ventilator running to the roof on the south side, about thirty feet from this end. Can you get hose and a bellows?"

"I think so. Why?"

"Get a crew," McMahon murmured. "Hickerson will understand. So will Chambers. Run a ladder, put a man on the roof, find that ventilator, run a hose in, then pump all the smoke you can make. Can you do that?"

"Now I see," Abe Bloom said quickly. "Yes, we can do that, John. I'll get a piece of tin. We'll make a funnel, start the hose in the top, hold it over a fire, and fan it up."

"Try that," McMahon said. "If it doesn't work within ten minutes, I'll thump on the south wall. Then kill the fire, bring the pumper, and keep throwing water down the ventilator until I say stop."

"Give me ten minutes," Abe said.

McMahon closed the shutter and crossed the warehouse floor to the same position he had held beside the small door. Now, listening with an ear against the planks, and hearing Buchanan moving and whimpering once more, he withdrew ten feet and placed himself at full length behind a packing case, one gun balanced carefully in both hands, covering the unseen door. Here McMahon waited with a patience born of years spent in exactly this sort of life. The minutes passed, small sounds came to his ears from outside the warehouse, and then he heard the cough. Buchanan kicked a chair over inside the room, coughed three times, and then cursed horribly. McMahon visualized smoke pouring into that tiny space and Buchanan floundering about the darkness, trying to plug the bottom of his stovepipe with anything at hand.

Buchanan was coughing steadily, a sound of strangulation begun deep in his thick chest and expelled in hacking gusts and then his coughing tapered off and was followed by a low and nearly hysterical laugh.

"Plug it up?" McMahon called.

"Damn you!" Buchanan shouted.

McMahon lifted his voice and called loudly, "Abe!"

"Yes?" Abe Bloom answered from outside the south wall.

"Turn on the water," McMahon said. "Let's get this over and done."

He heard the pumper start, a dozen men manning the handles, the man above them on the roof guiding the hose and calling directions, now that McMahon had canceled the order of silence by his own verbal command. That unknown man on the roof shouted encouragement, then called in triumph, "She's going down all the way. Pour it on, boys, pour it on!" and with his words the small door

creaked and came open, and Buchanan made his rush,
firing blindly to right and felt, then straight ahead, as he
came from the room that had been his sanctuary. He ran
directly toward and past McMahon, stumbled over a box,
fell full length on the rough floor, groaned and then cried
out in complete terror, and came to his feet like some
crippled beast, clawing with his fingers, then regaining
traction and continuing his blind rush toward the rear
door. McMahon held his own fire in this moment, suddenly sick of it all, and called,

"The rear door, Abe. Wake up your boys!"

He rose and faced the river door and heard Buchanan
fumble with the latch, then tear it open and rush into the
fire-tinged night. He saw the broad width of the man for
a moment, framed in the doorway, and then the shots
came in a combined roar. McMahon holstered his guns,
rolled and lit a cigarette, and took his time moving through
the warehouse and outside. He saw the crowd gathered
around a dark object in the snow and shook his head sadly
at the waste of talent in that dead man. Abe Bloom and
Chambers came from the crowd and stood beside him,
and Abe patted his arm softly.

"It's a clean sweep," Abe said. "We owe you a great
debt, John."

"Did he have a valise?" McMahon asked.

"Yes," Chambers said. "Hickerson is holding it."

"It will have the bank's money," McMahon said. "And
Trumbell's papers. We'll get some sleep and clean this
business up tomorrow." He laughed shortly. "If the hotel
can stand my weight, I'll try a little sleep."

"The hotel stands," Abe said. "My store is off plumb
but I'll be open for business Monday."

McMahon dropped one arm around the small man's
shoulders and said, "You mentioned a debt, Abe. You
don't owe me a thing. You and the other decent men in
this town would lick Buchanan in time. I just gave you the

boost. Maybe I owe you a debt. Don't ask me to explain tonight."

He turned away and walked through a gathering throng, around the warehouse, across the alley, through the twisted wreckage of Jensen's livery barn, onto the blackened, boot-churned snow of Front. Behind and around him they were picking up the pieces and marking one chapter closed in the life of this town; once again he had moved into and lived with the closing scenes of a young town's wildness. Warbonnet had seen its last wild, rough days. The drifters, the gamblers, the men like Buchanan and Timberlake would move on now, were moving tonight while he walked down Front in the snow that was stained red with the reflection of the fire still burning in the yards. He had a dozen loose ends to tie together the next day and then—and then, he thought with finality—he would do what he had decided days ago. He would write the Colonel and send this resignation with Chambers. After that the town and the valley lay before him, a good place to start another way of life.

He reached the hotel and entered the lobby and saw the drunken cant of the walls, the strips of plaster torn and scattered over the floor, the deer head lying with glass-eyed calmness beside the big gaboon in the front window where the checker players had battled throughout the long, quiet days. Will Overton stood beside the desk with Alice Trumbell, both resembling well-dressed scarecrows with blackened faces and hands. Trumbell came from the dining room, carrying a tray of steaming coffee cups, his face smudged and dirty, his boots so wet they squished with every step. Trumbell saw him and extended the tray and said, "Coffee. You need it, man."

McMahon took a cup and said, "Thanks," and looked at the white cup and the black coffee. Trumbell paused beside him and said, awkwardly, "I'll see you tomorrow about all this."

"Very well," McMahon said.

"Concerning the railroad," Trumbell said. "I'm afraid it's too soon, McMahon, in case you're wondering about my future plans. Five years from now, perhaps ten, and I'll try again. Not now."

"You're wise," McMahon said. "Let these people forget what happened before you try again."

"Mason is dead," Trumbell said bitterly. "They found him in the bank. It could mean but one thing."

"I saw him," McMahon said. "He sold you out."

"Yes," Trumbell said. "Well, I'd better pass this coffee around."

Trumbell went to the desk and offered two cups to his daughter and Will Overton, and continued around the big stove into the alcove. McMahon walked to the desk and smiled at Will Overton.

"My thanks, Will," he said wearily.

"John, why don't you get some sleep?" Will Overton said.

"I will," McMahon said. "Miss Trumbell, you did right well tonight. My congratulations."

Alice Trumbell said, "Thank you. It was mostly Will's doing."

"I see," McMahon said. "Well, good night."

As he walked to the alcove, Alice Trumbell's voice came softly, speaking across the desk to Will Overton, "When will you come to St. Louis?" and then he was facing Sam Fletcher and Mary, watching their eyes change and lift with some quality of admiration he found difficult to accept.

"All through?" Fletcher asked.

McMahon said, "All through. We'll clean it up tomorrow."

Fletcher nodded, forming an unspoken question with his eyes. Mary said, "Are you . . . ?"

"We'll talk in the morning," McMahon said. "After

that, if you'll put up with me, I'd like to come up on the farm with you for a while. If you still need that hired man."

Her face moved with emotion and she touched her father's arm. Fletcher said, "We'd be proud to have you, John."

She had to ask her question. She said, "How long—how long will you stay?"

"That depends," McMahon said. "That depends on you."